RESURRECTION
Primordium – Book 4

William E. Mason

RESURRECTION

DOUBLE DRAGON

Dedication

to Tanner, Gunnar, Axel, and Leo

Acknowledgements

I would like to thank members of my critique group, who, over the years, have devoted countless hours reviewing my work.

Robert Spiller
Beth Groundwater
Barbara Nickless
Maria Faulconer
M.B. Partlow

PROLOGUE

Justin Rasmussen leaned back in the low hanging crook of a baobab tree. *Adansonia digitata*. Legend said the devil pulled it out of the ground and shoved it back in upside down. Justin didn't dwell on how he knew this. He knew a lot of things, but unlike the baobab tree, which knew how to put down roots, sprout leaves, survive from season to season, most of Justin's knowledge was useless in this time and place.

He was satisfied for now that the tree provided a good view over the surrounding savannah. Dry grass spread out before him spotted with dense thickets and thorn bushes. He drew the palm of his hand across his forehead to forestall a rivulet of sweat that threatened to slide off his balding pate before cascading down through thick brows and into his eyes.

Jamani, ever faithful, squatted below on a low knoll. He had chosen more level ground, which still gave him a view without the necessity of expending the energy to climb a tree.

The grass of the savannah bent to a gentle breeze. It was almost wheat-like in color, punctuated here and there with leaning acacias, their dark trunks gnarled, their tops splashed with sprays of small green leaves. The rainy season was yet to come, which would urge forth bursts of red and orange blossoms.

A denser jungle crowded with towering palms, laced together by twisted vines, clustered in thick competition following the course of a river that flowed across the plain and emptied a kilometer away into Lake Turk.

An iridescent blue, the lake spread from lapping waves on the near shore to an extended line at the horizon. Justin could only surmise where it emptied. His learning said the lake was drained by a great river that flowed north all the way to a large sea. But he had never ventured far from what he called home. So he was unable to confirm or deny what he had been taught.

To the far south Mount Ken rose. Near its summit a faint dusting of white was a reminder of the cold that had gripped the region a generation ago.

Justin rubbed his hand dry against an animal hide that served as a loin cloth. He twisted his shoulders in a stretch of his lanky body, bronzed by the sun. "I can't decide," he said to Jamani, shifting a spear from one shoulder to the other, "whether the cold we experienced forty years ago was better or worse than the heat that assaults us today."

"Like heat." Jamani threw a stone out over the grass, as much in boredom as to check no saber cats were creeping up on them. "Like food. Like trees and grass."

We were just children, Justin thought. Glacial ice melted in a matter of months, forcing a scramble for survival. Devastating floods followed, swelling the lake beyond ancient shores and scouring the landscape. Years of famine followed until the land

8

rejuvenated. Vegetation now grew in the open, and game grazed on the flat plains. It had all happened so quickly.

A tug at Justin's foot drew his attention to a diminutive primate. An australopithecine was its scientific name. The creature pointed a crooked finger at the remains of a banana Justin held in his hand.

He tossed the banana and watched as the primate snagged it. "Good catch for a being without an opposable thumb. But they have time for that to develop."

With a tired, forgiving look, Jamani raised his hand and wiggled his thumb. "Oppos...I have thumb."

"Yes, you do."

The rest of the primate troop foraged farther out on the savannah in the waist high grass, oblivious to the noon day heat. They dug for tubers recent rains had spurred into growth.

An odd, swishing sound distracted Justin. He looked around, bewildered, wondering where the sound could be coming from.

Jamani pointed overhead.

Startled, Justin almost unbalanced himself.

A bright light fell out of the sky, descending rapidly.

The primates scattered, then huddled together at a distance as the light slowed and came to ground with a soft touch. The grass around the object smoldered, giving off a whiff of smoke that drifted south but did not ignite.

9

What had landed was ovoid, twenty meters in diameter and three meters thick with a textured outer surface. It had dug a short groove into the loamy soil, and now lay steaming, dirt pushing one side up at an angle to the ground.

An orifice sagged open on its top. From the orifice an arm extended, first one, then another. Pale, white and thin, the arms grappled against what appeared to be a slippery edge. A head emerged.

Justin leapt from the tree, his spear gripped tightly and raised.

A slender female, naked and pregnant to all appearances, levered herself out of the craft, for that is what it must have been. She slid to the ground, all the time shouting at someone or something.

The object's coloration darkened morbidly. If it were organic, Justin could have concluded it was dying, at least all movement from it ceased. That the object exhibited any indication of dying made Justin wonder. How could something organic survive such a fiery descent?

After a moment's hesitation, the female staggered to her feet and began slicking a slimy, clear mucous off her body. While doing so, she glanced often at the stunned primates who stood thirty meters from her. She didn't see Justin or Jamani in the dark shadows of the baobab.

Her distress was obvious.

She kicked the craft in disgust and simultaneously gripped her swollen abdomen. Her face contorted in pain.

Justin waved his spear toward the leader of the primates, Wakuru, indicating he should help her.

Wakuru, who had a basic knowledge of commands, shook his head and motioned as though Justin should do the approaching himself.

But Justin had been told in his youth of a craft like this. His instincts urged caution.

He motioned again making a slicing gesture across his throat, something he knew Wakuru would interpret to mean Justin was serious.

Wakuru stepped toward the pale female and stopped three meters from her. He sat on his haunches, broke off a stem of grass and picked his teeth. After surveying the situation, he looked back over his shoulder a couple of times to Justin, who motioned he should proceed.

With what could be interpreted as a primate sigh, Wakuru tossed the reed aside and stood. Stepping gingerly on bowed legs, he closed the distance between himself and the female.

She didn't flinch at his approach, but instead grabbed her abdomen again and groaned. Another contraction.

Wakuru stretched out his hand.

The female grasped it.

Wakuru made an awkward up and down motion that in another time would have amounted to a handshake, but now might have meant *let go*. He motioned with wild sweeps of his other arm they should go to the jungle by the river. Presumably, he hoped to communicate it would be cooler there, maybe safer.

The female gave the craft a last look as Wakuru led her toward the jungle. Her long strides forced him to double-time to keep up with her.

Another contraction gripped her, and she faltered.

Wakuru grasped both hands as high as he could to reach her upper arm, supporting her awkwardly until the spasm passed. Then, huddled together, they disappeared into the leafy growth.

Jamani eyed the craft. "It be Shepherd."

"I believe so." Justin looked from where the female had disappeared with Wakuru, then back to the craft. He felt an odd sense of déjà vu. He had only vague memories of the Shepherd from tales told to him during his youth. And now it lay in front of him seemingly dead. "I wonder what he expected to accomplish by coming here."

12

Chapter One

Gilomir's first utterance was a cry, the kind normal babies make when they exit the womb. Whereas his mother may have taken this to mean he was healthy, he screamed instead his frustration at still being in a hominid body.

The slick fluids of a human birth surrounded him. *This is degrading. Why am I still here*? He opened his mouth to cry again and gagged on blood and soggy tissue.

He lay on dirt, his mother's legs spread wide, rising like pillars, bloodstained and slick with the detritus of birthing. The orifice to the womb he had just exited gaped open, a red sore.

Mid-scream, he turned his head and stared through eyes still filmed over at his mother. His vision distorted a pleasant face. She must be all of twenty years old, pale and slender with wide spaced dark eyes and close-cropped black hair. Mia. He had spent nine months in her womb listening to her every conversation, her prattling, feeling her every emotion, absorbing her every thought. She was a host. But if he had any choice in the matter, he wouldn't be here at all. *But what next?*

Mother picked him up, wet and slippery, and cradled him in her arms. "He's beautiful. I shall call him Humanus to honor my master and acknowledge His debt to the hominid John Lohner, his father."

13

As far as *Gilomir*, now presumably Humanus, could tell no one in attendance but himself had any idea what she had just said. Large eyes in flat simian faces peered at him more in curiosity than with any sense of being in the presence of a lord and master.

Unceremoniously, Mia dumped him from her chest. Someone chewed the cord connecting him to her. He could only hope it would be tied off. These primitives--he peered as best he could--were more like monkeys. They could bleed his essence onto the ground before realizing such basics.

Someone laid a rough skin on him, providing a warm cover. Not that he needed it. The air was hot and humid beyond his expectations. An attending female wiped a leaf across his eyes, and his vision improved.

A tangle of growth climbed chaotically overhead, green and brown, all the while buffeted by the sound of faraway rushing water. Off to one side, a view corridor revealed waving yellow grass that caught the slanted rays of the sun at what must be the close of day. In the distance, purple hills darkened in the dwindling light.

An elephant trumpeted. A familiar sound, not one he must learn. After all, this age was not that different from where he had originated six million years in the future. Elephants were still elephants.

A far off huffing cry of a saber-toothed cat slid low to the ground. Now that was different. That kitten would have the lions of north Kenya for lunch. But Humanus didn't care. He was alive and better yet, looking forward to rescue.

A few days later, he was roused from a sleep in Mia's arms.

Her breathing had become labored. The lines around her eyes had darkened, giving her a hollowed-out look.

He knew she was synthetic, a product of the Shepherd. And therefore, it was of no surprise with the Shepherd gone, she had run out of energy and was going to die.

"My little man." She smiled down at him.

He tried to respond, but managed nothing more than the abrupt passing of air from his stomach.

She waved a hand.

Humanus tightened his cheeks, drawing his lips wide and exposing his gums.

"Your father was a strong man. Not just physically, but in what he believed. And all the while he was assaulted by that alien A4-Ni. I think it drove him insane in the end, so much destruction, so much death." She paused and took several deep breaths. "He was caught in the middle of a confrontation between A4-Ni, the guardian and the Shepherd, and what they wanted everyone to do."

Mia wasn't making a lot of sense. Humanus had a good grasp of what had happened while he was being carried around in her womb and even before, but that was still not a whole lot. Most of the time she was in a slumber as the Shepherd had transported them around a black hole and deposited them here, six million years back from where they had taken off.

"Your father was a paleoanthropologist."

15

As if he didn't know, but she seemed to have to say these things. Maybe this was what people did before they died.

"He made love to me on a night like this--" she gazed through the branches overhead where a full moon cast its ghostly rays. "--it was my first and only time. The Shepherd tricked me. I thought I was sterile, but I wasn't. When he could not extract your genome any other way, he said you and I were his backups."

I'm a backup?

"At first I was incensed I had been deceived, but upon reflection, I decided I didn't mind." She suppressed a cough. "John was dead or dying and I would have you to remind me of him."

Humanus would have nodded in agreement if he had control of his neck muscles.

"You are a composite of our master *Gilomir* and John, the hominid. And as such you are more than you could ever hope to be as *Gilomir* alone." She drew in a breath with what seemed like all her remaining strength. "I..."

And that was the last word she uttered. Her head flopped forward, and Humanus, who had been sucking on her breast, struggled to free himself from being suffocated by a doughy press of flesh.

Wakuru hurried to her side. Distress showed in his simian eyes, and Humanus knew the primate was feeling much of what he felt. Death was a known quantity. It had claimed members of Wakuru's tribe. It had certainly befallen others known vicariously by Humanus. The gloom of it descended upon him like a dark enveloping blanket.

As it closed about his psyche, a swift movement caught his attention.

Gomo, a surly, aggressive male lunged forward. He grasped Humanus' foot and dragged him from Mia's limp arms, then thumped him onto the jungle floor and headed for the plain.

With a screech, Wakuru leapt onto Gomo's back and rained fierce blows about his head.

Gomo blinked as though surprised by the attack. He dropped Humanus and shrugged Wakuru to the ground, then turned with a snarl, his mouth wide with a dry hissing, his long incisors glistening. The skin on his nose wrinkled. His eyes closed to mere slits.

Wakuru rolled away and regained his footing.

The two bluffed and blustered, Wakuru the larger and ten years Gomo's senior.

The other members of the troop danced around in agitated witness.

Finally, Gomo seemed to have had enough and simply stopped his assault and sauntered out of the clearing toward the savannah.

Wakuru limped over to Humanus and cradled him in his arms. He walked back to where Mia lay prostrate, the gray of death making her look dried and worn.

Wakuru muttered under his breath, nothing Humanus could interpret as intelligible words, but certainly sounds of mourning and sorrow. Had Mia known the commotion she had caused she probably would have been embarrassed.

Behind the grieving primate, a tall male figure appeared. He was definitely human with bronzed

17

skin and a short wrap of animal hide around his waist. His face was lean and chiseled with stringy graying hair falling long from his temples and bald top.

He gazed at Humanus with deep set eyes that projected an air of wisdom. The man placed a hand on Wakuru's shoulder and squeezed. "You must now care for this child."

Wakuru nodded and returned the gesture with a long string of gibberish.

The tall figure stroked Humanus' forehead. "You have come a long way. I pray your journey will not end here."

Humanus heard the words and understood them, but he didn't comprehend what the tall figure meant. Nor did he understand what a human was doing here millions of years before they were presumed to have evolved.

The tall figure smiled at him, then turned and disappeared into the jungle.

The other members of the troop gathered around Wakuru and Humanus, offering their own toothy smiles and little pokes with their fingers.

***

As the years passed and still no rescue, Humanus often wondered about the tall human, but the man never appeared again. Humanus tried on occasion to locate where he might have lived, or died, but found no trace.

Days blurred into each other with little to do but lounge in the trees, move onto the savannah for foraging, retreat into the shade during the noon day

18

heat, and sleep at night high in the canopy to be roused by the dreadful cries of predators.

One day, Humanus crouched, as he was inclined to do, on the ground savoring a clutch of plums he had just twisted from the tree overhead.

He held one high and dangled it over his upturned mouth, all the while stifling a laugh as a snarling Gomo scampered close trying to snatch it.

Humanus couldn't remember a time when the offending primate hadn't been around making aggressive sorties into the peaceful life Wakuru oversaw.

The runt-like Gomo lunged again but this time not at the prized fruit but at Humanus.

Humanus stood, a motion that demonstrated his superior height to the troubled primate. At twelve years of age, Humanus was two heads taller than Gomo.

He surmised the physical height advantage impressed Gomo, setting off a deep seated respect for a being that was taller. Humanus also knew that given a hand-to-hand fight, Gomo would have been the easy victor. The primates around Humanus developed their coordination and strength far faster than he did.

Fortunately, the evil Gomo hadn't come to the same conclusion. He always retreated, much to Humanus' relief.

But this time, Gomo's renewed assault exhibited something more sinister. It was as if over the years, Gomo was slowly piecing it all together and was now exhibiting his learning. He had become a more threatening menace.

19

Rather than take on Gomo directly, Humanus climbed into the plum tree and plucked fruit at random. He threw the ripe orbs at Gomo. "Here's one. And...oh, here's another."

Gomo fumbled at the cascading fruit, but managed only to deflect a few of them. The rest pummeled him.

With an angry snarl, he batted away the fruit and loped into the forest, giving a couple of quick looks over his shoulder to see if Humanus would follow.

With Gomo gone, Humanus eased back and dropped a plum into his mouth. As he savored the fruit, a young male primate scampered up to him and reached for the clutch of plums Humanus held.

"What have we here?" Humanus said, gazing at the eager primate.

Mewing sounds issued from the primate's open mouth.

Humanus tossed a plum into the air, and the primate twisted and bent backward to snag the fruit.

Humanus smiled. This was a very engaging primate, perhaps ten years old. Humanus wondered he hadn't seen him before, but there were so many, and when young, they all looked alike. This one distinguished himself by being eager, full of life and trusting. "What is your name, little one?"

The primate made an unintelligible sound and was silent, staring at Humanus with big brown eyes, which shifted from Humanus to the plums he held in his hand.

"I don't know the meaning of that sound, and--" Humanus smiled. "--I'm not going to try to learn how to say it." He held up a plum, teasing. "Your name shall be Kesi. That's easy enough to say. Even for you."

The primate peered trustingly at Humanus and drew back his lips. "Kesi!" he said on the first try and reached for the plum.

"Very good." Humanus handed Kesi the plum.

A dry rattling of brush distracted Humanus. Off to his right, Wakuru staggered into the small clearing. He was getting old, and with the constant harassing of Gomo, very tired.

Wakuru limped up to them. He stroked his hand over Kesi's head and nodded as though to indicate Kesi was a good primate, one Humanus could trust.

"I have named him Kesi," Humanus said.

Wakuru kept on nodding.

In a quandary about what to do, Humanus decided an embrace was in order. He didn't know why he thought that, or whether or not the action would elicit anything positive from Wakuru, but he climbed down from his perch and clasped his arms around him.

The elder primate went still, causing in Humanus an apprehension that he might have misjudged Wakuru's reaction, but then Wakuru responded with an embrace of his own. He grunted. Something Humanus took to be an acceptance, maybe even an acknowledgement of their relationship. Be that as it may, Humanus was encouraged they had advanced deeper into a meeting only the two of them could comprehend.

21

Wakuru was the first to break the bond. He nodded up and down in an idiot like motion, then ambled out of the clearing.

Gomo barged in, thwacking a long stick against the ground. If he thought this would intimidate Humanus he was wrong. Humanus leaned back and smiled. "So, odious Gomo, you have found a stick."

Gomo glared at Humanus and then at his stick. He threw the slender rod away and snarled, as though admitting he had chosen a weapon too frail and was enraged by the sarcastic putdown Humanus had delivered.

But none of this passed through Humanus' view of the scene. He was more worried that if he showed Kesi the least bit of attention, Gomo would realize the primate was favored by Humanus and then project any aggression onto Kesi instead of himself.

They stood facing each other, neither one about to give or show an edge of weakness.

Humanus stared into Gomo's eyes, trying to decipher what might be going on behind them.

"Do death," Gomo uttered to Humanus' surprise.

He blinked and leaned forward shocked. "What did you say?"

Gomo for his part seemed just as surprised at the utterance. "Do death," he repeated, then turned and stomped out of the clearing.

Gomo was supposed to be a primitive. His peer group had never uttered anything intelligible. But here was Gomo in full voice.

Who was teaching him?

22

Chapter Two

Nothing seemed to change as one day, one month, one year led to another. There were the odd encounters with predators, but other than that Humanus thought less and less of being saved, and more and more of just surviving for the next sunrise, a full moon, a heavy meal, the ministrations of the female primates.

Across the still waters of the lake a dark island loomed. It was obviously of volcanic origin with jagged spires that rose skyward. Not a trace of vegetation graced its slopes.

Humanus had long thought about the island, its remote austerity so different from the savannah grass and jungle of the mainland. Being too short to wade to the island, he had always put off investigating, until now.

This morning he woke Kesi. "You know, before my mother died she said a magical object was buried somewhere on that island over there. I don't know how she knew that, or what it might be, but today, I'm going to check it out."

An indolent Kesi roused himself enough to show total disinterest.

"If you aren't coming, I'll go alone." Humanus marched off toward the shore.

"Manus, wait!" Though there was still a lot to learn, at the urging of Humanus, Kesi had grasped the rudiments of language.

Humanus had only gone thirty meters when padding footsteps fell in behind him. "I thought you weren't coming?" he said to a downcast Kesi, who obviously didn't want to come, but perhaps out of some sense of loyalty decided he had to.

Humanus didn't take overt notice of Kesi's reluctance, but smiled to himself. "You may come, then."

At the shore, Humanus sloshed his way into the deepening water until it came halfway to his chest. *Now what?*

Kesi, ever loyal, followed, then stopped when the water sloshed at his neck.

"Okay, that's far enough for you." Humanus gripped Kesi under his armpits and lifted him onto his shoulders. "It's not that deep that I can't walk to the island."

He had been right about the depth of the water. It never came higher than his neck. The lake bottom beneath his feet felt smooth, a thin layer of silt on sand.

Eventually, he and Kesi came to the island's shore and confronted a shear rise of lava rock. He let Kesi stand in the shallow water.

"We'll have to circle to see if there is a way up," Humanus said.

Kesi nodded. "Circle." He glanced apprehensively at the looming wall.

Eventually, they came to a cracked lava tube. The edge of the tube appeared fragile with a loose jumble of rock holding back the still waters of the lake.

"We'll try this tube. But first it looks like we will have to descend a bit." Humanus climbed over the rock barrier and waved to Kesi.

After an apprehensive look over his shoulder, Kesi followed.

Humanus descended into the tube, discovering it went deeper than was immediately apparent from above. The ceiling of the tube kept getting lower, forcing him into a crouch as he proceeded. He waited every few meters for Kesi to catch up. "It's got to angle upward."

"Good," Kesi said.

But Humanus wasn't at all sure Kesi understood.

The little light they had at the entrance quickly gave way to an all-encompassing darkness, forcing Humanus to slow and feel his way forward.

"I think we're coming to the bottom," he said, though his enthusiasm was born more from hope than any certainty. He splashed into stale, knee deep water confirming they had reached the bottom of the tube. He pushed forward, and the floor of the tube ahead began to rise.

Humanus guided his hands along the walls. "I can't see a thing." He touched emptiness. "I think there's another tube joined to this one."

"No like," Kesi said into the dark. "Hurry out."

"We'll explore that one another day." The fear Kesi exhibited took hold of him. "God this water smells. A good thing the tube is angling upward."

A clatter traveled down the side tube.

"Hold on, Kesi. Something--"

25

"Hurry." Kesi splashed out of the stale water and headed up the dry tube.

An odd rushing sound and the push of air came out of the side tube. With a blinding insight Humanus realized that water was entering the side tube. How far away he couldn't tell, but for sure they were about to be submerged. "Get out, get out," he screamed.

Kesi was nowhere to be seen.

A gush of water exploded from the side tube, hitting Humanus and throwing him against the opposite wall.

Stunned, he gulped for air as water engulfed him. The darkness about him was complete absent any sounds but the faint bubbling of trapped air. *Where's the surface.* Humanus barely knew which direction was up.

He felt his lungs would burst. He lashed out, trying to orient himself. *Where is Kesi?*

Total darkness.

Kesi! A silent cry for help seared Humanus' brain.

A hand gripped his arm and pulled.

He kicked, and Kesi guided.

They clawed their way to the surface.

Air exploded from Humanus' gaping mouth. He leaned on a heavily breathing Kesi. "What hap--"

A light shone from the top of the tube. Then the light dimmed and the outline of Gomo framed in the opening.

"Aha, aha, aha!" he cried before disappearing.

26

"I'll get you for this!" Humanus screamed, then fell into a hacking cough up of water from his lungs.

Kesi leaned back against the side of the tube and seemed to be resigned to the whole sequence of events.

"You okay?" Humanus asked.

Kesi showed a thumb up.

"Then let's get the hell out of here." Humanus led the way upward, toward the light.

A gleam off something shiny caught his attention. "Hold on. What have we here?" He picked up a small silvery sphere. It wasn't any bigger than the eye of an antelope. Its surface was faceted, and tiny colored lights shone in a tight configuration.

"Where did this come from?" Humanus examined the sphere as he stumbled from the tube onto a flat gravel-strewn plateau. *Could this be the magical object of which Mia spoke?*

"Gomo?" Kesi asked.

Humanus glanced around, but the wicked Gomo was nowhere to be seen.

"Give." Kesi took the sphere and bit it with no observable effect on the surface. He handed it back to Humanus with a shrug.

Humanus closed his hand around the object. It felt warm to the touch, then a sudden jolt.

"*I see you have come a long way, Gilomir.*"

"It spoke to me," Humanus said, astonished.

"No hear."

"I mean--" Humanus tapped his forehead. "--it spoke to me inside my head."

Kesi took the sphere again and clamped his hand around it. "No hear."

"Maybe it doesn't want to respond to you." Humanus took back the sphere and held it tight.

"*You want answers. Everybody does, but in your case those answers are much more provocative.*"

If I think a question, will this thing respond?

"Yes."

What are you? What is going on here?

"*You have forgotten much in your sojourn through hominids. I am the guardian. If you open your mind to your past you will remember me.*"

The guardian. A force that could only be compared to an explosion hit Humanus. Memories slammed into his mind, and he saw a small sphere with the supernatural powers to see into the future or recall the distant past, and change either at will. *I remember.*

"*Good. Then we won't have to waste time refreshing memories.*"

You have been here all this time?

"*I have been here all this time. I am everywhere all the time.*"

You speak in riddles.

"*I don't mean to. But my primary concern is you. I brought you here. I am responsible for you.*"

You seem different than the guardian memories bring to mind.

"*Your memories are clouded by misinformation from the Shepherd and Mia. They had only a rudimentary understanding of what I really am. I would have hoped your own genetic memories would have been better preserved."*

Humanus did a search of what he remembered about the guardian and came up with nothing new. *Well, they aren't.*

"Have *you forgotten Zug?"*

I-- Humanus felt faint. *I--*

"*I didn't think so. You and Zug had a confrontation, one in which Zug prevailed."*

I remember Zug, but not the confrontation.

"*Then allow me remind you."*

A vision flooded Humanus' mind. He was pulled into a long-ago moment.

He screamed. Sweat poured off his brow and stung his eyes.

Zug. Tears streamed down Humanus' cheeks. He collapsed to his knees on the rocky ground, clasping his head tightly, squeezing. In anguish, he looked up and gazed at the infinity of sky overhead.

I remember now. I reached the abyss and peered in, everything lay before me, then he rose out of nowhere. A suffocating fog, he swept over me. I struggled. After he passed, I lay barren and alone. Now I am here and I am nothing.

"*You are who you are not. Look in a mirror and see a ghost. Look in a mirror and see Zug. Emptiness is out of balance. Only you can put it right."*

Humanus shook his head in despair. *I can't. I don't know how.*

"*We shall find out. You forget you are here not because you wanted to be. You are here because I brought you."*

29

"Wake up." Kesi shook Humanus.

He returned to the moment. The cloudless sky, a pale blue, met the line of the horizon. The sun reflected low off the slick waters of the lake. "How much time?"

"Time?" Kesi shrugged.

"I was asleep. This...this thing took me on a journey."

Kesi signed they should return to the mainland. It was getting late.

Humanus hefted the sphere. "It told me things about which I had chosen to forget." He slipped the sphere into a small pouch hung about his neck. "I need to find the human who came to me when I was born. He must know something of what is happening."

Kesi shook his head. "Leave alone."

"Easy for you to say. You didn't experience what I just did."

***

The next day, Humanus and Kesi went to the place in the river that Kesi said was frequented by two old men. Kesi said they drew water there and hauled it off to somewhere.

While waiting, Humanus and Kesi chased one another along the river where the banks narrowed, forcing the water to slide swiftly over flat rocks and comb into frothy depths. Arching branches reached out to close overhead, leaving a crooked opening to the sky where bright sunlight poured through, setting rocks aflame with glistening light and sending up shimmers on green leaves.

Entranced by the crashing water, Humanus failed to notice the approach of the two old men.

With his head turned to see if Kesi was catching up, Humanus ran headlong into the taller of the two.

"Whoa, little man," the stranger said. "You have grown so much since I last saw you."

Humanus struggled to free himself from the stranger's grip, then realized the man wasn't a stranger, but the tall being he had hoped to meet. That the man was tall went without saying. If Kesi was stacked upon himself he would have come to the man's chin.

"Who are you?" Humanus demanded, pulling away.

"You speak old English." It was as if the man had only left him yesterday. He looked the same, very lean with bronzed skin, gray hair, perhaps thinner, the hint of a gray beard. "I find it intriguing you speak at all, but old English?"

Humanus felt a burgeoning impatience. So many questions to ask, and the man was musing on a choice of language. Humanus thought to spew sentences from the hundred odd languages, all useless now, that he could speak, but decided not to confuse the issue. "I asked you a question."

"Indeed you did." The man patted Humanus on the head, a condescension Humanus found annoying. "Blond, blue eyes, a short muscular build." Before Humanus could object, the man looked to Kesi. "And what is your name?" The man accompanied his speech to Kesi with sign.

31

Kesi looked bewildered at first, probably from being asked a direct question by the stranger. "Kesi," he said finally.

"A fine name. I believe it means rational one in the language of the Swahili." The man smiled benevolently at Humanus, as a wise sage might smile upon a slow learning pupil. "You must have given him this name."

"I did. And I know what it means in Swahili. When did you learn to sign?"

"I signed as a child. For a while it was the only way I could communicate."

"The more I talk to you the more questions I have, but you keep avoiding answers."

"I don't mean to. It's just I seldom get a chance to talk with someone on this conversational level. Jamani--" he indicated the other old man, who had sat down and was cooling his feet in the river. "--is loyal and kind and caring. But he has limited mental abilities. He--"

"I'm leaving." Humanus' patience had come to an end. He wondered why he ever thought the old man could shed any light on his predicament.

The man waved his hand. "Calm down, boy. You need to learn indulgence."

Humanus hesitated.

"My name is Justin." He spread his hands expansively. "I am a friend. And I think you will need all the friends you can get."

Do I need friends? Humanus had Kesi, but if this Justin knew something and declared himself a friend then perhaps that was a good thing. "I have been here for a while now and know only your name."

Justin smiled. "I was here when you were born. But of course you remember that. You are now twenty years old and have grown to be a fine young man. But there are mysteries surrounding your existence."

My existence? That was an understatement coming from a fully developed human. "I, too, could wonder why a hominid of advanced Homo sapiens attributes exists in this time."

Justin peered at him and chuckled. "You could, but I would ask the same question of you."

"Then here's your answer. I was conceived one night near the fossil fields of Kanapoi. My father was the hominid paleoanthropologist John Lohner. My mother was a synthetic construct of an artificially intelligent self-replicating organic craft known as the Shepherd. The Shepherd fled Kanapoi with my pregnant mother six million years hence and ended up here."

"And I am an old man, who has difficulty understanding any of this." Justin eased himself down onto a rock and smiled wistfully. "I was born sixty years ago, or so I believe. I became me, but was a child of ten years at the outset. But it seems to me we are of the same stock. Whereas you come from future humans with artificial DNA thrown in by the Shepherd, I come from the Maraia who superseded humans, but were also brought forth by the Shepherd. Presumably, we also had some of the same god in us, at least that is what Sedroth taught."

"I know nothing of Sedroth."

33

"Sedroth was a hominid, born to the name Truman Justis, who was lifted up by the Shepherd and made a martyr. We followed his teachings."

"Either way, Sedroth or Truman, I've never heard of him. I do know the Shepherd. He nurtured me and my mother during her pregnancy. He died soon after depositing us in this time."

"You have an amazing understanding of events that must have happened while you were still an infant, more so only a fetus in your mother's womb."

"I am more than the flesh and bones you see before you."

"Alas, I think we all wish we were."

Humanus felt a flash of anger. "But I am!"

Justin smoothed back his graying locks and looked off into the distance as though he could quell the anger of a problem child by ignoring him.

Jamani tugged on Justin's arm. "I go. I no like. Kanapoi. Shepherd. This man. All bad."

Justin seemed pained. "You may go, Jamani. But I have waited a long time to have this conversation."

Jamani nodded and padded silently into the bush.

"Be that as it may," Justin said after Jamani had left, "here we are together, you and me. A redundancy of sorts. Now that's a mystery, don't you think?"

Humanus fingered the pouch that contained the guardian. How to find out what the old man knew? "Yes, it is a mystery. Have you heard of...*Zug*?"

34

Saying the word made Humanus' insides convulse involuntarily.

Justin gave a start, then eyed Humanus carefully. "I thought you didn't know about Sedroth?"

"I don't."

"Sedroth teaches that *Zug* is evil. *Zug* stalks us all. He has strewn the universe with his players to hunt down the guardian, his Shepherd and our lord. You have heard of players?"

Humanus searched Justin's expression, but got nothing from the effort, no indication of whether this was a trick question. "No. I have never heard of players."

"Sedroth teaches they are agents of *Zug*, informational smears injected into our space and time. They usually take human form to do his bidding."

"Our space and time?"

"Am I getting too far ahead of what I think your intelligence must be?"

"I know space and time." Humanus visualized the warping of time that must have occurred if a human sixty plus ten years old and born into this place was now confronting the child of a woman constructed six million years in the future.

"I thought so," Justin said, interrupting Humanus' train of thought. "If we are to get to know one another, then you'll have to trust me."

Somewhat piqued, Humanus reached into the pouch and retrieved the guardian. "Okay. I'll trust you. Do you recognize this?"

Justin gave a start, but recovered quickly. "Yes, that looks like the guardian. How do you come to have it?"

"I found it while exploring the island in the lake."

"That makes sense. It was the last time anyone saw the guardian. The synthetic, Michael, threw it there."

"Michael?"

"It is a long story and best saved for another time." Justin seemed impatient.

"All right, let's forget this Michael for now. Tell me what you know about the guardian."

Justin looked out over the flowing river and took on a very serious countenance. "The guardian is a small sphere of a size that belies its importance. Though I have been told it is simply a reservoir of knowledge, past, present and future, I don't think those who encounter it, really understand what it can do."

"I suspect the guardian knew all this would happen," Humanus said. "I even suspect the guardian caused it to happen."

"Long ago, during my youth, I was told the guardian contrived events in a way that was not at all conducive to the survival of my family. The guardian came to be a despised entity."

Humanus frowned. "But how can that be if the guardian was associated with the Shepherd? The Shepherd was very nurturing."

"That is also my conclusion. Though I was taught to fear the guardian, I have come to believe it is our salvation out of a world we do not

36

understand. Don't you harbor thoughts about what is to become of you?"

Images of his birth, Mia's pain, his initial crushing disappointment, then resignation all pushed into consciousness. "When I was born I had a fleeting idea I was somehow still trapped in this existence. Since then, all those ideas have long faded away. I am now quite comfortable here, although I could wish Gomo would meet up with a saber cat."

"Ah yes, the enigma, Gomo."

"Gomo isn't an enigma. He's a pest."

Justin scratched the gray stubble of his beard. "I suspect he is more than just a pest. He certainly doesn't fit into the normal australopithecine mold. Has anything strange happened that has caught your attention?"

Humanus felt a fleeting exhaustion. Justin seemed to be probing, always on the offensive. "Australopithecine." Humanus stalled. "I know this word and its reference to these beings that preceded the evolution of humans."

"I have asked you a question, and you are being evasive."

No deterring the man. "All right. How's this? Gomo spoke to me years ago in clear language."

Justin's face clouded with concern. "What did he say?"

"*Do death.* I have no idea what he meant, but was amazed he was able to articulate."

"Do you think Gomo could be a player?"

37

Gomo a player? An agent of Zug here? "I'll leave that to you. You know more about them than I do."

"I really know very little about them. In my youth, we were assailed by a player, quite an evil one. Of course they all are. Cardassin was his name. Some of Gomo's characteristics remind me of him. It was Cardassin threats that drove my people to build A4-Ni, in the hopes of saving their souls. I can only pray she achieved their goal."

Humanus stared. It was the second time in his life he had heard the word A4-Ni, the first being during Mia's death speech. But that hadn't carried any context. There were residual memories of an A4-Ni from Kanapoi and before that. But he didn't know if she was good or evil.

"I have heard of A4-Ni."

Justin brightened. "In what context?"

"My mother uttered the name as she was dying."

Justin's countenance clouded. "I'm sorry about your mother's death. But I'm sure you understand it was inevitable."

"I do."

"What did she say about A4-Ni?"

"Not much. A4-Ni hounded my hominid father, probably driving him crazy."

"You speak of her as playing a part in your time," Justin said, looking confused. "This I do not understand."

"I will tell you what I know," Humanus said. "A4-Ni has much to do with what has come to be. She first confronted the Shepherd two million years

38

from now and stole *Gilomir's* DNA. She inserted it into the descendents of these australopithecines. I told you I am the product of a hominid father and a synthetic mother but my lineage goes back farther than that. I am directly descended from that initial implant of *Gilomir*."

Justin laughed. "Sedroth taught we each carried in our genome the DNA of a god. But his name was Humanus, not *Gilomir*."

"Then you should know this. Before my mother died, she named me Humanus."

For a moment, it seemed Justin would faint. He leaned heavily on his walking stick. "There is much for an old man to understand here. I have enjoyed this conversation. It has cast some light into my own origin, and why I am in this place at this time. But indeed, it has raised more questions than answers. I will have to think about what you have said. We must meet again after I have had time to digest this information."

The old man gave Humanus a bewildered smile and trudged into the forest.

Humanus felt an oppressive weight of disappointment. The man appeared, cast ominous words about time and space, then disappeared.

"Come play," Kesi said.

"Where does he live?" Humanus asked.

Kesi shrugged.

"Surely you know. Someone must know."

Kesi smiled and skipped away along the river bank, then paused to induce Humanus to follow.

Humanus scowled. Another Homo sapiens here was mystery enough, but what about the old man's companion? The latter was obviously not a fully evolved human, but something stuck in-between, a man of the Neanderthals, but they inhabited the Earth millions of years hence.

Humanus palmed the guardian.

"*I see you are confused,*" it said.

That is an understatement.

***

Humanus trudged along a faint animal trail leading back to the tangled grove the primates called home. He hefted the guardian, trying to figure out what he was supposed to do. On the one hand, the guardian had laid down a challenge to him, one he abhorred. Confront *Zug*? Every fiber in his being told him to stay as far away from *Zug* as possible. And wasn't that just about where he was? Unless *Zug* suddenly appeared out of nowhere, what was the problem?

Justin's presence threw more confusion into the situation. What convolutions to time and space could offer up a man like Justin in the here and now? For his part, Humanus knew full well how he had arrived here. But something else was at work if Justin had been wrenched out of the future 8,000 years beyond what Humanus had left, rather, Mia and the Shepherd had left and slid without interruption to six million years in the past.

Zug? Humanus didn't think so. *Zug* would not be so coy. His tactic was frontal, laying waste to anything that opposed him.

What about the dead Shepherd? But the Shepherd had seemed more of a servant in the scheme of things than an initiator. By elimination,

40

that left the guardian. From what Humanus had gleaned from Mia, she thought the guardian was not an overt instigator but more a repository of events with the power to see into the future and replay the past. Those who used it believed the scenarios it projected. But what if it wasn't what it seemed? What if it were some sort of manipulator? After it convinced its users it was telling the truth, it could say anything it wanted.

Humanus' suspicion coincided with Justin's. The guardian was far more than anyone suspected. Perhaps it even had the power to intervene in events and control their outcomes. It might even be able to grab hold of time and space in a way Humanus didn't understand and twist it such that future and past could meet in a continuum.

But what kind of space and time would allow that to happen?

A scream, like a white hot light, seared across Humanus' thoughts.

He crouched reflexively and turned to see if Kesi was all right.

Kesi lay flat on the ground, his hands covering his head. He stared at Humanus and indicated with a shift of his eyes that the sound had come from up ahead.

The initial scream degraded into a terrified wailing, accompanied by a loud thrashing in the bush, a heavy thump, and then quiet. When nothing further happened, Humanus stood and eased himself through a thick tangle in the direction of the sounds, his spear at the ready.

He peered into a small clearing. At its center, Gomo lay on his back. A bear-dog straddled him.

Upon seeing Humanus, the bear-dog hunched down. A snarl pulled back blackened lips tinged with blood, showing gleaming teeth.

Normally, Humanus would have been no match for the animal, but Kesi barged in behind him and raised his club.

Vacant eyes flicked to Humanus, then to Kesi, probably calculating odds--take the kill and risk an attack, attack what seems to be a superior group, retreat and await another day.

The bear-dog chose the latter, turning and bounding into the cover of the bush.

Humanus dropped his spear and rushed to Gomo's side.

The evil one contorted in agony, emitting mewing sounds while pushing ineffectually at the ground beneath him. His stomach had been ripped open. Intestines lay strewn in ropey chaos. A long gash to his neck oozed blood. His arms twisted at unnatural angles.

Not knowing what to do to help, or even if anything could be done, Humanus leaned in close. "What happened?"

Surprisingly, Gomo was still conscious. "Dog. Dog." He twitched, trying to raise his hands but only managing to flop them onto his face where they smeared blood into his eyes.

Humanus suppressed his surprise at hearing Gomo's clear speech. He hadn't uttered another intelligible word since that long ago breakthrough. All that didn't matter, if he was about to die. "I

42

don't know how to help you. Your wounds are severe." Humanus thought to shove Gomo's intestines back into his stomach cavity when Gomo coughed a laugh that bubbled blood out of his mouth.

"Do death." He grimaced as he drew a bloodstained hand across his lips.

There it was again, an utterance that didn't make sense. It was as if someone or something was repeating a phrase, hoping to pound it into Humanus' mind. "Yes, you're dying." Humanus reached for Gomo's hands, thinking to still them. *What else can I do?*

Gomo yanked with a force that surprised Humanus. "I no fool!"

At first, Humanus felt a wave of panic as his emotions locked up. Then his mind stuttered to catch up. *Gomo in clear speech?* It was worse than before, or more accurately, better than before. *Where does this come from?*

The words wormed their way into his brain and pushed away all other thoughts. All compassion evaporated.

There is truly something evil here.

As Humanus looked on in wonderment, Gomo's wounds began to close. His intestines crawled back into his abdominal cavity. The edges of the gash on his neck pulled together.

Gomo stared the whole time at Humanus, a wry smile playing upon his lips. "Heh, heh, heh. I do death."

This time he said it with less force, almost a whispered affirmation of what was happening. Maybe of what was to come.

Humanus stood abruptly, almost knocking over Kesi, who had crowded close to see what was happening.

"Bad man," Kesi said.

"I do death," Gomo said, barely audible. He was now almost totally whole. He sat up and flexed his arms, pumped his legs and scratched his fingers across his taut torso.

"Let's get out of here." Humanus had witnessed a confirmation of Justin's surmise. Gomo was a player.

A shiver went up Humanus' back. He felt lightheaded. The contents of his stomach rushed out from his open mouth.

Kesi draped an arm over Humanus' shoulder. "Be sick?"

Another dry-heave contracted Humanus' diaphragm.

Zug was closer than he had figured.

Chapter Three

Humanus ran. He didn't care whether Kesi was able to keep up or not. All he wanted to do was get as far away from the evil Gomo as possible. Finally, out of breath, he stopped, hunching over his knees, gulping for air.

He had left the forest for the savannah, not a good place to be given it was the favored hunting grounds of carnivores like the saber cats and bear-dogs.

He sat on matted yellow grass and tried to control his breathing. Maybe he'd get lucky. Maybe no predator had witnessed his flight.

The sun sank toward the distant hills, touching their tops and sending bursts of light to reflect off low-lying clouds. Those dense with moisture remained gray blobs, but others lit up in a colorful array to the dying day, heralding the encroaching night.

He fumbled the guardian out of his pouch and clasped it.

What's going on?

He waited impatiently. *Why the delay?* Could one shout a thought?

"*Are you sure you want to know?*"

I wouldn't have asked if I didn't want to know.

"*It seems you are of many minds as regards the challenges that lie before you.*"

Many minds? Humanus snorted his derision. *I'm here. There's been a space and time manipulation that has placed Justin here, too. I just confirmed that Gomo is something other than a normal australopithecine, most probably a player, and you say I am of many minds?*

"*You needn't get so worked up.*" The guardian paused as if to ascertain whether or not Humanus was calming down. "*We have discussed Zug.*"

Humanus felt the now familiar contraction of his stomach. *You have discussed...Z...Zug. I'd rather forget all about him. It's bad enough that Gomo appears to be one of his players. You never said anything about players.*

"*Given our last conversation, mentioning players would only have made you more defensive. I hope you will still stand your ground, in view of what is about to befall you.*"

That sounds ominous.

"*Do you have any concept of where you are?*"

I know where I am relative to where I came from, Kanapoi, 1985. This place precedes 1985 by six million years. I also know I am in a universe I avoided with my every fiber before you brought me here. It was always a forbidden zone, a place once entered that was almost impossible to leave.

"*I am gratified you remember as much as you do. I brought you here to recuperate, to rehabilitate. Your confrontation with Zug was decimating. You needed a time and a place to regroup, to...how shall I put it, re-arm. Your sojourn through these hominids has enhanced who you are. But that enhancement has not been tested.*"

What am I to do? Confront Gomo?

46

"Forget Gomo. Zug has always had players strewn about this universe. They have searched for me, the Shepherd and you. Their success has been minimal and in the end of little consequence since they are not the ultimate challenge you must face."

I don't want to be tested. I'm fine just the way I am. I can deal with Gomo, he's a primitive.

"You only think you can deal with Gomo. Look at him as a preliminary test."

Humanus lay on his back and gazed at the darkening sky. The first stars winked on. What had seemed an infinite space now struck him as finite. Though he couldn't imagine an edge to the depths he contemplated, he knew if he were able to go far enough in one direction he would only end up where he had begun. Worse than that, according to what the guardian was saying, he would end up repeating what he had set out to do, endlessly, round and round. World lines curved into circles. No wonder it was called the forbidden zone.

Are you still there?

"Yes."

Tell me about Justin.

There was a long pause, one so long that Humanus thought he'd been forgotten.

"I will try."

***

I see a tree silhouetted against a dark looming sky. Its branches spread unnaturally. Its blossoms glow pink.

The primitive Jamil stares in wonder. But his wife, Rafiya, calls to him. She stands with their

47

young son, Jamani, and the clone, Justin, who is the same age.

Jamil trudges up to them and embraces Rafiya. Jamani clings to Jamil's legs. The clone remains detached. *Will he always be of blank mind*? Jamil wonders. How does one measure the age of a clone that came forth a child of ten and not an infant?

"Akilah lies dead," Jamil says. He motions back to the way he has come. A soft rise of a body disturbs the otherwise flat line of ice near the unnatural tree.

"Where Michael?" Rafiya asks.

Jamil points to the unnatural looking tree with the pink blossoms. "He be tree. Cardassin make him."

Rafiya nods with understanding.

Even though Cardassin is gone with the Shepherd, the results of his actions remain. The devastation he visited upon Jamil and his family has no excuse. Jamil knows he is harmless. He only wants to live out his days in the frozen waste. Fish in Lake Turk. Watch his son grow to manhood. He wants nothing to do with the mutants Cardassin fostered, the mutants who killed his parents and laid waste to his home.

Jamil does not understand why he is caught in the middle of a conflict between the forces of Cardassin and the Maraia. Jamil's people made the decision long ago to forego their Maraia roots and interbreed with sub humans. Being bad Maraia wasn't so bad until Akilah and the others appeared.

"I get body," Jamil says.

"Not safe."

48

"All dead." Jamil smiles despite his sorrow for the loss of Michael. He is now free to pursue his life, to spend time with Jamani and Rafiya. He looks over to the clone. What is Jamil to do with him?

When he reaches Akilah, he is startled by her appearance. He has seen dead people before, but she is different. Her features are corrupted by the mutating genes Cardassin sowed inside her. He wonders about the wisdom of even touching her.

In the end, he takes out his ice razor and melts a hole in the ice, then with his foot he nudges her body into the freezing water.

She sinks slowly, and the water dulls as it re-freezes. No ashes to ashes here in this frozen wasteland.

A yelp from Rafiya startles him.

He races back to her, his heart pounding as he sees a looming shape of a man standing next to her.

As he comes up to her, he takes out his razor and is prepared to cut the being in half.

"Wait," the being cries. "Don't hurt me."

Jamil recognizes Trudal, the Maraia traitor who was a seer for the hated Cardassin.

"I think you dead," Jamil says, ice razor pointing at Trudal's mid-section.

"I almost was. The mutants carried me away when they learned Cardassin was gone. They headed for Kanapoi, and at first I thought they were celebrating as I was. Then I realized they wanted to kill me because of my association with Cardassin."

"Should have," Jamil grumbles.

"We all had to survive the beast," Trudal pleads, spreading his hands wide. "Please don't kill me. Not now. I can help."

"How help?"

"I know things you do not. I can guide you. I can--" he glances at the immobile Justin. "--I can educate the clone."

Jamil isn't so proud as to dismiss the knowledge Trudal has. And if the odious worm wants to tend to the clone, then that would be one less person Jamil has to worry about.

"You can live. But I no want bother."

"I'll be no bother. Definitely, not a bother." Trudal smiles and extends a hand Jamil ignores. "That's okay...Jamil, is it? Yes, I thought so. Might I suggest we retire to the ruin and take stock of what supplies remain? There will be nothing left of Cardassin's compound at Kanapoi after the mutants are finished ransacking it. There won't even be any mutants left after a few days. With the nano-assemblers gone, they'll quickly die off."

"Nano..." Jamil reaches into his pocket and withdraws the cylinder he picked up earlier off the floor of the ruin. "Know this?"

Trudal stares, dumfounded. "That's a nano-assembler. Where did you get it?"

"Ruin."

Trudal reaches for it, but Jamil pulls it back.

"It will save our lives," Trudal says. "You know it has great powers."

"Don't know. It be a stick."

"It's hardly that. Here, let me see it."

Jamil is reluctant.

"I'm not going to run away with it," Trudal says. "I just want to see if it still functions."

Jamil hands the nano-assembler to Trudal, then peers as Trudal turns it over and thumbs flush-set buttons on its surface.

"It responds. We are saved." Trudal hands the nano-assembler back to Jamil with a broad smile.

***

"Whoa. One second," Humanus said out loud. "Who's this Trudal?"

"Trudal was a Maraia, who went over to the side of the player Cardassin."

If he was a traitor to his own people, then why is this Jamil trusting him?

"That trust hasn't been established. I thought I was clear on that point. Trudal did have a change of heart at the last moment, coming back over to the Maraia, but he still must prove himself to Jamil."

I guess Trudal did take Justin in and was responsible for his development and education.

"More than that, Trudal helped Jamil and his family survive the coming events, since he alone knew how to operate the nano-assembler."

That was my next question. What is a nano-assembler?

"It's a device that was designed and built by the Maraia. Properly programmed it can create just about anything. When the Maraia realized they had opened a...Pandora's Box...are you familiar with the expression?"

Yes.

"Good. When they discovered that, they put strict limits on what it could produce, things like no

51

lethal weapons and such. They didn't constrain its ability to alter genes, and soon it became very popular with those seeking to improve their genetic lines. Of course that led to disaster. The Maraia belatedly tried to shut down nano-assembler use, but it was too late. As a counter to the free-wheeling culture that indulged themselves with designer genes, the cult of the TrueMen was enhanced to keep the Maraia genome pure at all costs."

Okay, I get the nano-assembler. What's this ruin they keep talking about?

"The ruin was built shortly after your time in Kanapoi. Soon after you and Mia and the Shepherd left, a joint operation between the United States of America and the Kenyan government constructed an observation post to track the departure of the Shepherd."

The ruin still existed in 10,000 A.D?

"Yes, of course. By then it was obviously in ruin, but the original concrete and steel, stainless no less, was intact and probably good for another ten thousand years."

Humanus sat up. Justin and Jamani were ten years old in 10,000 A.D. Yet they were here, now, older. This was the first amazing fact of the whole narration. *Then the ruin could exist today.*

"It does. To the west."

Though astounded, Humanus forced himself to file the information away. Keep to the subject, he told himself. *You said the Shepherd had taken off with Cardassin, thus ridding these people of his threat.*

52

"The Shepherd left before Michael could reach him with Akilah. She had been mortally infected by Cardassin, and Michael had hoped to get her to the Shepherd for a cure. But the Shepherd left for the past with Cardassin on board."

Why would the Shepherd carry Cardassin away?

"To neutralize him. Players like Cardassin exist in specific time frames. Some of the time frames can be quite large. But Cardassin's wasn't. His spanned a mere 10,000 years. By transporting him out of his time frame he would cease to exist as an agent of Zug."

How far into the past did the Shepherd travel?

"About six million years, give or take a few."

Humanus was stunned. That would put him here, now, in this time frame assuming he traveled back the same way.

But that would deposit two Shepherds here in close proximity, the one that brought me and Mia and died, and the one that carries Cardassin. Are there two Shepherds?

"There is only one Shepherd. Actually, I'm surprised he hasn't shown up yet."

This didn't compute. *But he has. He's dead.*

"World lines, Gilomir. World lines. They might become tangled, but they never exhibit paradoxes."

So I could possibly see the Shepherd again in this time carrying Cardassin.

"I thought that assumption was implicit in what I said?"

Why would the Shepherd travel back here, anyway?"

"To insure your genome is preserved."

Humanus laughed. *Well, he needn't worry about that. Here I am.*

"Cardassin terminated the Gilomir/hominid genome the Shepherd carried. The only pure source that still exists is, as you have so astutely pointed out, you."

Something doesn't seem right.

"What might that be?"

The Shepherd had the Gilomir/hominid genome right where he was in Akilah, assuming he could have neutralized Cardassin some other way.

"Negative. Akilah had already been corrupted by Cardassin."

What about Jamil, or Jamani?

"Negative again. They represent primitives, or Maraia who mingled their genomes with devolved hominids in a hope to escape the control of the player Cardassin."

Humanus thought for a moment. *There were other Maraia. I presume they were killed when the mutants took over the ruin, but certainly the Shepherd could have extracted whole DNA from them.*

"They had been dead a while. There was no certainty their genomes would have remained intact, or pure given the trauma of their death."

Humanus did a mental double take. He wasn't a geneticist, but it seemed to him viable DNA could have been extracted. *What about Justin? He was alive and well and standing right there.*

"The synthetic Michael dumped organic material into a barrel and dropped in a nano-assembled pill of DNA. There's no confirming Justin is pure."

I don't buy any of this. There were plenty of ways for the Shepherd to restore the genome Cardassin destroyed, yet you have denied all of them.

"Very perceptive, Gilomir. If you must know the truth, I instructed the Shepherd to abandon his position in 10,000 A.D. and come here."

You did what? Why?

"I think you understand what I instructed the Shepherd to do. You may not understand the full reasoning for that instruction, but I don't expect you to, just yet."

But...but...

"Do you want me to continue the vision regarding Justin?"

Humanus slumped with exhaustion. It hadn't been easy absorbing the fast paced flow of information the guardian presented. He took in a deep breath and before he could let it out the vision continued.

***

I see Jamil pocket the nano-assembler. "We go to ruin. Take supply."

"That's an excellent idea," Trudal said. "There should be enough equipment in the ruin to provision us in the near term. When we have found a more permanent place to live, I can embellish it using the nano-assembler."

Jamil frowns at Trudal.

55

"Of course with your permission." Trudal gives a short laugh and looks away.

"Come." Jamil waves his arm over his head at Rafiya and the boys, then stomps off toward the ruin.

Climbing the escarpment to the top of the plateau proves to be more difficult than Jamil has imagined. "Ice melts."

Trudal thrusts his hand into a patch of slush. "I don't understand what is happening. We have thaws at this time of year, but nothing like this. Nothing so precipitous."

Once inside the ruin they begin to take stock of what supplies are left.

An ominous groan shakes the whole structure.

"An earthquake here?" Trudal looks about, alarmed.

Rafiya clutches the children.

Jamil rushes to the entrance and peers out. "No good. Must go. Now!"

They fall in behind Jamil as he scrambles on crumbling ice and stands atop the plateau. To his horror the ice on the plain below fractures. Long cracks rip parallel to the rock of the plateau, then the shards of ice slide toward Lake Turk.

"What happen?" Jamil turns to Trudal, for once relieved he has someone to ask about what is going on.

"I don't know. It appears to be a massive melt. I've never seen anything like it."

The ice beneath their feet trembles and shifts.

"We have to get out of here. If we stay we'll be swept into Lake Turk."

"Come." Jamil leads the way across the decaying ice on top of the plateau. He heads south, hoping to gain higher ground.

***

Humanus stared at the guardian in the palm of his hand. *So they abandoned the ruin. Where did they go?*

"They found higher ground. It was a wise decision. The waters of Lake Turk expanded with the ice melt, completely submerging the plateau and the ruin."

How did they survive?

"Fortunately, Trudal was true to his word. He operated the nano-assembler, so they never wanted for anything. He also took a personal interest in Justin and his education."

What happened to them, I mean the others?

"Years later, Jamil took sick and died. Shortly thereafter, Rafiya died. It was said her heart broke with Jamil's passing. Trudal lived to see Justin and Jamani into young adulthood, then he too succumbed. By then, the waters had receded and this land experienced a resurgence of growth."

You did this.

"As I said they returned to the ruin where they live to this day."

The guardian had ignored Humanus' accusation. Why? *Perhaps another time. But...did you say where they live to this day?*

"Did you not understand me?"

You said the ruin existed, but I didn't know it was home to Justin and Jamani.

57

"No, you wouldn't have known until I told you. Now you know."

I have traveled far and wide and never come across any plateau, much less one with a ruin atop it.

"You haven't gone far enough."

***

"Humanus." Kesi called low into the night.

"I'm over here." Humanus pocketed the guardian. Every time he visited the damn thing it showed him something troubling. At least this time he had learned where Justin and Jamani lived. The morning couldn't come soon enough so he could set out and locate the plateau.

Kesi stood over him. "Not good you here."

"I know. I just had to get away." Humanus stood and looked over the expanse of dark grass. "I guess we had better not press our luck. Let's get out of here."

"We hurry."

They walked side by side toward the jungle, glancing apprehensively left and right as they went.

"Did Gomo come back to the glen?"

"No see. No Gomo."

"You realize," Humanus said, "he's not like you. He's not even like me."

"Not like. Bad man."

The moon edged above the far horizon, sending ghostly rays across the landscape. At a distance, the dark shapes of elephants swayed, certainly asleep and not at all worried about predators. Of all the animals on the savannah, they alone had no natural enemies. Not much would change in six million years.

Somewhere in the far distance a saber cat huffed its throaty cry. Instinctively, Humanus checked the direction of the wind. They were downwind from the sound of the cat, not that it would help if there were a slight shift in the direction of the wind. Cats could sense prey from over a kilometer away.

Nearer by, birds called to one another in preparation for the night. Insects and tree frogs filled the air with a rhythmic pulsing. Normally, Humanus let the sounds pass through his mind barely noticed. But tonight the constant chatter was an irritant.

They came to the clearing that was home.

Humanus headed directly for his own shelter. Over the years he had become tired of what the other primates accepted as home. Buffeted by storms, assaulted by predators, Humanus had climbed into the forest canopy, dragging broken tree limbs behind him. These he had lashed together into a semblance of a tree house. It had a floor. It had walls that supported a roof structure that was covered with dried grass and palm leaves. Humanus' only regret was that he didn't have the tools to build something more substantial. What he had been able to garner from the forest was rotted trees that had fallen and other vegetation ripped from dead and dying plants.

The other primates hunched in a close circle as though they had been waiting for Humanus.

"What has happened?" he asked.

"No thing," Kesi said. "They wait. They be afraid. Want you make heat flower."

In the past, Humanus had lit a fire on cold nights to push back the chill. Since then, he had used fire to cook food and sharpen spear points. He was otherwise frustrated by his lack of resources. Even with the knowledge of how to improve their lot, he was handicapped without the requisite materials. But he also suspected any so called improvement would not necessarily be well received. They were still moving through the stages of evolution at an excruciatingly slow pace.

"I'm tired," Humanus said, hoping they would leave him alone.

"Baa!" Wakuru stepped to the center of the circle. He raised his hands over his head, then dropped them to clutch himself. He was obviously signing he was cold.

Humanus approached the elder primate. "You're cold aren't you?"

Wakuru nodded.

"And you want me to make a fire."

Wakuru nodded again. This time he cast a watery gaze up at Humanus.

Wakuru might have been a pet dog that gave its master everything and when it didn't get what it wanted knew the buttons to push to gain its ends.

"Okay. You win. How can I refuse a look like that?"

Wakuru pulled back his lips in a wide smile and bounced up and down in anticipation.

Humanus went to the clutch of rocks he used to keep embers alive, but someone had dislodged them and the coals were cold. He retrieved a hardened stick and a soft wood slide and some fine kindling. As he rubbed the stick back and forth, the others clustered around in awe. He soon had the slide smoking, then an ember leapt from the end of his stick and ignited the kindling. He carefully rolled the kindling to catch the heat of the ember and it burst into flame.

The assembled primates released a pent-up sigh.

Wakuru stepped to the fore and reached his arms out, fingers spread toward the rising glow. "Baa," he said.

Humanus wondered why that was the only sound Wakuru could utter, but he was an old primate and wasn't about to change what had worked for him in the past.

Humanus transferred the kindling to larger twigs and when they caught he blew on the fire. He sat back and let Kesi, who was much pleased by all of this, add larger branches. The light pushed back the looming dark and gave immediate warmth. The primates circled around and stared unfocused into the fire.

Humanus wondered if it had always been this way. Man's fascination with fire.

"I'm going west tomorrow to find the plateau where Justin and Jamani live," Humanus said to Kesi. "Do you want to come?"

Kesi pulled his gaze away from the flames. "I come." Then he looked into the fire with a sad expression, perhaps one of resignation about things to come.

Chapter Four

The morning dawned gray and damp, the tail end of the dry season, the beginnings of the monsoon. The rains would come, the rivers would swell and the savannah would turn green. The grazing animals would also return, as would the carnivores that preyed upon them.

Humanus roused Kesi, who slept draped over a branch high in the tree canopy. "I'm going now. Are you coming or not?"

Kesi opened his eyes and stared, unfocused. "Eat?" he asked.

"I've got food." Humanus thrust out his hands to show a clutch of bananas and a pomegranate. "We can eat as we walk."

Kesi glanced at the offerings and didn't look too happy about it. He stretched, yawned, then scratched under his armpits. After relieving himself off the branch, he swung easily to the ground and waited for the more clumsy Humanus to join him.

Humanus shoved his friend's shoulder as much to acknowledge Kesi was the better climber as it was a playful sign of their camaraderie. He glanced at the sky with its low-hanging clouds. "I hope the rain holds off until we get back. I don't much like walking wet."

By mid-morning the clouds had lifted. The sun baked the land with suffocating heat made worse by the moisture in the air. Now and then, distant thunder rumbled across the plain, followed often by the cry of a startled animal, a saber cat huffing in the distance, an elephant trumpeting nearby, or a baboon barking for some unknown reason.

Humanus took it all in. This was the world he inhabited, a veritable menagerie of sounds, underlain by the steady buzz of cicadas.

"Why are they always there?" Humanus asked Kesi in frustration.

"Don't know. Buzz is buzz."

"Sometimes I forget it's there, then I hear it and can't focus on anything else. It can drive you crazy."

Kesi lagged behind, forcing Humanus to stop periodically for him to catch up.

"Hot," he'd say each time he came abreast of Humanus, then without changing stride he'd continue past on a line west where the elusive plateau was supposed to be.

At mid-day they came to a shallow gorge that cut across their path. At its bottom a trickle of water flowed, one of the many tributaries to Lake Turk. In another week, the gorge would swell with runoff from the rains and be almost impossible to cross.

Now, crossing would be easy, but they'd still have to be on the lookout for predators. Where there was water, there were always animals.

Humanus held up a hand that they should stop. They were twenty meters from a watering hole and still in high grass.

"We can take water from there if it is safe."

Kesi, ever vigilant, scanned the surroundings. "No animals."

"I don't see any either."

Humanus stepped from the cover of the grass and approached the pond.

A bear-dog lunged at him from out of nowhere.

Bear-dogs. They seemed to be everywhere.

Humanus stumbled back, knowing a bear-dog could be negotiated with. This one seemed immature.

"Arrf! Arrf!" Humanus cried, regaining his footing and feinting at the snarling beast.

It recoiled. Its resolve seemed to dissipate.

Humanus waved his spear and sent the animal on its way.

Kesi came up behind him and clapped him on the back. "Gone."

"Yeah, he's gone. But I think we were lucky this time. Let's get our water and be on our way."

"On way."

The savannah rose to the northwest of them. A herd of ugly, ungainly wildebeests ranged like a dark cloud across a field of dry yellow grass. The low rumble of their pounding hooves could be felt even at this distance.

"Good," Kesi said.

"Yes, it is good for you and your people. There will be more meat in the coming days. But where there's game there are predators."

Kesi nodded. He crouched down, looking from one side to the other.

"I don't think we have to worry, just now," Humanus said with some humor.

Kesi stood upright and frowned as if offended.

"At least," Humanus said, "if there's a saber cat lying about, he'll be more interested in those cows than in us."

They trudged on through the all-encompassing heat. Humanus gave in to Kesi's pace and eventually both of them pushed through the tall grass abreast of each other.

A green canopy of trees loomed before them. It was a welcome barrier for buried in the depths of such foliage must be a river, a river that would cool them, a river that might offer a fish or two.

Humanus pushed through outlying bush and skidded to a halt when he came to the river bank. "I knew it."

Kesi flopped down on the sloping bank of the river and scooted his feet into the water. "I like."

"Yeah, I like it, too," Humanus said, sliding down beside him. "There are fish here." He pointed.

"Much fish."

Humanus stepped into a calm eddy. "Watch," he said. "I'm going to fetch us lunch."

Kesi peered intently as Humanus raised his spear and thrust it at a fish.

The spear missed the fish by a wide margin.

Kesi grunted, the lowest form of communication, a sound easily interpreted as disapproval.

"It's tricky," Humanus said defensively. "The water refracts the image of the fish, so it's not where you think it is. You have to spear a little higher, sort of where the fish isn't. Like this!"

The spear darted into the water and came up with a fish flapping at its end.

Humanus was well pleased at his effort. "Now, you try."

Kesi gripped his spear, his eyes darting back and forth, following the abundant swarm of fish in the pool. He stabbed, then brought the spear out of the water with a fish at the end.

He drew back his lips, exposing his teeth in a wide grin.

Humanus clapped him on the back. "Good job!" It always amazed him, the dexterity of these primates and how quickly they learned complex tasks.

Kesi pulled the fish off the end of the shaft and tossed it onto the bank next to the one Humanus had caught.

He had turned his attention back to the water, when a cracking twig on a bush gave him pause.

A saber cat moved in silent slow motion out of the undergrowth toward their fish.

"Hey! Get out of here," Humanus cried waving his arms, then immediately regretted the action.

The cat's dull eyes shifted from the fish to the two of them, presumably calculating that either one would make a better meal than the fish flopping on the river bank.

The cat lunged at Humanus.

He threw his arms up, as the force of the attack propelled him backward and deeper into the river.

Water closed over his head. The saber cat pressed down on him, a dead weight pushing him under.

Air escaped Humanus' laboring lungs. He fought to regain the surface.

The cat twisted. Strong claws thrust at Humanus' body, then jerked frantically, followed by a stiffening.

Humanus swam out of the way of the cat that was suddenly immobile and sinking. His head breeched the surface.

A fishing spear stuck vertically out of the lion's back, a clean kill, through the shoulder blades penetrating to the heart.

Humanus gasped for breath, wiping water from his eyes.

Kesi crouched on the shore, gripping his knees and looking forlorn.

Humanus clambered out of the river and rushed to Kesi. "You did it!"

But Kesi wouldn't have anything to do with the comfort Humanus offered. He began to shake and made a mewing sound.

The lion's body floated out of the pool and into the main flow of the river.

Humanus crouched next to Kesi and put his arm around him. "You saved my life."

He nodded.

Humanus sat for a long time with Kesi until he stopped shivering.

The sun had reached zenith and begun its descent when they crossed the river and continued their trek.

The outlines of a distant plateau came into view.

At first, the formation seemed an inconsequential line on the horizon, but as they marched, it loomed larger.

Shear walls of red rock rose from the flat plain. Its north end pointed toward Lake Turk, then scaled back to the south until the rising elevation of the savannah merged with its top.

About a third of the way from the north end, an unnatural looking structure crusted its surface. The ruin.

***

Humanus levered himself over the last meter onto the top of the plateau, then he turned and gave Kesi a hand up.

He stood and viewed the surrounding countryside. It seemed he was standing on the deck of a ship, surrounded by a yellow sea of grass. In the far distance to the north, the waters of Lake Turk shimmered in the afternoon sun. A ribbon of dark green jungle, following one of the rivers that fed the lake, snaked away to the east. Low hanging clouds, laden with the monsoon rains, bunched farther south.

The plateau itself was bare of vegetation and strewn with broken rock and sand. At its northern end a squat gray structure stood out in contrast to the red, iron rich ground. The ruin bulked low, with black rectangles showing where windows must have once been.

"There it is." Humanus pointed. "It looks ominous."

Kesi shook his head. "I stay. No like."

68

"Come on. The only ones who are supposed to be there are Justin and Jamani. I don't think they will hurt us."

"You go. I wait." Kesi sat down.

Humanus realized there would be no arguing with him, so he started off toward the ruin. He'd only gone a short ways, when Justin emerged from what must have been the ruin's entrance.

He waved a greeting and hollered. "I wondered when you would find me."

Humanus didn't know what to make of the man's ambivalent reclusiveness. Perhaps it was born of having lived alone with Jamani so long, surrounded by a hostile environment and other primates less intelligent. "You said you wanted to talk again."

"I did. But I'm not sure I'm prepared to learn any more than what you've already told me. It's only slightly past midday. Won't you and Kesi join us for a meal?"

"Thanks, but we've eaten, and Kesi doesn't want to come any closer than he is." Humanus indicated Kesi, who remained on the edge of the escarpment thirty meters away, staring at the landscape below.

"Then let him be," Justin said. "He's much like Jamani, wants to keep things simple. But you and I both know things aren't always simple."

Humanus glanced at Justin, wondering what he meant by that. Probably that things were about to change and it would be best if they could act in concert rather than at cross purposes.

Humanus fell in step with Justin. "You've never used the guardian, have you?"

"Of course not." Justin smiled down at him. "It was long gone by the time I had any clear knowledge of it. I'm not sure I'd want to use it even if I could."

"I have used it since we last talked, and it has told me much about what has happened here. It has told me about the rapidly changing climate and your exodus. It told me the ruin survived the floods and storms, and that you now live here."

"If it can tell you that, then it must know everything."

"It probably does. But getting information out of it is another matter."

They came to the ruin's entrance.

A heavy wooden door hung from steel hinges anchored with metal spikes into the aged concrete. Humanus had only a moment to wonder about the construction when Justin stepped aside and indicated he should enter.

Humanus scanned the interior of the ruin. A sense of shock was his first impression. Here were things from another time, another world.

The windows which had seemed dark rectangles from afar were indeed windows, sealed with a translucent material that resembled glass, but looked less clear. Thick but well-worn carpets covered the floor. Positioned about were wooden chairs, tables of rather ornate design, potted plants, what looked like a cooking area given the stack of pots and pans, and two beds covered with garish spreads and a cluster of embroidered pillows.

Humanus found himself reaching back through memories gleaned from Mia for the earthly words needed to put these objects into context. "Where did you get all of this?"

"Some of it is very old. Some of it we made with Trudal's help using the nano-assembler. Some of it we scavenged from Cardassin's Kanapoi." Justin peered at Humanus. "You do know about Trudal?"

"Yes. The guardian has told me." Humanus spied some things that looked decidedly metallic. "What's over there?"

Justin gave a detached look to where Humanus pointed. "Just assorted knives and forks we hauled from Kanapoi. I didn't see much point in doing it, but Jamani had some fixation with metal."

"Could I have a look?"

"By all means, look. It's a pile of junk as far as I'm concerned."

Humanus knelt and sifted through an assortment of knives and other implements, the uses of which he could not identify. He clutched and raised what might have been called a machete in 1985. So much for knives and forks. "Could I borrow this for a few years?"

Justin laughed. "Of course. This stuff is already rusting to bits. If you can use anything here, take it."

"Thanks." Humanus slid the long blade into his belt. When Justin looked at him quizzically, he thought to divert the conversation. "Cardassin lived in Kanapoi? Why? It was a dump."

71

Justin dragged his gaze away from the long blade, a smile on his lips. It was obvious he knew what the knife must represent to Humanus.

"What you knew of Kanapoi in 1985 might have been a dump, but when Cardassin lived there it was a paradise supported by the fruits of nano-assemblers."

"The guardian told me the climate was severely cold. Kanapoi a paradise?"

"But it was. An artificial bubble enclosed the entire place. A faux sun shone night and day. Liquid water gurgled from artificial springs and fed a lake where water fowl swam. Kingfishers and cormorants glided through the air. On the banks, trees hung with fruit. Cardassin and his cohorts lived in lavish tents up from the water's edge."

"These nano-assemblers seem to be wonderful tools."

"They are if used properly. But they can also be the instruments of evil."

"I learned you still have one."

"I do. But I was never taught how to use it. Trudal kept that knowledge to himself."

"Why would he do that?"

"He probably didn't trust us to not turn on him, given his history, his close association with Cardassin. I tried to dissuade him of those fears. But his paranoia ran deep."

Jamani emerged from a tunnel at the back of the ruin.

"Ah, Jamani, we have a guest."

Jamani grunted and walked past them. "I go hunt."

Justin shrugged and lifted his hands in resignation. "Kesi is outside. Why don't you take him with you?"

Jamani didn't indicate he had heard and continued out the entrance.

"We'll probably get more said if we are alone. Would you like to see the rest of what we have here? There's a lot of history associated with this place."

"It's odd you should say that. Everything that happened here was after my time. But thank you. I'd like that."

"You'll have to excuse an old man. I tend to forget your exact place in the time line of things."

"I excuse you." *What else can I do? The old guy is rummaging around my brain and coming up with all sorts of stuff.*

Justin walked to the end of the passageway Jamani had just exited. "This leads to a tunnel that penetrates the plateau west to east. It was built a long time ago and remarkably still survives in this age. Personally, I don't go here very much. I was told I was born there, in the depths of the tunnel, though of course I have no memory of the event. It's also the birth place of A4-Ni and her launch site."

"What is this A4-Ni? I've heard her name put forth, and I still don't know what she is."

Justin scratched at the stubble of his beard, a gesture Humanus interpreted as the prelude to very serious talk. "My ancestors built A4-Ni and primed her with their genome. They hoped A4-Ni, who was nothing more than an artificially intelligent, self-replicating machine, would carry their heritage out into the universe to prosper."

"That seems a very noble effort."

"Of course it was," Justin said. "But no one ever knew what became of A4-Ni. That you spoke of her is still a point of confusion."

Humanus looked around at the confining walls and ceiling. "If A4-Ni launched from here, how did she get out?

"Good question. The roof there--" Justin pointed. "--opened and A4-Ni was able to take off."

"It looks intact to me, now."

"Yes, I suppose it does. I don't know what happened to this place after we abandoned it. Perhaps the roof collapsed back on itself."

Humanus raised an eyebrow. It wasn't that Justin was stupid, but there seemed to be memories he chose not to revisit.

"You returned to this ruin when the waters receded. Things had changed that quickly?"

"They did. The weather warmed to what it is today. The grasses returned. So did the animals that feed on the grasses and then the animals that feed on them."

"There weren't any animals during the ice age?"

"There were animals then," Justin said, "but not like these. I don't know where the grazers came from."

"They just started popping in out of nowhere?"

"They must have, though I never saw any of them do it."

Humanus pondered what must have happened. The guardian hadn't been explicit about its control of events, but it was obvious the guardian somehow reached in and wrenched the world around to its liking.

"I think I understand," Humanus said, "though even I don't know how it can be done. The part of me that is not human was brought here by the guardian. When I say here, I mean what you call this universe. It was known to me as the forbidden zone, a place to be avoided. But something happened to me that I cannot elaborate on for lack of human words to explain, and the guardian had brought me here to recuperate. I needed a refuge. The guardian deemed this was the place to go.

"It is not a normal place, and hence its moniker as the forbidden zone. All world lines here curve in circles and begin again. There is no *out* here, only *in*. Everything that happens here will happen again, not in exactly the same way, but well within the variations allowed by the closed world lines."

Justin scowled at the information. "I'm trapped in an eternal cycle?"

"Worse than that, you, and I mean all Homo sapiens, are trapped in an eternal cycle you were not meant to see or given the intellect to comprehend."

"But we are conscious beings."

"You were not meant to be. It is only the introduction of my DNA that has made you conscious and given you the sight to look out at this abomination of a universe and wonder."

Justin stared at Humanus for a long time. "I have often questioned why we are here. If what you say is true, and I have no reason to doubt you, then we humans and the Maraia are a mistake, a fortuitous creation."

"You could look at it that way, and you wouldn't be far from the truth. You Maraia built A4-Ni, who spiraled out of control and arrived two million years from now, your Maraia genome dead. She encountered the Shepherd and the guardian who carried my alien DNA, stole it and inserted it into the descendants of these primitive australopithecines you see around you now. They evolved into conscious humans and then the Maraia. So it isn't so much as a mistake, as a tragedy, endowing beings with a sight they do not know how to use."

"And what is to become of us?"

"That remains to be seen. You are the last of the Maraia. I am the last of a pure *Gilomir*/hominid combination. The guardian has plans for me, but I don't know what they are."

Justin stared, an old man trying to understand complex things. "Come. I tire of this history." He waved a hand into the air as if to say he didn't understand any of what Humanus was talking about, then retraced their steps to the main room of the ruin and showed Humanus to a chair beside one of the tables. He took another chair opposite and pushed a bowl of fruit toward Humanus. "Help yourself."

To Humanus, Justin seemed to have aged in the short time Humanus had known him. Was all this information bearing down too heavily on the poor guy? Humanus reached for a banana. "You said you had a nano-assembler."

76

Justin took a small cylinder from a sack at his hip.

"Here it is. If I knew how to use it, we could make this world an even better place to live. I don't even know if it still works."

"May I?" Humanus reached for the nano-assembler. It seemed simple enough, but advanced technologies always looked simple and usually never were. At least that was the residual memory he held from his hominid father, Lohner.

Humanus slid his thumb over flush set buttons.

The cylinder lit up and a small screen started to scroll text.

Startled, Humanus handed the cylinder back to Justin.

"That's as far as I've ever gotten with it," Justin said. "It's easy enough to turn on and off, but what does one do with it when it starts going crazy?"

"A pity." Humanus felt unnerved. "Maybe the guardian knows how to operate it."

Justin brightened. "I'd bet my life the guardian knows. Ask it."

Humanus withdrew the guardian and clasped it.

Can you tell me how to operate the nano-assembler?

"*Yes.*"

How? Silence. *I asked how?*

"*There is no need for you to know.*"

But it would improve our living conditions.

"*Perhaps.*"

Humanus thought some more, but didn't receive any further response from the guardian. Frustrated,

77

he returned the guardian to the pouch around his neck. "It knows but doesn't want to tell me."

Justin looked bewildered. "I wonder why."

"I do, too. I suppose you and me knowing how to work the nano-assembler at this point in time doesn't fit in with its plans for us."

"A manipulator."

"Exactly," Humanus said. "That corroborates what I know about you being here. You said the Shepherd left you and your family in 10,000 A.D. shortly before the ice started melting."

"That is correct. I have no idea where the Shepherd went."

"The guardian told it to come here."

Justin looked queasy. "With Cardassin?"

"It seems a player like Cardassin can be neutralized if he is transported out of the time frame in which he was initially programmed to exist. From what the guardian said, Cardassin's time frame was rather limited, maybe 10,000 years."

"Then the Shepherd didn't have to come all the way back, or is it up, to here to neutralize Cardassin."

"The guardian said the Shepherd had to come here because that is where I was, and I represent the purest form of the *Gilomir/*hominid amalgam."

"But we Maraia are also pure. The Shepherd made us and we, in accordance with our faith, kept our genome pure. Granted, the others could have been corrupted. But I am pure, at least as pure as one can be. Maybe the guardian thought you would be more pure?"

"I came here directly," Humanus said. "Your Maraia genome has been moving through thousands of years. Even if your ancestors didn't do anything to adulterate it, it could have degraded through natural causes. I never got a straight answer out of the guardian. When pressed, it simply said it wanted the Shepherd here. We are both here. Maybe we reinforce each other."

"I don't like the sounds of any of this. It's as if events are converging, and you and I are at the resulting focus and don't have a clue about what is going on."

Humanus hefted the guardian. "Want to give it a go?"

Justin eyed the guardian suspiciously. "You think it would respond to me?"

Humanus shrugged. "You'll have to try."

"What do I have to do?"

"You just hold it and think about whatever you like."

Justin took the guardian into his hand and closed his fingers over it. "Like this?"

"Like that."

"I'm not feeling anything."

"Maybe if I clamped my hands over yours." Humanus took Justin's hands in his and squeezed.

A dizzying rush followed.

"Yes, yes, I believe it is working now." Justin sounded alarmed. "I'm glad you are with me on this. I wouldn't be able to do this alone."

"What is it you want the guardian to show you?"

"I've always wondered about my namesake, Rasmussen." Justin looked like he might tear up. "I am Rasmussen, at least a clone of Rasmussen, and I know nothing about him except he died a horrible death at the hands of Cardassin. He also had a daughter."

"Akilah."

"Yes, that was her name. He had a wife, too. Her name was Cristina. No one ever told me what happened to her."

"Ask."

Justin asked.

***

I see the Truman Light, a fast flyer, descend precipitously out of low hanging clouds. It comes within meters of the icy plain below, shooting fast, heading south toward the ruin that was once Nairob.

At the controls is Gregory Rasmussen. He should be seated, but instead he stands, feet spread wide in a solid stance, his fingers moving rapidly over flush set keys.

"We have to gain altitude," the first mate shouts. "We can't maintain this speed and course in this storm without crashing."

"Trust in Sedroth," Rasmussen says calmly. He pushes a lock of brown hair from his forehead and parks it over an ear. "We may die with this flight, but we would certainly die at the hands of Cardassin's mutant pilots who pursue us."

He glances at a monitor hanging from brackets bolted to the low ceiling. Vibrations rattling throughout the craft make seeing the monitor's image difficult. "It looks like the mutants have broken off their pursuit." Rasmussen gives the first mate a self-satisfied smile. "You may take her up to fifty meters."

"I will, Doctor, and be glad to do so."

"You best watch your tongue," Rasmussen says. He casts a glare at the first mate, a man twenty-five years younger than Rasmussen's forty-five.

"My apologies," the first mate says. "We are coming up on Nairob."

"What is the status of the storm?"

"The snowfall is intensifying. Cross winds at forty knots. We'll have to rely on the auto-guide to land us."

The craft levels at a height of fifty meters and skews sideways, but gives them a view of what was once a bustling city, once, thousands of years ago, a whole climate change ago. Now, nothing remains but gray rubble, locked into a matrix of snow and ice.

But there is hope for the future here, despite the existence of proto-humans, the devolved remnants of Homo sapiens. They have long occupied the city, living under its collapsed walls, running through dark tunnels like rats.

Rasmussen hopes to join forces with other Maraia, who earlier rejected his rule as the leader of the cult of TrueMen. They immigrated south to establish their own colony. He knows he now has no better hope of escaping, much less repelling Cardassin's mutants than to form an alliance and seek refuge in the one place few were willing to inhabit.

Rasmussen points to a screen showing the layout of the city. "The airport is to the west. It will probably afford the smoothest place to land." He taps a finger on the screen. The auto-guide locks onto the coordinates.

"The tarmac must be long gone by now," the first mate says.

"No doubt it is. But the ice should be smooth. We'll have to retro-boost quickly to not overshoot."

A diminutive woman enters the control room and leans heavily against the doorway. She is very pregnant and near term.

"How much longer, Gregory?" she asks. "My contractions are coming once every two minutes."

"We'll be down in three. Buckle yourself in for landing."

"But you are still standing."

"Cristina, please."

The woman returns to the passenger compartment.

"You are risking a lot here, if I dare to say so," says the first mate.

Rasmussen nods grimly and steps to his crash chair, lowers his athletic frame into the seat and pulls the harness over his shoulders. "Buckle up."

"Aye."

The auto-guide system engages, and the Truman Light descends precipitously toward the surface. A moment later, the craft lands with a heavy bump and slides across slick ice. Retro-boosters thunder, turning the craft almost sideways before computers adjust the thrust and bring it to a stop.

"Quickly now. We can't trust that the mutants haven't found another way to track us."

The first mate presses an alarm button that releases a repetitive pinging, signaling evacuation. The emergency door opens, and the Maraia in the passenger compartment pile out.

Rasmussen is well ahead of them on the ice. He is met by a contingent of Maraia men.

"We are holed up in the ruin of the terminal," one of them shouts. He points to a hulking collapse of concrete walls. Dark corridors penetrate into the interior. "This way."

"Get the women and children safe," Rasmussen calls back to the TrueMen in the flyer. "Then we must push the flyer into the lee of that collapsed hanger and unload what supplies we have. We'll melt ice onto the top of the flyer to camouflage it."

The group hurries toward the dark corridors, some dragging their young by the hand, others carrying them.

"We'll set up a perimeter, just in case," a Maraia says. He motions at three Maraia men in the crowd and indicates they should square off around the flyer, ice razors drawn.

Five minutes later, after securing their women and children, the TrueMen return. As ants will converge on a large crumb of bread, they attach themselves to the flyer and heave. Once the initial frozen contact with the surface is broken, the flyer slides easily toward the hanger and bumps to a stop.

Quickly, men swarm across the flyer, removing supplies and piling them on the ice. When the craft is empty they climb on top of the wall and melt overhanging ice onto the flyer. In moments the melt refreezes.

With the flyer secure, Rasmussen heads for the terminal.

A shot from an ice razor cuts into the blowing storm.

Rasmussen runs to a clustered group of men who stand staring down at a body on the ground. "What has happened here?"

A young man steps forward and extends his hand to Rasmussen. "Welcome to Nairob, Doctor. My name is Ferral." He shakes Rasmussen's hand.

"I asked what happened here," Rasmussen repeats.

Ferral shrugs indifferently. "A proto. He came out of nowhere, yelling and screaming and waving his arms. I cut him down. Better safe than sorry."

Rasmussen peers at the downed figure. "A proto. It's not a good sign they're already on to us. Let's hope he isn't the head man's son or something. We have enough trouble on our hands with the mutants. We don't need protos gnawing at our backsides."

"We best be getting inside," Ferral says. "All the corridors that give access to the outside have been sealed. It's a defensible space."

Rasmussen wonders about the lack of compassion from Ferral, but chooses not to address it. After all, this terminal is going to be their home for a long time. It is away from the city proper and should give them a good distance from the protos.

He enters the ruined terminal with Ferral and climbs a broken stair at the southern end to what was once a mezzanine. From there he has a view of the ruined city beyond.

Nothing remains but gray tumbled shapes, drifts of snow and ice. Here and there a light glows briefly, probably an unguarded fire from a proto hangout. They remain intelligent enough to make fire, but that is about all.

A broad avenue cuts through the distant ruin and disappears into the mist. An avenue like that in its prime would have been lined by blocky buildings. People and vehicles would have crowded its lanes. Purple and red bougainvillea would have cascaded from balconies. Bright flowering trees, yellow acacias, flame trees, *peltophorum africanum*, red and orange would have lined the boulevard.

Overhead, the sky would not have been dark and brooding, but blue, with puffy white clouds carrying moisture that would have fallen as rain, to thicken the air with an ensuing humidity.

A world lost long ago. Rasmussen shivers in the evening cold. The temperature has dropped below freezing. It warms during the day to slightly above freezing if the sun is out, otherwise, life is made miserable trying to keep warm.

There is reason to know what has come before if only to put into perspective what they have inherited. With any luck they will be able to change this world, defeat the mutants and their master Cardassin and reclaim this frozen waste for the Maraia.

A scream, coming from the depths of one of the dark corridors, pierces the air.

"Cristina!" Rasmussen returns to the main floor of the terminal, brushes past gaping women and falls to his knees beside his wife.

"It's a girl," she says.

A pale squirming infant lies cradled in Cristina's arms.

"She's very active," Rasmussen says. "Are you all right?"

"I'm fine. She entered this world quickly, like she was on a mission. We shall call her Akilah. You promised we could."

"Akilah is a good name." Rasmussen leans close and peers at the tiny figure. "She has your eyes." He brushes his hand over Cristina's sweat dampened forehead and gives her a kiss.

"I fear for her future, Gregory," Cristina says.

"I fear for all our futures. These are not the best of times, and I don't think they will be getting much better any time soon. But we are here and we will make of it what we can. Our faith must remain strong. Praise Sedroth."

"Praise Sedroth." Cristina lifts Akilah to a breast and induces her to feed.

Chapter Five

I see a razor shot fry the ceiling above Rasmussen's head.

He ducks amidst a cloud of pulverized concrete and a shower of sparks from ionizing reinforcing steel.

"Here they come!" Ferral shouts.

In the dim light, on the far side of the ancient tarmac, a shuffling line of mutants advances toward the Maraia defensive positions. As they come closer, individual mutants stand out. Some of them wear brightly colored vestments, here and there a red sash drapes diagonally from a shoulder, a chest hangs with military ribbons stuck directly into skin, a triangular hat cocks on a head.

The mutants jostle one another, their breath puffing in great clouds, their eyes bright belying the effects of drugs. Some stumble and fall down only to be stepped on by those advancing behind.

Rasmussen estimates over a hundred of them arrayed in ranks of a ten across and ten deep. Most of them carry ice razors. Some carry sticks. Others carry large chunks of ice.

With only twenty-five Maraia men including his own to go up against the hoard, Rasmussen begins to wonder if Ferral has though of an exit plan. The ragged line breaks into a shuffling run, ice razors blazing chaotically.

"They're crazy," Ferral says without emotion.

"Mutants don't think." Rasmussen checks his razor. "They do what Cardassin tells them to do."

Ferral twitches in anticipation. "Once they reach the perimeter we'll blow the explosives, then cut them down."

The line of disfigured beings closes on the outer markers the Maraia have set to indicate the line of explosives.

Their advance reminds Rasmussen of the way war was waged a long time ago, a rather quaint outdated form, where the goal was to survive withering fire and attrition, then triumph. They just might have given their four to one advantage in manpower.

"Steady," Ferral says.

The leading mutant line reaches the outer marker and crosses the perimeter.

The explosives blow.

The advancing line degenerates into disarray, littering the ice with limbs and other body parts, some flying through the air to plop grotesquely near the hunkered down Maraia.

Gaps in the front line fill with mutants from the rear.

"Open fire," Ferral says.

Rasmussen marvels at the calm in Ferral's voice, his lack of any emotion.

Red and blue streaks from Maraia ice razors meet the flashes from the mutants and weave a tightly stitched pattern across the intervening ice, the cascade of light almost festive, carnival-like.

Mutant razors rake the Maraia barricades, sending chunks of concrete flying, instantly vaporizing ice to steam. Cries of anguish rend the air from unlucky souls, who lurch backward, legs seared, and crawl to the rear.

Ferral glances to Rasmussen. "Interesting, they have industrial strength razors. They'll be able to breech our defenses."

"Then we have to fall back," Rasmussen shouts.

Ferral has binoculars to his eyes. "Who the hell is that over there? He looks to be a Maraia."

"It's probably Cardassin's seer, a Maraia traitor named Trudal. He went over to the other side before I was born."

"Did he mutate his genes?"

Rasmussen worries Ferral will get them caught if they don't start moving. "That's not been reported. He simply chose Cardassin over his own flesh and blood. Come on. We've not much time."

"Fokkin' traitor," Ferral sneers. "I'd like to take him out now."

"Don't waste your energy. Trudal is slime who's not worth the effort." He grabs Ferral's arm and heads for the terminal.

On the way back, a TrueMen emerges from a dark corridor and meets Rasmussen. "They've split up and surrounded the terminal. We've no way out."

"We'll set up defenses inside," Ferral says. "I don't think they'll try to enter. It's too defensible a space."

The Maraia regroup at a central space that was once an arrival hall. They split up into teams of five to ten men and set up to blast anything that emerges from the entrances.

89

The battlefield goes quiet.

"What's happening?" Rasmussen asks Ferral after they have climbed to a mezzanine that has a view over the hall and to the outside.

"It's hard to see." Ferral pans with the binoculars. "Great Sedroth, will you look at that guy? He must be two meters tall."

Rasmussen grabs the binoculars. "I've heard tales about a giant mutant. Cardassin must have gotten something right using the nano-assemblers."

"We could certainly use a nano-assembler about now," Ferral says.

"The situation is dire, Mister Ferral, but that is no excuse for blasphemy."

Ferral smiles cynically. "You TrueMen never were very realistic."

Rasmussen glares but does not want to engage Ferral in a debate as to why his parents chose to immigrate to Nairob and leave the cult of TrueMen behind, alone in Kanapoi, to contend with Cardassin. "Tend to your station, Ferral. I'll tend to mine."

The hulking mutant stands above the horde that has gathered around him as though he is going to ready them for another charge.

"He's waving a white flag." Rasmussen hands the glasses back to Ferral. "I think he wants to negotiate?"

"It could be a trick."

"We don't have much choice. It's only a matter of time before they overwhelm us."

"Then let's meet him somewhere away from the women and children." Rasmussen points to a clear area near the outer wall. "That has a corridor leading directly to it. We could meet him there, and if we're betrayed, still have a chance of bolting to safety."

Ferral draws a white cloth from his pocket and waves it in response.

A minute later they stand face to face with the giant in the close confines of the clearing.

"You obviously have us surrounded," Rasmussen says. "Why talk?"

"Me Igor," the giant replies with a grin. He thrusts out his hand and seems disappointed when Rasmussen refuses to shake it.

"What do you want?"

"How want to die?" Igor keeps the grin pasted on his face. "Fast? Slow? With pain?"

"Is that all?" Rasmussen takes a step backward toward the corridor, his hand out, sweeping Ferral along with him.

Screams of pain, sizzling blasts from razors echo out of the corridor.

Rasmussen turns as two mutants bolt from the dark interior.

Triumphantly, the first mutant holds the swaddled Akilah above his head.

Cristina staggers ahead of the second mutant, her arms outstretched, her garments torn and stained with the blood of afterbirth. "My baby," she wails. She falls and struggles to rise.

The second mutant grabs her hair and pulls. "Up!"

Rasmussen wheels and looses a bright beam from his razor that severs the mutant in two at the waist. He swings the razor in an arc to bear on the first mutant, who has stopped to gape at his twitching comrade, the baby Akilah still held high over his head.

A heavy sizzle from Igor's industrial razor flashes between Rasmussen and the mutant. "Enough."

Rasmussen thumbs his razor down and edges over to kneel beside Cristina. "Go back inside. We'll handle this."

"Not without my baby!"

Ferral comes to Rasmussen's side, razor drawn.

The steady burst from Igor's industrial razor cuts into the concrete floor, sending up an acrid smell of burnt lime.

He motions for Rasmussen and Ferral to step away from Cristina. When they refuse, he plays the beam to within centimeters of her head. "I kill her, then you, too." He motions again.

Rasmussen and Ferral take a step back.

Another mutant races forward and pulls Cristina farther away.

Igor snaps off his razor and relieves the first mutant of the swaddled Akilah. "Now talk." He beckons behind him and the robed Maraia traitor, Trudal, steps from the shadows.

"Good work, Igor." He holds up a restraining hand when Rasmussen starts to raise his weapon. "Let's be civilized here, Doctor, or is it Professor Rasmussen. There's no need for further bloodshed."

Trudal sets a small black box on the floor, flips a switch and steps back.

A wispy holographic image appears in front of them. A thin, dry man, wearing an oversized great-coat and wearing yellow boots trimmed in purple fur struts back and forth.

"My lord Cardassin." Trudal gives the image an elaborate bow. "We have captured the wife of the outlaw and his infant daughter."

Cardassin stops mid-stride, almost unbalancing himself. "You have, have you?" He claps his hands melodramatically, awkwardly as though he is on drugs. "That is excellent, my dear Trudal. What shall we do with them?"

"I thought you might tell us, my lord."

"Quite right. You are my seer, but you can't see so far as to see my intentions...or can you?"

"No, of course I cannot, my lord. And even if I could, I wouldn't."

"Well spoken, Trudal. Now, let's play a game."

"Me like games," Igor says without looking up. He is busy poking his finger at the infant.

Cardassin shifts his gaze to where Rasmussen stands. "Mister Rasmussen," he says, "or is it Doctor, or shall I just call you Gregory?"

"You can call me anything you want. I'm not going to deal with you. Give me back my wife and daughter."

"My, my, such impatience coming from such a learned person. I perceived you were smarter than that." He frowned in thought while stroking the end of his short beard. "Tell you what, I'll give you a choice. You may have one of these hostages back, your wife or your daughter. You decide. I will take the other and...what shall I say, toy with her."

"You beast. They are non-combatants. They have no part in the quarrel between us. I...beg you, if you wish. Please return them. You can take me instead."

"No. That's not in the rules." Cardassin picks his teeth with the side of a fingernail. "I don't have a lot of time to devote to this diversion. Miss Cristina, what say you? I do need an answer quickly."

"Gregory, I'll go! Take Akilah!"

"I can't let you do that."

"You have little choice," Cardassin says with a sneer. "I'm trying to be reasonable, here, but I feel resistance coming from you to play this game."

"Wait," Cristina cries. "You must take me. My husband means well but has been given an impossible choice. Take me!"

"Well, Gregory, I guess the woman has spoken. She would have been my preference, anyway. Not much one can do with an infant." Cardassin turns to Trudal. "Trusted seer, wasn't that an interesting game to play?"

"My lord, it was indeed. But I don't see why you should have to give up either one of the hostages, much less let this worrisome band survive intact."

"My, my, my, Trudal, you always did have a foresight that has been the object of my envy...what is it, Igor?"

"Sire, I have been told we are being attacked from the rear by protos."

Cardassin waved a hand in the air. "Please kill them."

94

"They swarm like rats. There must be thousands of them."

"Then we shall retreat and play another day." With that his image begins to fade. "Igor, do bring the lady along as well as the swaddled one, I have plans..." Then he is gone.

The massive mutant stomps over to the kneeling Cristina and grabs her hair with his free hand. The cradled Akilah squirms in his other arm.

Cristina buries her teeth into Igor's forearm.

The giant hisses with pain.

Cristina lunges for Akilah, grabs the blanket wrap with one hand and slides the bundled Akilah toward Rasmussen.

Razors drawn Ferral and Rasmussen converge on the tiny package.

Igor hesitates.

A rising crescendo of razor fire comes from outside.

"I go now." Igor back-steps, pointing his industrial razor at Rasmussen and dragging the hapless Cristina. He grins. "Goodbye."

Trudal is long gone, and Igor slips out of sight around a concrete abutment.

Rasmussen races after the giant.

Ferral tackles him before he can get through. "You can't go out there. That's just what they want."

"Screw what they want. I want my wife back."

"You'll only get yourself killed. Then where will your daughter be?"

Rasmussen struggles to stand and makes another charge for the corridor.

Ferral trips him, crawls over his struggling body and hits him hard in the face. "You stubborn fool."

Rasmussen's shoulders heave with sobs. "I'll never see her again."

"We've all known for a long time that death stalks us. Bide your time. Care for Akilah. We'll get Cardassin."

Rasmussen nods vacantly, tilting back his head to staunch the flow of blood from the blow to his nose. "I don't know if I'm a selfless hero or a spineless coward."

"We can decide that later. Right now, we have a terminal to secure."

***

Justin shook uncontrollably. He pulled away from the guardian and Humanus. "I didn't know. Yes, I did know. Cardassin was a beast. Trudal said so. But to that extent? And Trudal...he was no better, maybe even worse given he was one of us. I can't watch any more of this."

"I understand." Humanus started to pocket the guardian.

"What happened to Cristina?"

"I thought you were finished?"

"Yes...yes I am. I don't want to know. Yes, I do. Akilah survived. And the Maraia survived, at least long enough to come north and build A4-Ni. It took them over twenty years before they left Nairob. Why?"

Humanus fingered the guardian. "I could ask."

"Yes, do. But I don't want to be a part of it. Just tell me what it tells you."

Humanus closed his fingers around the guardian for a few moments. "It doesn't take long in real time." He tried to smile, but what was pouring into his mind wasn't pleasant.

"Well?" Justin clasped and unclasped his hands.

"They set up in the ruined terminal."

"We know that!" Justin shouted. "Sorry. I'm a bit out of sorts here. Please, ignore my outbursts. Proceed."

Humanus eyed the old man. *Is it worth telling him this? Will he gain something from it other than a lot of pain?*

"They continued to fortify the terminal," Humanus continued. "All the while the mutants mounted periodic attacks, which lessened over time as Cardassin probably lost interest. The protos always roamed the perimeter, looking for protein. A dead mutant or Maraia was as good a source as the rats they were used to.

"The nights were the worst. Protos slipped into the terminal despite the Maraia's best efforts to keep them out. Women disappeared without a trace. In desperation, some of the Maraia men snuck out to look for their women. Nothing was ever heard of them again. Maybe they were accepted by the protos. Maybe they were killed and eaten. It is known a mixed breed of Maraia and proto grew out of the exchange, a breed with the intelligence of a Maraia, the cunning of a proto.

"In the face of these kidnappings and defections, Rasmussen became more and more adamant they stay together, that they preserve their Maraia heritage and keep their genome pure.

"Eventually, the mixed bloods left Nairob, shunned by both groups. Cardassin's mutants didn't bother them, since it was the Maraia they were after. And the Maraia considered them damaged goods.

"Over the years, the Maraia managed to survive, but barely. Rasmussen became obsessed with the myths surrounding the burial place of Sedroth in the frozen north. It was said Sedroth was buried along with the guardian in a cave in a plateau beside Lake Turk.

"With his Maraia slowly dying off, he believed if he could discover Sedroth's grave and retrieve the guardian he would be able to build an artificial, self-replicating, universal constructor. If primed with their remaining genome, it could be sent out into the universe to sow the Maraia seed.

"The rest you know."

Justin wiped his eyes. "Jamani's people. They called themselves bad Maraia, a Maraia and proto mix."

"Yes, that's probably true. Have none of them survived but Jamani?"

"I wish they had." Justin shook his head, his face showing despair. "We barely survived. If there were any others, then they must have perished in the floods."

Humanus pocketed the guardian.

"You never answered my question about what happened to Cristina."

Humanus looked Justin in the eye, searching, wondering if the man was strong enough to know

98

the truth.   Perhaps it would be too much. "Cardassin transformed her genetically, then he toyed with her for years as he stated he would. Then she died."

Justin's eyes clouded with tears. He struggled for composure. "Yes, I see. Rasmussen and Ferral knew as much and could do nothing to save her. How did she die?"

"She suffered greatly.   In the end, after the Maraia had stormed Cardassin's Kanapoi, Akilah killed her."

"Akilah?"

"She was in her early twenties at the time. She didn't know the Maraia mutant she dispatched out of pity was indeed her mother.   Of course Cardassin and Trudal set it up, and chortled over the event."

Justin seemed shaken.   "To think I spent all those years with Trudal.   He knew what had happened all along. But he took a special interest in me, he schooled me, made me what I am today."

"Maybe it was a penance of sorts."

"It bedevils me how evil can transmute into good into evil."

Humanus placed a sympathetic hand on Justin's shoulder. "It's Yin Yang."

"Who?"

"It's an ancient Taoist expression describing the unity of opposites."

Justin shook his head in seeming disbelief. "How do you know these things?"

"I spent nine months in Mia's womb. When the Shepherd built her, he programmed her with all the knowledge and history of the planet he had been able to absorb, intercept, impugn, or learn. Mind you Earth, once hominids crossed the electro-technological threshold, became a prodigious emitter of everything and anything."

"Interesting," Justin said, looking up to the ceiling as if remembering. "Trudal seemed aware of the concept, this duality or at least something very similar. He was a thoughtful man, very much concerned about the evil derived through *Zug* and the latter's manifestation in Cardassin. He also knew about you from Sedroth, the *Gilomir* you, whom we Maraia embraced. He considered you good. And though the two seemed to me to be mutually incompatible, he spoke of them as mutually rooted. The two always making a whole."

"Trudal was indeed prescient. The guardian has reminded me of the same duality, of which the maximum effect of one has imbalanced the effect of the other. He has challenged me to reconcile the two."

"Of what you speak of is beyond my comprehension. But if the guardian has put this task before you, then it must have its reasons, and you must comply."

"I am thinking long and hard about what to do. In many ways, my life here has reached equilibrium, the days pass peacefully. Nothing save the occasional interference of Gomo mars my existence. I can deal with Gomo. Why should I take on *Zug*?"

Justin rested both his hands on Humanus' shoulders and looked him in the eye. "I can only offer passing counsel. If this imbalance, as you put it, exists, and the guardian has set it before you to fix, then I think you've got to do it. If Gomo and Cardassin are any indication of what the unopposed rule of *Zug* portends, then it is every good man's duty to rise against it. You are human, too. You owe it to the race, to the Maraia, to confront *Zug*."

Humanus frowned and pulled away. "I don't know that I owe anyone anything."

"You needn't be so cynical. If we are all trapped here, you are also here for a reason. You cannot be complacent."

Humanus blew out a breath of frustration. "You are wise in ways you cannot imagine."

"I only wish." Justin seemed to revert to the memory of the guardian's vision. "Dear god, Cardassin was an evil being. I beseech Sedroth that we never see the likes of him--"

Kesi rushed into the ruin.

"I thought you were afraid of this place." Humanus stood to receive him then realized from the look on Kesi's face that something had happened. "What is it?"

Kesi gesticulated out the entrance in the general direction from which they had come. "Smoke, Manus. At home."

"This doesn't sound good," Humanus said to Justin. "We've got to go." He grabbed his spear, checked the long steel blade at his belt and hurried out the door.

On the far horizon a column of light gray smoke curled upward against the pale blue sky.

Someone has messed with my embers.

***

101

By the time they had crossed the expanse of the savannah, the smoke had all but disappeared.

At the edge of the forest, Humanus slowed, indicating Kesi should fall in line behind him.

A thrashing sound came from the grass in front of them, then a male primate burst clear and ran past them, waving his arms hysterically.

Having sidestepped the crazed primate, Humanus looked quickly to Kesi, but he had flattened himself on the ground.

"We must hurry," Humanus said. "Something terrible has happened."

Throwing caution aside, Humanus ran to the glen. He clawed his way through the surrounding bush and skidded to a halt.

Vegetation smoldered, sending drifts of smoke across the clearing and making it hard to see what was going on. A break in the gray fog showed a cowering clutch of primates off to one side. On the other side were a number of the younger males. At their center and in front stood Gomo, his arm wrapped around the neck of a sagging Wakuru.

Gomo pressed a sharp stone against Wakuru's stomach and angled it up under his rib cage. He did not plunge the blade home, but its pressure was enough to breach Wakuru's skin and let loose a thin trickle of blood.

Wakuru's eyes darted wildly as though he knew something ominous was about to happen but was helpless to prevent it. He let out muffled barks, which only made the situation seem more surreal.

"Heh, heh," Gomo laughed. "Wakuru be do death."

102

Humanus drew the machete from his belt and raised it overhead. "Release him, Gomo, or you're the one be do death."

"Eh?" Gomo cocked his head and shoved the sharp stone another centimeter upward.

Humanus froze with indecision. He was too far away to deal a swift blow with the machete, and he wasn't so accomplished with his spear that he could hit Gomo and not Wakuru.

"Eh?" Gomo gave the stone a shove. It slid effortlessly into Wakuru's chest cavity.

Wakuru emitted a sharp yelp, then sagged in Gomo's grip. A gush of blood emptied over his hips and legs.

Gomo pulled his arm away and let Wakuru sink to the ground, his eyes fluttering, his limbs twitching.

Humanus screamed, giving vent to his rage.

"Heh, heh." Gomo picked up a stick and threw it at Humanus, who ducked.

Humanus lunged at Gomo, aiming the long blade at his neck.

Two of Gomo's young bloods leapt in front of him, arms raised, ready to give up their own lives to save his.

Humanus stopped his charge and stared in shock. "What's this?"

"They be mine." Gomo showed stained teeth in a wide grin as he peeked over the shoulder of one of his men.

"Kesi." Humanus motioned for Kesi to come up alongside him.

Kesi moved in close in a crouch, rigidly alert, club raised. "Gomo bad, Manus. These be bad. We go."

Humanus did a quick survey of the other primates. They seemed ambivalent, not knowing with whom to take sides.

Gomo jumped up and down in a taunting dance. "Kill me. Heh, heh. Kill me." He back-flipped once, then again, and tumbled into the bush. After frenetic thrashing, the sound of his retreat lessened, followed by silence.

Cries of anguish rose from the other primates as they rushed to Wakuru.

Humanus pushed through and fell to his knees next to Wakuru's still form. An ache clutched at his chest, an ache he had not known even when his mother had died. Wakuru had been a father to him. "You're a dead man, Gomo." Tears stung his eyes and streamed down his cheeks.

Others in the group were also crying. Two of them drooped their arms over Humanus' shoulders in a show of sympathy.

"Where did he go?" Humanus demanded, standing abruptly and grabbing his spear.

Kesi gave him an anxious glance. "Leave for now, Manus. Not good." He grasped Humanus' spear with both hands and struggled to take it away from him.

Humanus yanked the spear back. "I'm going to kill him."

He ran out of the clearing and into the forest in the direction Gomo had taken. Thick bush impeded his way, scratching, clawing, slowing his pursuit.

In frustration he screamed and slashed at the vegetation with his knife in a fury that did little to help his progress, but managed to dissipate his anger.

He came clear of the forest and fell into the tall grass of the savannah. He rolled onto his back, letting cool wind caress his body.

His chest heaved as he gulped for air. He stared unfocused at the sky, black with puffy clouds illuminated by the full moon.

An odd hissing sound drew his attention. High overhead, out of the constellation Cygnus, a bright light descended rapidly. *A meteorite?* But it seemed not to slow or burn out.

Humanus covered his head with his arms, yet still peered out, unable to keep his eyes off the light, which grew brighter.

It swept down with a rush, came to an abrupt pause a meter above the ground, then settled quietly the rest of the way.

Dear god, he thought. *It's the Shepherd.*

***

In the light of the moon, the Shepherd was dark colored with a tint of green. Its exterior was rounded, perhaps twenty meters in diameter, slightly textured and seamless. A faint drift of smoke rose from where it touched the ground.

There was no movement, or any other indication the Shepherd was alive or dead. It just sat there.

Humanus approached the craft, and would have closed the distance to touch it if Kesi hadn't appeared from the woods and restrained him.

"Stay here, Manus." Kesi grabbed Humanus by the shoulder. He pointed to the ground, pushing Humanus down to sit.

"Wiser than me, as always," Humanus said. "There's no rush. We'll just wait until something happens." He sat cross-legged on matted grass.

Kesi sprawled beside him.

Humanus soon found himself bored with the passive observation. He picked up a stone and prepared to heave it at the still form.

Kesi stayed his throw. "What do?"

"It's all right. I'm just going to see if I can rouse it."

Kesi didn't look convinced.

Humanus threw the stone.

It bounced off the resilient surface, but that was all. The Shepherd remained quiet.

Humanus shrugged. "Nothing. We should get some rest. We'll probably need it."

Kesi nodded and lay flat on his back on the matted grass. He closed his eyes and folded his hands upon his chest as though nothing bothered him.

Humanus caught him opening one eye to peer around. "Relax," Humanus said. "I don't think the Shepherd poses any danger to us." *Maybe not the Shepherd, but what it might carry.*

He had dozed off when a nearby rustling awakened him.

He reached for his spear, as Justin, followed by Jamani, emerged from the tall grass to join them.

Justin glanced at the Shepherd, then hunched down next to Humanus. "We saw it come down. Has anything happened?"

"Nothing. It hasn't moved since it landed. I threw a stone at it about an hour ago and got no reaction."

Justin took a seat between Humanus and Kesi. "I suppose given the magnitude of this event, we should be patient. I'll sit here, excuse me Kesi, and wait with you if you don't mind."

"I no mind." Kesi rolled onto his side away from the two of them.

"What happened back there with the smoke?" Justin asked.

Humanus' eyes stung, and he was thankful for the dim light. Despite the Shepherd's arrival, Wakuru's death was still in the forefront of his mind. "It was Gomo again. This time he really did it. He killed Wakuru."

Justin gasped. "Why would he do that? Wakuru was the gentlest primate of them all. He was like a father to you."

"He was. Maybe that's why Gomo killed him." Humanus brought his knees up to his chest and hugged them. He didn't want to talk about Wakuru. "I wonder what is going on inside. You think Cardassin is in there?"

"I don't see why he wouldn't be if all we've been told is true. I don't think the Shepherd would have dumped him into empty space. I mean, I would have, but perhaps the Shepherd doesn't operate that way."

Humanus brushed his cheeks. "Who knows how the Shepherd operates?"

Justin scratched at the stubble on his chin. "I'm trying to figure out the Shepherd's time line. You said the guardian told you there was only one Shepherd. You were deposited here by a Shepherd that died, so we can take that to be the end of the line for the Shepherd. There was a Shepherd in my time in the future, presumably the one we see before us. He left my time with Cardassin and came back here. But what happened between now and the far future?"

"I don't know what happened in my own time after I left in 1985," Humanus said. "A4-Ni was still very active. The guardian was still there. You said the Maraia were created by a Shepherd three thousand years before your time. We don't know when or where that Shepherd or this one was created. Some myths have him created outside the anomalistic locality, but that seems contradictory, the insertion of matter into a closed universe."

"What about the guardian?"

"That's a good question. But we both know the guardian seems to make up the rules as it goes along."

"This is all very confusing to an old man." Justin yawned. "It's getting very late."

"I had fallen asleep just before you arrived. I think I'll catch more rest. You should, too."

"I will." Justin indicated Jamani. "He'll keep watch and alert us if anything happens. I don't believe I've ever seen him sleep."

"It's almost the same for Kesi, but he does sleep. It's just not a deep sleep." Humanus leaned back on the grass and closed his eyes.

Uncounted minutes later, he was roused from a fitful sleep in which he had been dreaming about Mia. As soon as he opened his eyes, his dream evaporated. For a moment he tried to recall its details, then reality intruded.

"Wake up," Kesi whispered.

Dawn was fast approaching. A thin sliver of the rising sun had already crested the far horizon, sending shafts of red light across the golden fields of grass. The trees in the forest behind them lit up with a dull glow sparkling with dew encumbered leaves.

On the top side of the Shepherd, a lump formed, then split. The edges drew back.

After some internal movement, a membrane of some sort burst and something was thrust upward.

Humanus pointed. "What is that?"

By this time Justin had also awakened and sat gaping. "I believe it's a boot. A yellow boot."

Chapter Six

A second yellow boot joined the first. They waggled back and forth spastically, then, with a mighty thrust from somewhere deep inside the Shepherd, the boots and the body they were attached to cleared the outer surface. The rest of the body followed only to fall back onto the textured surface, slide slowly off the edge and drop to the ground.

Justin gasped. "It's Cardassin. What shall we do?"

Humanus stared at Justin for a moment, then they both grabbed their spears and rushed to the struggling form on the ground.

Cardassin stood and began wiping away the thin mucous membrane that encased him, finally getting it off his head. He began shucking it from the rest of his body when he glanced up and must have realized Humanus and Justin were about to make a kabob out of him.

"Wait! Don't kill me, for Zu...Zedroth's sake. I'm cool. I mean, I'm okay. I'm not me." He did a little shuffle dance. He looked ludicrous, dressed in a long, red coat trimmed with black and white matted fur, a bank of military style ribbons sagging off his chest. "See. I *look like* him, but I'm not. He went his way, and I'm here now going mine. Ha, ha."

The laugh isn't convincing, but the creature seems innocuous. Humanus looked at Justin and

110

shrugged. "There's no point killing him until we find out what is going on."

Justin nodded and lowered his spear.

"Whew," Cardassin sighed. "For a moment there I thought I was a goner, and by all estimates I've been a goner before and certainly don't want to be one again." He thrust out his hand to Humanus. "My...name...is...Cardassin." He spoke slowly as though talking to an imbecile, or perhaps a native who didn't understand old English.

"We know who you are." Humanus ignored the proffered hand. "I'm Humanus and this is Justin. Over there are Kesi and Jamani."

A spear sailed through the air.

Cardassin leaned to one side and let it pass to the left of his temple. "Ha. That Jamani was always a hot-headed little fella."

Justin turned quickly and held up a hand to Jamani.

"I remember some precious moments." Cardassin waved his hands in the air like an old time preacher. "Way back when, mind you, when I hosted that there primitive and his mother for a short while. But on my mother's grave--" He held his hands over his heart. "--I never laid a hand on either of them, so I don't know why that youngster all grown up now, has it in for me."

"Maybe it's because of what you did to everyone else who lived at that time," Justin said. "What about his grandparents?"

"Ah, yes...there was something that went on with the grandparents. Did they survive?" Cardassin blinked rapidly while looking over one shoulder then the other, probably to see if an assault was coming from another direction.

Justin drew himself up to his full height. "You know damn well they didn't. I have a mind to give Jamani back his spear and let him tickle your heart with the end of it."

Cardassin's shoulders slumped and then started to heave.

Humanus couldn't believe his eyes. The one who had been foretold as being some sort of beast was now convulsing in sobs.

"I'm not me," Cardassin whimpered. "I'm not me. Have pity."

"What happened to you?" Humanus asked.

Cardassin wiped at his cheeks and looked around sheepishly.

"I used to be a player," he said sullenly, then released a sudden smile. When no one reacted, the smile dampened. "But the Shepherd took me out of my zone, and now I am just *me*."

He said this with a slight flip of his wrist that gave Humanus pause. *Is this guy for real*?

"Who this?" Kesi said close to Humanus' ear.

"He is, was, a bad man from another time and place. We aren't too sure who or what he is now."

"Kill him." Kesi looked to Justin and when Justin didn't respond he sought out Jamani.

Jamani marched up to the rest of them. "Agree. Kill now."

Justin looked perplexed. "We can't just kill him in cold blood. It wouldn't be right."

"He bad," Jamani said. "He say anything to live."

112

"I'm not so sure." Humanus stepped between the others and their possible target. "If indeed the player has been drawn out of him, then Cardassin is simply another being, like us, caught up in a drama he doesn't really understand. I suggest we don't kill him right away. If he is benign and willing to work with us, then there might be a benefit to keeping him alive."

"I'm benign!" Cardassin thrust both arms into the air. "And I can help in many ways...I'm really good with kids." He smiled hopefully.

Humanus didn't know if the guy was a predator or just a simple being trying to get a foothold in a world none of them understood. "We'll hold off for now."

The others didn't look convinced, but probably because Humanus held a semblance of authority, they all nodded grudgingly.

"Well, Cardassin," Humanus said. "What have you got for me?"

"Got for you, got for you." Cardassin furrowed his brow, sucked in his cheeks and pulled on his ear. "I've got plenty! Though I'm not a player anymore, I can spot one a kilometer away. I can smell them close up. I know how they think. I know their motives."

He stopped and blinked rapidly again. "I think that could be useful. Couldn't it?" He leaned forward expectantly.

"Yeah, I guess that could come in handy," Humanus said. "What do you think, Justin?"

Justin nodded, but didn't take his gaze from Cardassin, causing the latter to squirm.

113

"Why does this man hate me?" Cardassin whined. "I never did anything to him."

"You killed Akilah," Justin thundered, suddenly letting his emotions get the better of him. "You contrived to have Cristina killed. You killed Rasmussen, my gene donor."

Cardassin cringed. "Huh?"

"Yeah, you bet. A big, huh." Justin stepped forward but was restrained by Humanus.

"I know how I got here," Cardassin sneered. "How did you get here?"

"That's none of your business."

"Okay, okay." Cardassin held up both hands defensively. "I don't want to make waves, send you into orbit, or mess with your karma. Rasmussen. Odd fellow. Always had it in for me. I heard through the grapevine someone cloned him."

"I'm the clone. What about the dead--Akilah, Cristina?"

Cardassin looked down at his boots and scuffed the ground with his toe. "Yes, yes, yes, I admit that, yes, I did all those terrible things. But I was a player then, and that is what players were supposed to do." He looked up pleadingly.

"We understand your argument," Humanus said. "I think this interrogation has run its course for now." He turned to Justin. "We'll let him live. Let's reconvene tomorrow, and talk again. I think the heat of the moment might be clouding our judgment."

"Where are you going to keep him?" Justin asked.

"I hadn't intended to keep him anywhere. It's not like we have bars to put him behind. On the other hand, I don't think he'll go anywhere if we just set him free. He wouldn't survive a night in this environment if he wanders off."

"Hey, I'm not going anywhere," Cardassin crowed. "When do we get breakfast around here?"

Justin pulled Humanus to one side. "I'll go along with you for now. He seems imbecilic enough to not be a threat. But if he steps out of line just a little bit, I'll let Jamani deal with him."

"Fair enough. None of us really knows what is happening here. I've gained insights from the guardian, but how it's all going to play out is beyond me, and the guardian isn't saying.

"Maybe we should take Cardassin up on his boast he can smell players out. Have him check Gomo."

Justin nodded, then motioned to Jamani. "It's best we be getting back to the ruin. I'll see you in the morning."

"Actually," Humanus said, "I've got a problem. Before Gomo killed Wakuru, he won over some of the young bloods in the troop. I'm not sure I'm safe going back there. Kesi isn't either. I was wondering if you'd mind us staying at the ruin?"

Justin laid an arm around Humanus' shoulders. "I'd like that. We have so much to talk about. Having you close would make it a lot easier."

"I'm deeply indebted." Humanus turned to Kesi. "We'll go with Justin and Jamani to stay in the ruin for a while."

115

Kesi nodded and looked back to where the glen lay hidden amongst the trees. "Goodbye home."

"It's not home if you don't feel safe there," Humanus said.

"Gomo bad."

"Yes, Gomo is bad."

The four of them headed for the ruin.

"What about me?" Cardassin wailed.

"What about you?" Humanus asked. "Talk to the Shepherd. He brought you here."

***

The next morning, Humanus stepped from the ruin. The sun was still just below the eastern horizon, giving the sky a pale blue-black color that was quickly intensifying with yellow and orange. Heavy clouds hung here and there, auguring the approach of the rainy season.

The air was fresh and thick with the scent of dew-soaked earth from the fields below. Birds squawked and chirped chaotically, an elephant trumpeted, the ground vibrated from the thudding of wildebeests on the run--a noisy chorus welcoming the new day.

A movement at the base of the escarpment drew Humanus' attention. An animal in distress? He walked closer to the edge and peered over.

Cardassin lay on his back on his coat, gazing up at him, his arms and legs spread-eagled.

"What's the problem, Cardassin?" Humanus called down to him.

Cardassin didn't answer.

Disgusted, Humanus found a path and descended the escarpment with long strides. He came up to Cardassin. "Are you all right?"

"I haven't eaten in twelve hours. I'm hungry. One of those abominations, those long-toothed cats, almost made a meal of me."

"Saber cats. They can be a problem." Humanus didn't feel any sympathy for the skinny man. The guy deserved every discomfort that came his way. Still, he didn't like leaving him there begging for help. "If you can make it up the escarpment, then I'll give you something to eat. We'll have to ask Justin if he wants to put you up in the ruin."

Cardassin leapt to his feet.

Miraculous recovery, Humanus thought. He climbed back up the trail. At the top, he waited for Cardassin who, despite his initial energized recovery, was taking the ascent slowly. He had left his coat behind.

At the top, Cardassin bent over, hands on knees, breathing hard.

"What about your coat?" Humanus asked.

"Later. I'm not used to these sorts of exertions. In the old days, I never had to lift a finger."

"I guess times have changed."

"Yes, yes...obviously they have. I'm still trying to decide if it's for better or for worse."

"Aren't we all."

They came to the ruin's entrance.

Jamani was awake and filled the doorway, blocking their way.

117

"Cardassin is hungry," Humanus said. "I offered him some food."

"No like him here."

"I know you don't, but we can't let the man starve to death just because we don't know what to do with him."

"I know to do. Kill him."

Humanus decided he wasn't going to get anywhere with Jamani. "Is Justin awake?"

"Yes, I'm here." Justin came up behind Jamani. "I feared something like this would happen. Are we now to be Cardassin's caretakers?"

"I'll go if you don't want me." Cardassin turned to leave, paused when no one stopped him, then continued with what was obviously a bluff.

Humanus laughed. So did Justin. Jamani scowled.

"We can give him some fruit," Justin said. "After that, he'll have to prove his worth before I'll dispense anything more."

"Sounds fair," Humanus said. "What do you think, Cardassin?"

Cardassin turned. "Great. It's a good deal. I'll try to think of a way to prove my worth."

Inside the ruin, Justin ushered them to a table. Kesi sat slurping on a guava. Jamani remained near the entrance, refusing to join them.

Cardassin sat on a stool set apart from the other stools at the table. "This is wonder--this is my stool!"

"It well could be," Justin said. "We were able to scavenge furniture from Kanapoi after the ice started to melt."

"The ice melted?"

"Yes. All of it."

Cardassin winked. "Must have had something to do with how you got here."

"It might have." Justin indicated the bowl of fruit. "I thought you were hungry."

"Quite right. I am hungry. Where do you get all this marvelous fruit?"

"Actually, we have Jamani to thank. He gets up early, and when he returns he brings this. I confess I really don't know where he gets it."

"I'm still getting used to the climate being so changed. In my day, back then when I was not me--" Cardassin glanced around nervously. "--and it was very cold, we had nano-assemblers to provide us, me and my mutants, excuse me, with a controlled environment. We could sure use a little controlling now. It's hot, wouldn't you say?"

"Yes, it is," Justin said. "When the world changed, we, too, had a nano-assembler. If it hadn't been for that we would have perished."

Cardassin's jaw dropped down. "You had a nano-assembler?"

"Yes. Jamani's father took it up from the ruin at the end of times."

"So that's what happened to my missing nano-assembler."

When everyone stared at him, Cardassin rushed on. "Not that I wanted it. It's a good thing you had it. Especially if it saved your lives...how did you know how to use it?"

"Actually, we didn't. Trudal used it for us."

"Trudal?!" Cardassin looked perplexed.

"You do remember Trudal," Justin said.

"Of course I remember Trudal. That lying, thieving, double crossing low life, if I could have I would have..." Cardassin glanced from face to face. "You know," he said with a smile, "Trudal wasn't such a bad guy after all. Shucks, he saved your lives didn't he?" The laugh that followed started robustly, then spiraled to silence.

"For a moment," Justin said, "I thought you might be reverting to your former self."

"No, no, no. That's not possible. I was just remembering that Trudal hadn't been really forthright with me. You understand. A bit of betrayal. Ah...tell me, do you still have the nano-assembler?"

"I do," Justin said. "But it's useless since Trudal never taught anyone how to use it."

Cardassin stood and let a wide smile cross his face. He stretched his arms out to his sides as though he were about to embrace something big. "But I know how to use it!"

Humanus squirmed where he sat. The conversation was getting out of hand and Cardassin, benign or not, was taking it there. "I think we should back up a bit here, and rather explore what you have become, Cardassin. What do you think of that?"

"I'm quite prepared to tell you everything. You know. But please, be discreet with your questions. There are youngsters hereabouts." He gave an exaggerated glance to Kesi.

120

"I'm not interested in your peccadilloes," Humanus said. "I'd like to know more about your transformation."

"Ah, the transformation. I'm glad you gave me a pass on the peccadilloes." Cardassin giggled. "At first I thought you were talking about an Italian sausage, and I was at a loss as to what to say."

Justin looked confused.

"The transformation," Humanus repeated.

"Yes. After the Shepherd took off from...here actually--" Cardassin gazed about in wonder. "--six million years into the future, I knew I was a goner. Gone, gone, gone as an agent for the master of the univer...for *Zug*. He had commissioned and sent me into the anomalistic locality as an informational string with a paltry time span of ten thousand years. I was crushed when I came into being. Ten thousand years! Others had hundreds of thousands and overlapped my own, no less."

"Did that cause problems?" Humanus asked. "The overlapping?"

"You bet. It was a huge problem. We felt no reservations about killing one another. All these players competed to get the guardian or the Shepherd or a line on *Gilomir*...I'll be damned. You're Humanus, you're *Gilomir*."

"Correct. Part of me is *Gilomir*." Humanus wasn't interested in getting into his genetics with Cardassin. "So the Shepherd took off from Kanapoi six million years hence."

Cardassin was obviously still thinking about Humanus as *Gilomir*, but then recovered quickly. "That's exactly what the Shepherd did. And within

121

nanoseconds I, as a player, was history. I fully expected I, as a hominid form, would also be history. But that wasn't the case. I don't know why, but here I am whole. Isn't it wonderful?"

Everyone just stared at the wretched beast.

"I guess we can say you have come a long way," Justin said.

"Thank you for saying that, Mister Justin. I have. And I remember every second of my ten thousand year service."

"I don't think we want to hear about it in that great a detail," Justin said.

"No?" Cardassin pouted.

"Is there a period that was more, shall I say, productive than any other?" Humanus asked.

"So kind of you to be interested, *Gilomir*. I mean Humanus." Cardassin shook his head in wonderment, then crossed his legs, laid an elbow on one knee and put his hand to his chin. "Actually, my time in the late twentieth century was the most enjoyable. I believe that is a time concurrent with your own background."

"John Lohner and Mia met in Kenya in 1985."

"That's perfect, except I was not in Kenya. I was actually going to school. I wanted to be a writer, and I wrote my first book then, based on my experiences in higher education."

"You were a writer?" Justin was nonplused.

"Yes. I wrote *Cardassin goes to Harvard*. Have you ever heard of the book?" He looked to Humanus for a reaction.

"No, I haven't," Humanus said. "My hominid father went to Harvard. He never mentioned you."

122

"I was just a small fish in a big pond. There was a lot of agitation in those days. The war and all. Not the next war, that one in the middle east, but the one at the time in the far east."

"Vietnam."

"Yeah, that one. I read a lot about it. They came for me and wanted to put me in the army, but I couldn't pass the physical."

"What was wrong with you?"

"Something psychiatric." Cardassin wiped spittle from the side of his mouth. "I think they thought I was insane."

"How could they?" Humanus leaned back on his stool and suppressed a smile. He had been wondering about that exact same sanity in the man who preened before them.

"Later, I wrote another book, *How Cardassin Started the Iraq War*. But it wasn't well received. Everyone thought it was a work of fiction, when in fact I had put it out there as a non-fiction offering."

"Any other moments of clarity in the ten thousand years of your existence?" Humanus asked.

Cardassin glanced from face to face, as if realizing Justin and Humanus were putting him on. "You really want to know?"

"I wouldn't have asked if I didn't," Humanus said.

"Okay. There were lots of problem times. Times when other players were on the scene, and there was nothing I could do but recede into the woodwork."

"Other players?"

123

"Yeah. They usually manifested as dictators and tyrants. You'd recognize their names. They all seemed to know better how to make life miserable for humans. But I always thought that just because humans carried your *Gilomir* genome, that wasn't a reason to harass them. The guardian and Shepherd were here and there. If I had known they would all end up in Kenya, then I might have done some post doc as a paleoanthropologist."

"I think we've heard enough history," Justin said.

"You don't want me to continue?" Cardassin looked disappointed.

"No," Humanus said. "You've proved your point and we believe you. I think you are now, basically, a nobody."

"I like being that. There was so much pressure before to succeed."

"Here's the nano-assembler." Justin took it out of his pocket. "Does it still work?"

Cardassin immediately became all business. He took the proffered nano-assembler and examined it one end to the other, then ran his fingers expertly over the flush set buttons.

"It is still functional, but is low on power. These things last tens of years without the need for a recharge, and luckily too, since we, I, didn't have any idea how to do it."

"What can you get it to produce for us?" Humanus asked.

"I suppose the real question is what do you want it to produce?"

Humanus thought for a moment. "A vehicle for transport. I'm tired of slogging for hours across the plain whenever I want to go anywhere."

"Excellent," Justin agreed. "I'd like to see a vehicle, too."

Cardassin peered into the small screen of the nano-assembler. "There are choices here. We have tracked versus wheeled vehicles. Comfort models as opposed to more rigorous models. They all seem to be capable of carrying multiple passengers." He looked up expectantly.

"I think wheeled," Humanus said. "Tracked implies the vehicle would be moving rather slowly. It's flat out there. If having a vehicle isn't going to get me somewhere any faster, then why have one?"

"I agree," Justin said. "What does Kesi think?"

Humanus looked over at Kesi. "I think he would walk regardless of whether we had a vehicle to ride in or not."

Cardassin fairly danced with joy. "Okay. Here's what we've got." He held up a pellet that had dropped from one end of the nano-assembler. "I apply this to raw materials, hopefully iron rich, and after some time, we'll have our vehicle."

"There's a pile of knives and things over there," Justin said pointing. "Is that what you're looking for?"

"That would do splendidly."

"I don't think building a vehicle here in the ruin would be what we want," Humanus said.

They all looked at him.

"I mean, how would we get it out and onto the plain below?"

"Ah, quite right, quite right," Cardassin said. "We need to transport that pile of metal from over there--" he pointed. "--to the edge of the escarpment and toss it below."

"It will take a lot of time and effort." Justin glanced at Kesi, and peered over his shoulder to see what Jamani was doing. "I guess Jamani has left us."

"I help," Kesi blurted.

"Great!" Cardassin said. "I'll also get the nano-assembler to create a supply of fuel for the vehicle. Dear me, the charge is really incredibly low. I suggest extra fuel should be the last thing we ask it for. Better to ration our requests to things we think are vitally important."

"Can the Shepherd recharge it?" Humanus asked.

"I never thought of that," Cardassin said. "We'll have to ask him."

"Where is Jamani?" Justin said. "He always has a tendency to wander off when one needs him the most. But we can get Kesi started. You and Humanus can give a hand, too."

Cardassin frowned as though participating in actually moving the heavy metal hadn't been part of his plan.

Humanus, too, didn't see any way he could get out of the physical labor involved. After all, he had been quite enthusiastic about the prospect of having a wheeled vehicle.

Jamani's squat frame obscured the doorway to the ruin. "Shepherd here."

126

"Yes, Jamani, we know," Justin said somewhat impatiently. "He arrived yesterday."

"Shepherd here, outside."

***

Humanus led the way out the door and onto the rock-strewn top of the plateau.

The Shepherd sat a short ways south of the ruin.

"This is very fortuitous," Humanus said. "It appears he wants to interact. If that's the case and I can establish communication with him, I'll ask if he can recharge the power supply of the nano-assembler."

The late morning sun stood overhead, casting little shadow off of anything. The Shepherd's gray-green exterior was very apparent, so too, its texture. There were no indications of any openings.

"How do we communicate with this thing?" Humanus asked Cardassin.

"You're asking me? I do believe you have spent as much time in the interior of a Shepherd as I have."

"You're probably right about that, but I was a developing fetus. I was able to monitor what little, Mia, that's my mother, said to the Shepherd, but she, too, was unconscious for most of the journey."

"She was?" Cardassin looked bewildered. "The Shepherd never afforded me such luxury. I was awake and conscious the entire time it took to travel from the future, out to the Cygnus-X black hole, around it, and then back to here. I thought I'd go insane. I probably did."

127

"You were awake the whole time in the Shepherd's womb?" Humanus asked.

"Yeah. Kind of icky, if you really must know."

"Okay," Humanus said. "We agree we don't have a known way to communicate with the Shepherd. I will approach him and see what happens."

Humanus walked toward the Shepherd.

Almost immediately, the smooth exterior parted along a thin vertical line, as though someone had cut a wedge out of a round of cheese. A pink fleshy interior was exposed to Humanus. He looked over his shoulder at the others.

"I think he wants you to go inside," Cardassin said.

"No way." Humanus stopped his approach, then cupped his hands to his mouth to shout. "We want to know if you can recharge the nano-assembler we have?"

The Shepherd moved slightly. It was as if it had inflated a bit and then let air out. "You don't have to shout. I can hear you perfectly well. Why don't you come to me, and we can discuss the matter in a more intimate setting?"

Humanus couldn't pinpoint the source of the Shepherd's voice. It seemed to come from everywhere at once. "I know very little about you," Humanus said, "and I'm not willing to give myself up to you at this point until we get to know each other better."

"Very reasonable. You are a lot like our Mia. Despite the fact that I was her creator, she

128

developed a mind of her own, an unforeseen manifestation of her hominid base."

"You didn't answer my question."

"About the nano-assembler? Yes, I can recharge it."

Humanus returned to where Justin was standing. "Did you bring it with you?

"Yes, of course." Justin handed Humanus the nano-assembler.

He stepped back to the Shepherd. "Here it is. Where do you want me to put it?"

The Shepherd shivered. "I said I could recharge the nano-assembler, not that I would. Don't you want to come over here so we can talk about it?"

Suddenly, Humanus found the quivering pink flesh repulsive. "I think not. If you aren't willing to do this for us, then we can continue this conversation another day." Humanus turned around and came back to bewildered looks from Justin and Cardassin.

"You can't talk to the Shepherd that way," Cardassin said. "He can make a lot of trouble for you."

"I'll take my chances."

"What are we to do if we can't recharge the nano-assembler?" Justin asked.

"What we've been doing all these years up to now," Humanus said. "I don't see a problem."

Justin stared over Humanus' shoulder. "I think we have a problem."

Humanus turned around and nearly bumped into the Shepherd, who had risen silently and moved up behind him.

The Shepherd had closed its fleshy opening much to Humanus' relief, but what now?

"I have certain guidelines given to me by the guardian," the Shepherd said. "You, *Gilomir*, are involved in all of them. I cannot understand why you are being so obstinate."

"I am not being obstinate, just careful. Am I expected to throw myself at you when I don't know anything about you, or your motives, or where you've been all this time and why there's one dead Shepherd here already?"

A moment of silence. Humanus presumed his proclamation had caught the Shepherd off guard.

"There is a dead Shepherd here?"

Humanus was right. "Yes. A dead Shepherd. He arrived twenty years ago carrying Mia and me. Once we were deposited into this environment, he died. Could he have been you?"

"I have no way of knowing. I was created in 1985 by A4-Ni under the direction of the guardian."

"A4-Ni created you?" Justin said incredulously. "Why would she do that?"

"Let's not get off the subject," the Shepherd said. "I'm more interested in knowing whether this Shepherd that brought Mia and *Gilomir* here, was in fact me."

"Manus, I know grave," Kesi said.

"You know where the Shepherd is buried?" Humanus was flabbergasted. Kesi had never spoken of this before. Neither had Wakuru.

130

"It be over there." Kesi pointed southeast.

"I seem to recall," Justin said, "that after you arrived and the Shepherd died, the troop dragged the carcass away from the general area. It had begun to smell, so much so, that even the bear-dogs left off chewing on it. The primates probably decided it was easier to remove the carcass than for them to relocate themselves."

"You knew about this, too?" Humanus was becoming increasingly incensed. Things had happened he didn't know about.

"I just said I did."

"I want to see this grave," the Shepherd said.

Humanus shoved his hands to his hips. "I'd like to see this grave, too."

Chapter Seven

"What about the vehicle?" Cardassin wailed.

Humanus stepped close to him, finding an odious smell lifting off his coat. The man probably hadn't bathed for a number of days or was it months, years, and was still wearing the same red coat and yellow boots.

"Keep it down," Humanus said in a harsh whisper. "The Shepherd wants to see the grave. Perhaps some quid pro quo here will help get the nano-assembler recharged. In the meantime, you can help by throwing the knives over the edge."

"What about Kesi," Cardassin whispered back, falling readily into a conspiratorial mode. "Isn't he going to help me?"

Humanus recoiled from a wash of rancid breath. Cardassin had cut a pathetic figure from afar. Up close there was more to him than Humanus wanted to experience. "We need Kesi to direct us to the grave." He spoke in a normal tone, feeling foolish conspiring with Cardassin.

"Then Jamani can stay and help," Cardassin said petulantly.

The man can't be thinking straight. "Do you really want to be left alone with Jamani?"

"No...no, I guess not," Cardassin said. "I'll do my best. But mind you I've had a long journey and am not as strong as I used to be."

Humanus felt a rising impatience. "Were you ever very strong?"

132

"You don't have to get nasty."

But nasty was the way Humanus wanted to be, given Cardassin's history, the fact that he showed up unexpectedly, the way he insinuated himself into their lives. He waved Cardassin away and turned back to the others. "Okay, Kesi, lead the way."

"Wouldn't it be easier if you all just came into me," the Shepherd said hopefully. He floated like a green helium filled balloon. "I can take you anywhere we have to go."

"You don't give up do you?" Humanus couldn't think of anything he'd less like to do than to be bundled into the Shepherd's wet tissue. These two newcomers were beginning to get on his nerves.

"I am not going to push a solution upon you," the Shepherd said, as though he could sense Humanus' unspoken reaction. "I will follow at your pace."

Kesi set off with a childlike run of enthusiasm, a chance to show the grown-ups something only the kids knew about. He paused at the edge of the escarpment and located a path that took them at an angle to the plain below. As they descended, the Shepherd swooped back and forth mid-air, seemingly impatient.

Once on the plain, Kesi headed in a southerly direction toward the ribbon of green that encased one of the rivers flowing into Lake Turk.

The others followed.

After several kilometers of hiking through the dry grass, Kesi ran parallel to low bush where the jungle met the grass of the plain. He paused now and then to part the brush and peer through the

133

trees. All the while the steady gurgling rush of the river drifted to them from beyond.

Finally, he disappeared into the bush, then returned and waved to the others to follow.

Humanus closed up behind Kesi on a faint path that led across matted ferns between columns of ropey trunks that towered overhead and closed off the sunlight in a verdant canopy.

They came to the banks of the river. At this location, it had eroded the ground several meters deep.

Kesi pushed his way to the drop-off.

Just over the edge was an indentation, almost a cave. At the back of this indentation, rested a hulking, decaying shape. The outlines were still discernable. The Shepherd.

"How did they ever get it all the way here and then lowered into this cave?" Humanus asked.

"Not me, Manus. But much work."

As Humanus, with Kesi close behind, clamored down the bank, the live Shepherd hovered over the river. A small portal opened in his side, and a thin beam of light shot out to play over the carcass.

"Why didn't you tell me about this?" Humanus asked Kesi.

"Don't know. Important?"

"Yeah, this is really important." Humanus crawled farther into the cave. "Look at this."

He lifted what appeared to have been part of the Shepherd's exterior and fingered it. "Though much has deteriorated, this feels new." He brought it up to his nose. "God, what an awful smell." He dropped the sample.

It thumped to the ground, lifting a small puff of dust.

Justin crawled in beside him. "Maybe we shouldn't be poking around here."

"Why not? We might find something the Shepherd out there won't. I presume that light coming from the Shepherd is some sort of probe."

"Probably. Why don't we let him decide if it's him? I'm more worried about what these decayed remains might do to us. The Shepherd is, was, an advanced form of construction. Maybe there are radioactive power-packs or other toxic materials lying about here that will kill us if we paw through them. That awful smell could be full of contaminants. There's all this dust."

Humanus sat upright as much as he could and started to slap the dust off his hands, then thought better of it and rubbed them on his loincloth. "You're right. We may have already done ourselves harm rummaging around in this debris. Let's exit and see what the Shepherd has to say."

The light from the Shepherd went out.

Humanus stepped to the lip of the cave and confronted him. "Did you learn anything? I couldn't. These are the remains of something that might have been you, but I'm sure your diagnostics are sophisticated enough to determine if it is you."

The Shepherd swayed slightly as he hovered several meters above the raging waters. "These are my remains."

"Really?" Humanus was surprised. It would have been easier to comprehend, if the remains had belonged to a Shepherd that was like this Shepherd.

135

But if this Shepherd said it was him, then that raised all sorts of complications. Not the least of which was world lines, which the guardian waggled in front of Humanus almost every time he chose to question something.

"The dead Shepherd's remains are made up of atoms and molecules," Humanus said. "If you, the live Shepherd, are hovering here looking at you, the dead Shepherd, then how can all those atoms and molecules be in the same place at the same time?"

"You have a point, but it does not really create a paradox. In the course of your lives, and that includes you and everyone here, the atoms and molecules that make up your bodies are sloughed off and replaced in their totality every seven years or so. Since I am bigger, the replacement cycle is on the order of fifteen years, but is of no consequence regarding the anomaly of my being dead there and alive here."

"So, this is you."

"Indeed."

"How does that make you feel?"

"I...I don't feel. But the reality of it poses fundamental questions for which I shall have to generate answers."

"That's it?"

"What else do you expect me to do? Place a bouquet of flowers?" The Shepherd shivered in mid-flight.

Humanus suddenly wondered if the Shepherd had a primitive sense of humor that exhibited itself outwardly with shivering. "You think this is funny?"

136

"No, not at all. This is very serious business."

Humanus climbed the bank to the plain above and hurried to catch up with the others.

The Shepherd bore down on him, almost knocking him over. "You have been here a long time, alone, except for these primitive primates."

Humanus slowed to a walk, putting his hands over his ears. The Shepherd seemed determined to attain whatever it was that guided him. Here was a simple statement of fact, but where was he going to go with it?

"Yes, I have been alone." Humanus stopped and faced the Shepherd. "It's different now that I have made contact with Justin. Otherwise, I was finding that I talked to myself a lot. My thoughts did dances in my head, and with no outlet continued to dance."

"I can change all that."

"Could you now? And what price would I have to pay?"

"Nothing much. Nothing that would cause you any inconvenience. Nothing more than giving me some of your DNA. After all--"

"Never."

"You seem so sure of yourself. Why would you deny me access to your DNA?"

"My DNA is mine. I'm not prepared to give it up so it can be trundled everywhere in the universe by you."

"But you are not an isolated being. You are *Gilomir* and have larger responsibilities. I suspect your refusal is coming from your hominid side."

137

"At this point it could be either side. You aren't telling me something I don't already know."

"I do not mean to insult your intelligence. I am still collecting data as a means to achieving the goal the guardian set before me. At the expense of offending you further, can you tell me how you felt knowing that Mia was a synthetic construct?"

"I could say it's none of your business. But in the interest of gaining your cooperation regarding the nano-assembler, I'll tell you. She was my mother. I spent a lot of time in her womb. I have feelings about her, an attachment to her that transcends what she was physically. There you have it. Why did you want to know?"

"I was curious about the strength of an emotional attachment between an enhanced hominid, such as yourself, and a synthetic being."

"Now you know. The others are waiting."

"Go to them. I must retire and ponder the consequences of what I have learned."

"You'll get back to us?"

"Yes. I think that is only fair."

The Shepherd levitated and disappeared to the north out of sight.

"Shepherd gone." Kesi looked relieved.

"Yeah, he's gone. He's got a lot of thinking to do. The reality of his end here seemed to have disturbed him. You did good, Kesi." Humanus ruffled Kesi's hair.

"I be good, Manus." Kesi grinned.

***

Exhausted, Humanus trudged up to the base of the escarpment. "Am I going to have to climb that to get home?"

Justin pushed up close behind him. "You're the one who wanted to move in here."

"Guilty as charged." Humanus began the ascent.

At the top, he found Cardassin lying flat on his back again. He had discarded his heavy coat to one side and was bare from the waist up. The lower half of his body was covered by some sort of fabric pants. He was still wearing his boots. "Are you okay?"

Cardassin opened an eye and shaded it with one hand. "No. I'm exhausted. I have taken all the metal objects from that there remote room and have thrown them over that there precipice."

Humanus walked to the precipice and peered down. "I see. There's a pile of metal objects on the floor below. Whatever happened to the pellet that was going to transform these things?"

"You push, don't you?"

Humanus wagged a finger at him. "You best behave yourself, lest I remove your privilege of staying in the ruin."

"Okay, okay. I have it right here." Cardassin reached in a pocket and withdrew the pellet. "You want me to start the thing now?"

"Are we waiting for something to intervene?"

"No. I guess not. Did you want me to hike all the way down there to activate the pellet?"

Humanus stood back a step. "Be my guest."

Cardassin frowned, then grumbled, but levered himself to his feet. "Okay. If this is to be done, then I am getting the feeling that I must do it alone."

"You are most perceptive," Humanus said.

Cardassin limped to the edge of the escarpment, and followed the path to the pile of metal.

Humanus observed his progress from above. In the dim light Cardassin stretched out his hand, crumpled the pellet to a powder and sprinkled it over the metal.

Almost immediately the pile convulsed.

Cardassin jumped back as though he were alarmed by what was happening.

"I thought you had used a nano-assembler before," Humanus called down.

Cardassin looked up. He cupped his hands to his mouth. "I usually let Trudal operate the thing."

Humanus cupped his hands beside his mouth, finding humor in mimicking Cardassin. "Are we making any progress?"

But as he spoke he saw the pile of metal transform. It gave off a reddish glow as components bent, then melted. The liquid metal ran freely, but never seemed out of control.

Humanus looked on in amazement. "Justin, Kesi," he shouted over his shoulder. "You should see this."

Within minutes the contortions and convolutions of the material took form.

Justin and Kesi came out of the ruin.

Justin gaped. "I see the outlines of a vehicle. Where did the nano-assembler get its design?"

"I don't know. I thought you might know. After all, it was the Maraia who built the nano-assemblers."

"That was before my time," Justin said. "But the Maraia had advanced vehicles. We know they fled to Nairob in a flying craft, the Truman Light. I presume that long ago, the guardian showed them how to build wheeled vehicles, and a lot of other things."

"There was obviously a program for wheeled vehicles. They might have built and used them before snow and ice engulfed their world." Humanus led the way down.

"Look, it's really taking form, now," Justin said when they came up to the vehicle.

After another few minutes, all activity stopped.

"Is it finished?" Humanus asked.

Cardassin walked over to the vehicle and kicked one of the tires. "I think so."

The vehicle was a blocky cousin to what Humanus had learned from Mia to be a Land Rover. It was colored beige with four rubber tires, four doors, a canvas fold down top, real glass for a windshield and leather seats.

"What about fuel?" Justin asked.

Cardassin held the nano-assembler close up. "It has very little charge left, but probably enough to fill a couple of containers with fuel." He stepped to the rear of the Land Rover look-a-like and removed two metal containers that were strapped to the back. He placed them on the ground next to the vehicle.

"We'll need water and organic material," Cardassin said. "We could create fuel without

141

either one, but it would take longer and require a more complex pellet, thus running down the nano-assembler's charge even further."

"Jamani," Justin called to where Jamani had remained on top of the escarpment. "Would you please bring us two containers of water and some of that fruit that we didn't eat this morning?"

Jamani seemed reluctant to get involved, but he disappeared from the edge of the escarpment. Moments later he reappeared carrying the requested items. He strode down the path and placed the water containers and old fruit at Justin's feet.

"Thank you, Jamani," Justin said.

"I go."

"Yes, of course." Justin turned to Cardassin. "Will this do?"

"Excellently." Cardassin poured the water into the metal containers, shoved soft fruit in after the water, then dropped half a pellet in each one.

The water became agitated. After a short while, it calmed down and the air was permeated with the smell of what Humanus took to be the fuel.

Cardassin tried to lift one of the containers, but was unable to get it up high enough to pour the contents into the fuel inlet of the vehicle.

Humanus took the container from him and emptied it into the vehicle's fuel tank. "We'll just use the one for now," he said. "Do you know how to operate this thing?"

Cardassin smiled. "Of course. During my long history, vehicles of this sort have been popular at one time or another, and I have always been told that I was an excellent driver."

142

"Well..."

Cardassin opened the door on the side of a steering wheel and slid onto the seat. He fumbled with something under and near the steering column. "I can't seem to find the keys."

"It needs keys?" Justin asked.

"Unfortunately so." Cardassin began a search looking behind a sun visor, feeling under the seat. Eventually, he opened a compartment on the other side of the vehicle. "Aha. There they are."

He pumped the gas pedal twice, then inserted and turned the key.

The vehicle lurched forward, but did not start.

"What's the matter?" Humanus said. "We're not going to go anywhere like that."

"It has a clutch, which I forgot to depress. The last vehicle I drove more or less took care of these things on its own." Cardassin tried again and the engine coughed to life with a sputter that settled into a steady rumbling rhythm. "I think we're in business."

"Okay. Shut it off. We aren't going anywhere tonight in the dark. Tomorrow we can take it out and see if we can bag us a wildebeest."

***

Humanus awoke with the first light smudging through the translucent windows. Despite what Justin had said about Jamani, he was asleep. He had pulled a carpet close to the entrance of the ruin and now lay on his back, snoring. Kesi, too, was still asleep. Justin lay in his bed with a light cover draped over him.

In a far corner, Cardassin sat hunched against a wall, his knees drawn up to his chest, his chin resting on his knees. He was awake and stared at Humanus.

"Did you sleep at all?" Humanus felt slightly unnerved by Cardassin's stare.

Cardassin blinked, as though coming out of a trance. "I never was able to sleep much. I've been sitting here thinking about my situation. I don't know why the Shepherd chose to bring me here. He could as easily have dumped me somewhere in space."

"We wondered about that as well, but decided that wasn't the Shepherd's style. Or more to the point, it wasn't something the Shepherd had been told to do by the guardian."

Cardassin shuddered. "The guardian? That infernal device has caused me more trouble than I care to remember. I assume you've never had the privilege of using it."

Humanus debated telling Cardassin about the guardian, but decided against it. There was no reason to divulge any more information to someone still suspect than was necessary. "I understand it can tell the future."

"It can do more than that. I suspect it can create the future. I suspect it has powers that can't be imagined. I suspect it is responsible for what has happened here. Past and future bent around to meet."

"You have a point." Humanus wasn't about to get into a deep conversation with Cardassin about the warping of space-time this early in the morning.

Give me something simple. "How about us rousing the others and getting this hunt underway?"

Cardassin stood and dusted off his knees as though they needed dusting. He picked up his coat, which sat in a crumpled heap beside him. "I guess I won't be needing this thing anymore. It smells. Do you think it smells?"

"Like a week old warthog carcass." Humanus wondered about the unhinged way Cardassin always conducted his conversations. Always on the edge of whatever had to be said. Always pushing the limits of the recipient's capacity to accommodate what he was saying.

"I was never into hunting." Cardassin threw the coat off to one side. "I suppose I'll have to drive."

"Will that be so hard?"

"No." Cardassin stretched. At his motion, Jamani sprang into a crouch, his spear poised.

"It's okay, Jamani," Justin said from his bed. "We're all just getting up. We're going hunting today, remember?"

"I hunt." Jamani indicated Cardassin with a thrust of his spear. "Not with him."

"You can hunt any way you want to. I think the rest of us are anxious to try out the new vehicle." Justin rolled out of bed and laced on his sandals. "Jamani hasn't had a chance to get the morning's fruit, but perhaps we can find some on the way. It's best we get going while it's still early."

Humanus gave Kesi a tap to awaken him, then led the way out the door, across the plateau and down to the Land Rover.

145

The vehicle stood shiny in the slanted light, a fine film of dew on its horizontal surfaces.

Cardassin unlatched the canvas top and folded it back, then strapped it down. "I assume you want the top down."

"Makes sense." Humanus climbed in on the passenger side without opening the door.

Cardassin slid behind the wheel, and Justin sat in the back. Kesi hesitated.

"Come on, Kesi," Humanus said. "It's not going to hurt you, and we can't go slow enough for you to keep pace. You don't have to get inside if you don't want to. Just stand over there." He indicated the running board and a roll bar to hang onto.

Kesi climbed onto the running board and shuffled back and forth feeling for a foothold. After depositing his spear in the back, he gripped the roll bar with both hands. His face showed intense concentration, masking whatever fear he felt.

Cardassin started the motor and dragged on the gear shift with a loud grind before remembering to depress the clutch.

With a lurch, they were off. Jamani walked slowly after them and quickly fell far behind.

Cardassin revved the vehicle's engine to a high whine, then shifted gears. With another jolt it picked up speed.

Cardassin grinned maniacally at Humanus, who searched for something to hold onto and wondered if Cardassin was as good a driver as he claimed.

As the vehicle picked up speed, Humanus marveled at the blur of passing landscape. When he looked close he could not focus on anything. When he looked far, the whole world seemed to turn. An optical illusion. Dual tracks lay out behind them, pressing deeply into the damp soil, crushing dry stalks of grass as well as new green into the dark earth.

"We saw a herd of wildebeests off that way." Humanus indicated the direction, then quickly clamped his hand back on the handhold.

Cardassin swerved abruptly, almost tossing Kesi off the running board.

"Do we have to go this fast," Justin yelled.

Cardassin looked back to Justin. "What?"

The Land Rover hit a bump that lifted Humanus off his seat.

Kesi lost his footing and was dragged several meters before clambering back on.

Humanus tapped Cardassin on the shoulder. "There they are." He pointed. "Slow down. We don't want to spook them."

Cardassin hit the brakes and sent everyone lurching forward. The motor coughed and died. A whiff of exhaust laced with fuel smell slewed over them.

"What's the matter?" Humanus wrinkled his nose at the smell.

"I killed the engine. No problem. I'll start it again once you tell me what you want to do."

The herd was still a hundred meters away, grazing peacefully. A gentle breeze in the cool morning air brought the pungent odor of animal dung. Larger bulls, issuing grunts, roamed the perimeter, while the cows and their bleating calves clustered closely at the center. Tails flicking the ever present flies, the wildebeests grazed on lean pickings this early in the season.

Humanus estimated there might be two hundred animals in the herd. "I think they've been making their way across the plain toward that river beyond. If we circle to the right, then approach them, we'll have them between us and the river. Once they reach the river, it will take them some time to figure out where and how to cross. We can cull a bull or two then." Humanus readied his spear, as did Kesi.

Cardassin restarted the engine, over revved the motor, but after a worried glance from Humanus, gained control. He eased the Land Rover around the herd, then headed slowly toward it.

The herd became alert. After a moment of hesitation, they moved with an overabundance of braying and huffed protest in the direction Humanus had predicted.

Cardassin stepped on the accelerator, and the Land Rover gained speed, too much speed as far as Humanus was concerned.

"Slow down!" Humanus shouted. "You're spooking them!"

The herd launched into a trot that quickly developed into a stampeding run. Clicking hooves, snorting nostrils, they reached the banks of the river. There, they bunched up in a chaotic slithering mass. Some staggered over the edge and plunged into the silty waters. Waiting crocodiles slid from the shallows on the opposite bank to take a prize. Other wildebeests faltered, slid down the muddy slopes, regained their footing and struggled to rejoin the herd. The main mass veered away from the crossing and ran parallel to the bank.

The Land Rover hit a rock.

Cardassin over-corrected and sent Kesi flying.

He landed hard, his spear knocked from his hand as the Land Rover plowed onward.

Humanus cupped his hand and leaned close to Cardassin's ear. "We've got to go back for Kesi!"

But it was all Cardassin could do to keep the vehicle upright, much less slow it down and turn around.

The herd ebbed and flowed in front of them, then shifted abruptly and folded back on itself.

Above the din of thundering hooves, cries and shouts arose from a band of primates on the far side.

"Gomo!" Justin shouted.

"I see him," Humanus yelled. "It looks like he's got five of his guys with him. They're turning the herd. We've got to save Kesi."

Cardassin struggled with the steering wheel. It locked in an extreme turn, wheels spun in the wet soil, a spray of mud lifted.

The idiot will get us all killed. Humanus leapt out, hit the ground running, then doubled back to Kesi.

He stood, favoring his left foot. His eyes flashed. He knew full well the danger they were in. "Go back, Manus."

Humanus ran up to him. "Can you walk?"

Kesi took a step and winced. His ankle was red and swollen.

Thundering and bellowing, the herd bore down on them, goaded on by Gomo and his men.

"He's trying to kill us." Humanus unsheathed his machete. "I'll fell a lead animal and hope the others avoid trampling it."

Kesi nodded and braced the butt end of his spear into the soil.

A young bull, swifter than the rest, lowered its horns. Eyes wild, it lunged at Humanus.

He slashed with his machete, landing a superficial wound to the animal's neck. It stumbled on.

Another bull, older, careened forward.

Kesi's spear caught in the animal's chest and shattered.

The bull went down with an agonizing bellow. Its nose dug into the soil. Its legs splayed out.

An engine roared to one side as the Land Rover careened across the line of the stampede.

Justin held onto the roll-bar and leaned out of the vehicle.

"Grab Justin!" Humanus screamed to Kesi. "I'll take care of myself."

Kesi nodded grimly.

The Land Rover nearly hit them as it roared past.

Kesi latched onto Justin.

Humanus lunged and fell awkwardly into the back seat.

"Help me," Justin cried. "I can't hold him."

Together they dragged Kesi into the Land Rover.

Cardassin never wavered, never reduced speed. Knuckles white, he gripped the steering wheel, his teeth bared in a frozen grimace.

As they cleared the main herd, the Land Rover clipped another animal at the edge and sent him stumbling.

Cardassin stepped on the brake and lurched forward, hitting his forehead on the windshield.

As soon as the vehicle stopped, Humanus was out looking for Gomo.

He was about a kilometer away with his men, dragging the carcasses of their kill toward the jungle. As if he knew Humanus was watching, Gomo stopped and raised his spear, tauntingly, letting out a shrieking cry.

Humanus glared at him, but gave no other indication of a reaction.

Gomo's comrades then stopped as well, and after dropping the carcasses on the grass, hopped from foot to foot, making obscene gestures.

"I'm going after them," Humanus said through gritted teeth. He lunged for the Land Rover.

Justin grabbed him by the shoulder. "Don't be a fool. You're outnumbered. You can't get them all and they might get you. Where will that leave us? I'm an old man, here, defenseless, with a lame Kesi and a non-combatant." He nodded toward Cardassin, who had leapt out of the Land Rover at Humanus' approach.

"That animal killed Wakuru, the only father I ever knew." Humanus shrugged off Justin's hand and climbed behind the steering wheel. "How do I get this thing going?"

Neither Justin nor Cardassin moved.

"Damn it, Cardassin! Get over here and start the engine for me!"

151

Cardassin glanced nervously at Justin, then leaned over Humanus. "Press this pedal first, it's called a clutch. You have a choice of speeds with this lever here, the gear shift. Whenever you change speeds, you have to depress the clutch. When you want to stop, press the brake, here." He turned the key and started the engine.

Humanus raked the gear shift back as he had seen Cardassin do before, then let out the clutch.

The Land Rover lurched forward. The engine coughed, but didn't die.

He pressed the accelerator down as far as it would go.

The Land Rover moved forward, the engine topping out at a fierce whine.

Humanus pressed the clutch, shoved the gear shift forward, released the clutch, all without taking his foot off the accelerator.

The engine wailed, then caught the higher gear. The Land Rover shot across the plain toward the now astonished primates.

Okay, you son of a bitch. See if you can outrun this.

Humanus steered erratically toward the group.

At the last moment, they dived in different directions out of the way of the speeding vehicle.

Humanus slowed the Land Rover almost stalling the engine. He cranked the wheel over and came around for another pass.

One of the primates was slow to get to his feet.

Humanus aimed at him.

The Land Rover's front bumper caught the primate's head with a sickening crack, a spray of blood and his limp body was brushed to one side.

One down.

Gomo threw his spear.

It didn't come close to Humanus, but made a lucky hit on the right rear tire.

A loud hiss, then an erratic flopping.

The Land Rover slewed dangerously.

Humanus braked again, spun the steering wheel and prepared for another pass.

But his speed was much diminished.

The remaining primates and Gomo simply stood pointing and laughing, brandishing their remaining spears.

Justin had been right. It was a fool's assault. Suddenly the anger he had felt gave way to a near panic. He'd have to get out of there before the primates acted on their advantage.

He spun the steering wheel again, and directed the wobbling Land Rover back toward Justin and Kesi.

A spear barely missed his shoulder and cracked into the windscreen.

He came up to Justin and stood on the brake.

The Land Rover stopped. The engine coughed and died.

"I'm not going to say I told you so," Justin said grimly. "You're lucky they aren't in the mood to come over here and take us on."

"At least I got one of them." Humanus sought to cover his humiliation. "There will be other opportunities."

"I thought that was obvious in what I said before you took off. Now look at our poor vehicle."

"It'll repair itself," Cardassin said. "That's one of the good things about nano-assembled products."

As he spoke the tire sealed and re-inflated, the cracks in the windscreen disappeared.

"That's a relief," Humanus said. "I guess we're back to where we were a few minutes ago. He glanced over to where Gomo had been, but they had already taken up the carcasses and disappeared into the jungle.

Humanus put a lid on his anger and turned his attention to Kesi. "How's your foot?"

"Hurt big, Manus."

Justin gripped the foot gently, pressing the swollen tissue and moving the foot back and forth.

Kesi moaned.

"I think he just twisted it," Justin said. "Still, it's going to lay him up for a while."

Humanus glanced apprehensively to the barrier of jungle where Gomo had disappeared. "We'd best be getting back to the ruin. This isn't turning out to be as much fun as I anticipated."

Cardassin maneuvered the vehicle around, finally showing some coordination.

"Those there primates had it in for us," he said, rubbing blood from a gash on his forehead as he kept the Land Rover at a steady pace.

"They've become a problem," Humanus said. "Everything was going along well, until Gomo started acting up."

"Gomo. He'd be their leader, the one who taunted you?"

"That's him. Justin thinks he's a player. I've seen enough of him to also think he's a player. What do you think?"

Cardassin smiled. "He's a player all right. A pity he chose such a primitive form in which to express himself. It doesn't give him much to work with."

They came to the animal they had clipped.

Despite a leg broken, the young bull tried to stand. Its wild eyes betrayed a sense of impending death.

"We might as well end his misery," Justin said. "Not exactly a noble way to hunt, but food is food."

Humanus leapt out and approached the animal. He circled, raised his machete and stabbed the beast just back of its horns to sever the nerve stem leading to the animal's brain.

The bull jerked and was still.

Cardassin stepped out of the vehicle. "How are we going to get that beast back to the ruin? It must weigh two hundred kilos."

"I'm going to butcher as much as I can. We can load the pieces into the back of the Land Rover. The rest of the carcass we'll leave for the bear-dogs."

"Better kill small one, Manus," Kesi said, rubbing his ankle.

On the way back to the ruin, they passed Jamani, who trudged along with a newborn calf slung over his shoulders. Humanus offered him a ride, but Jamani refused, not much to Humanus' surprise.

"We'll have enough meat for a week," Justin said.

"Good." Cardassin waved a hand over his head. "I was getting tired of grains and fruit. It's a shame you don't have a freezer."

"I can guess what a freezer is," Justin said. "I wonder if the nano-assembler has a blueprint for one. It's terrible how one step forward leads to another and soon we're being pushed into a run, chasing needs."

Cardassin tried looking over his shoulder to answer Justin but only over steered sending everyone sloshing to one side, then the other. "At this point I don't think we have enough charge on the nano-assembler to make any more luxuries."

They came to the bottom of the escarpment.

Finally, Humanus thought.

Cardassin stopped the Land Rover without running into anything. He was the first out and headed for the trail leading to the ruin.

"Hey, Cardassin!" Humanus called. "If you want to share in this bounty, you're going to have to help us haul it up."

Cardassin looked to the top of the plateau and then back to the Land Rover, obviously calculating what expenditure of energy it was going to take for him to be included in the spoils later. Grudgingly, he came back to the vehicle and lifted out the smallest piece of the dismembered wildebeest.

Humanus shook his head.

Jamani caught up to them. He un-slung the calf and held it by its two hind legs, then he bent and hoisted Kesi over his shoulder.

Kesi made a face as though he was about to protest but must have realized that it was the only way he was going to get up to the ruin.

Jamani set off at a brisk pace, stumping his way effortlessly up the trail.

Justin manhandled a haunch of the wildebeest over his shoulder and began to climb. He stopped halfway up. "Here he comes." Justin pointed to the south.

Humanus scanned the distant horizon where Justin was pointing.

A speck grew in size, racing low to the ground.

A moment later the Shepherd hovered in front of him.

Humanus shielded his eyes with his hand. "Now what?"

Chapter Eight

"You have used the nano-assembler to build a vehicle." The Shepherd's voice resonated in the humid air.

The low sun backlit his ovoid form, making him look somewhat sinister, but maybe that was only Humanus' take on what could otherwise be a benign encounter.

"Was that wise," the Shepherd continued, "considering that the charge for the nano-assembler is so low? Would it not have been better to synthesize medicines, or perhaps a greater array of tools, perhaps ones that might be used as weapons or for hunting at a safer range?"

"You want me to stay?" Justin yelled from halfway up the path leading to the top of the escarpment. He staggered under the weight of the slab of wildebeest he had chosen, his sandals slipping on the loose gravel.

"No. I'll be all right." Humanus waved him on, then turned back to the Shepherd. "I will be all right, won't I?"

"You have nothing to fear," the Shepherd said, "especially from me of all beings."

"Still, it's reassuring to hear you say it." Humanus eyed the avocado-tinged, rugby ball-shaped object floating before him and thought about the absurdity of speaking to a fruit that talked. "As for the nano-assembler, no, we didn't think too much about what we should make. We figured you would eventually come around and re-charge the thing for us." This was not true, but Humanus still harbored the hope the Shepherd would comply.

"That was a reckless assumption of your part. I have no specific instructions from the guardian in that regard."

Humanus felt a flash of impatience. The Shepherd, for all his vaunted history, was coming off as a stubborn, honor-bound being, unable to make up his own mind on the simplest of requests. "Certainly, the guardian gave you leeway for decision making?"

"The guardian has foreseen all the circumstances I might encounter and has given me specific directions on how to proceed."

That's odd, Humanus thought. If the guardian had covered all situations, then it must have covered this one. "When was the last time you consulted the guardian?"

"Actually, it was thousands of years ago, somewhere along my world line, but that is irrelevant."

"I don't think it's irrelevant. If you haven't been able to use the guardian, its priorities might have changed."

"This is an academic discussion." The Shepherd sounded defensive. "We don't have the guardian to consult."

Finally. I have turned an advantage. Humanus withdrew the guardian from the pouch around his neck. He could have sworn the Shepherd retreated a full meter as though the display of the guardian's existence had taken him by surprise.

"Where did you get it?"

"I found it on the island in Lake Turk."

"May I use it?"

"Sure." Humanus tossed it hand to hand, relishing the Shepherd's presumed discomfiture. "But first I need you to recharge the nano-assembler." *Please let it be this easy.*

"I can't do that without authorization."

Back to square one. Dismayed, Humanus re-pocketed the guardian. "I'm not convinced that is true. You have my offer."

The Shepherd was silent for a while, probably computing scenarios again, maybe extrapolating action on a best guess basis from what the guardian had previously told him.

A high frequency sound suddenly emanated from the Shepherd.

Humanus covered his ears. "What the hell is that?"

"I am sorry. I did not think that frequency was within the range of hominid hearing. I must recheck my references."

"You didn't answer my question."

"If you must know, and I hope you do not take offense, I was simply calling for the guardian to come to me. It worked before. Now, for some reason it is not working."

"I do take offense." Humanus started to walk away. "I don't like the fact that you tried to take the guardian from me without my permission."

"Hold on. I computed it was worth a try, even risking your anger. I would then have to deal with your anger, but still have a sixty-eight percent chance of mollifying you."

Screw this. Humanus grabbed a wildebeest haunch and turned to hike up to the ruin.

"Why are you leaving?" The Shepherd sounded plaintive.

"We are getting nowhere with this discussion."

"But we are," the Shepherd said. "I have exhausted the simplest means forward and am now prepared to take a chance and re-charge the nano-assembler, assuming that by so doing I will not be compromising whatever the guardian has as its ultimate goal."

Fat chance. There's only one way to settle this. Humanus left the Shepherd and walked over to the compartment in front of the passenger seat of the Land Rover to retrieve the nano-assembler. He returned and held it out, wondering if and how the Shepherd was going to grasp it.

A thin pseudopod snaked out from the Shepherd and snatched the nano-assembler. The The pseudopod withdrew into the Shepherd and a moment later re-appeared with the nano-assembler still in its grasp. "It is charged," the Shepherd said.

"That fast?"

"That fast."

Humanus took back the nano-assembler with the uneasy thought that the Shepherd could have duped him, and he would have no way to know until Cardassin tried to use the nano-assembler. But would the Shepherd be deceitful?

The Shepherd bounced up and down impatiently. "The guardian?"

161

Humanus went through the routine again. He held out the guardian to the proffered pseudopod. "You *will* give it back, won't you?"

"Of course. You probably need it more than I do."

Like the nano-assembler, the guardian made a quick circuit inside the Shepherd and was handed back to Humanus.

"Interesting," the Shepherd said. "The good news is that I have not compromised the guardian's goal by recharging the nano-assembler."

"You must be relieved," Humanus said sarcastically.

"No hard feelings?"

Before Humanus could answer, the Shepherd embraced him in some sort of force field and a moment later, Humanus found himself on top of the plateau with a stack of the remaining wildebeest parts at his feet. When he turned to confront the Shepherd, all he saw was a dark green spot receding by the instant toward the southern horizon.

"How'd you get all that up here so fast," Justin asked, returning from the ruin.

"The Shepherd lifted me. I didn't know he had such powers. Did you?"

"That's news to me. What did he want?"

"I'm not sure, really. We argued about the nano-assembler and eventually he agreed to recharge it."

"He did? What made him change his mind?"

"I let him use the guardian."

***

162

The Shepherd accelerated away from the plateau, watching the solitary figure of *Gilomir* grow smaller and smaller.

I need time to calculate, the Shepherd thought. *Nothing is as it seems.* When he ascertained that he was out of sight, he stopped, hovered for a moment then dropped to the ground to be partially shielded by the tall grass.

So confusing. The guardian is not telling me everything. Not that it should, but how am I to function if I do not know what is going on?

The Shepherd activated a playback mechanism to review what had been a very troubling session with the guardian.

"You recharged the nano-assembler."

"It was the only way to gain access to you," the Shepherd said defensively. "I calculated that recharging the tool was a superior solution to simply grabbing it. I calculated that I should not divulge the full scope of my powers and risk alienating *Gilomir*."

"Having a functioning nano-assembler was not in my plans for *Gilomir*. It complicates matters."

"But surely you knew I was going to do it."

"It was one scenario with a high probability of happening. In retrospect, I should have paid more attention to it."

"You need not worry," the Shepherd said. "I didn't give the nano-assembler a full charge.

"I know. The point I am trying to impress upon you, is simply that you are not at liberty to do as you please."

163

"I should not have proceeded without explicit instructions," the Shepherd recited.

"See that such oversights don't happen again. Is there anything wrong with your computational capabilities."

The Shepherd did a cursory review of his circuits. "Nothing I can detect. I shall be on the alert for any malfunctions in the future."

"As for holding your powers in reserve, you have done well. However, it will now serve my purpose for you to demonstrate those powers. After I am returned to *Gilomir*, transport him to the top of the plateau along with his burdens. That will demonstrate you had the power to take me from him, but for some unexplained reason you chose not to."

"I will comply."

"Good. Let us move on. We shall continue to give *Gilomir* the impression his DNA is all important for us to regain. It is best he thinks this is our prime objective. It will distract him from recognizing the true goal I have for him."

"If I might ask, do you consider it wise to keep him from knowing your true intentions?"

"*Gilomir*, the superior being he is, will no doubt come to recognize my goal in due course. At some point, I will also enlighten you to them."

"How do you want me to proceed in the near term?" the Shepherd asked.

"Reinforce the idea you are stubbornly bent on obtaining his DNA. You will do this by creating a synthetic female hominid, whom you will program to become his companion."

"I have created such beings before." The Shepherd remembered Michael, whom he had left in 10,000 A.D. "But as you well know, my store of a viable genome, either *Gilomir*/hominid or simply hominid, was destroyed by Cardassin.'

"Before you return me to *Gilomir* I will download a suitable female hominid genome."

That surprised the Shepherd, but he dared not show it. "Shall I endow her with the usual fail-safe energy limitation and interactive metabase of knowledge?"

"This time her energy supply should approximate the average life span of a hominid. As for the metabase, I want something more subtle, something more hominid. Give her exceptional reasoning powers and a broad education, but not the depth and scope a metabase would provide. I want her as normal as possible."

"That will greatly simplify her construction. When do you want her ready?"

"As soon as possible. Her construction should take no more than an hour or two."

The Shepherd computed. "One hour and twenty-three minutes to be precise."

"Excellent. After creating the female, you will leave."

"Leave?"

"Yes. Here are the coordinates and time reference I want you to attain."

"These are the coordinates of the dark star Cygnus X-1," the Shepherd said, examining the information. "You want me present two million years from now?"

"Do you foresee any problems attaining the dark star at that place and time?"

"No master. I just I thought I was to be here to facilitate the recovery of the *Gilomir* genome."

"I do not know whatever gave you that impression. I believe my directions are clear. Please proceed. You may now return me to *Gilomir*."

"Guardian?"

"What is it?"

"May I ask a question?"

"Certainly."

"Why did you have me bring Cardassin back to this time and place? He is no longer a player. He is an empty vessel."

"Yes, he is no longer a player, and you are quite correct characterizing him as an empty vessel. Even empty vessels have useful purposes."

"Thank you, guardian. May I ask another question?"

"This is the last one. You have work to do."

"I calculate the only entity that could have effected the warping of time and space to produce the present circumstances is you. Consequently, you must be more than I or anyone else has assumed you to be up until now. Given that my calculations are correct, how could such a massive dislocation be achieved?"

"Very perceptive, Shepherd. You are aware of the anomalistic nature of this universe, the one I refer to as the forbidden zone, a region of space-time warped on a massive scale into a closed timelike curve. If you are so inclined you can

166

research the mathematical properties of a Klein Bottle to derive a geometric metaphoric, interpretation of the phenomenon.

"Be that as it may, a dissection of a Klein Bottle along its plane of symmetry produces a Mobius strip, which can serve as a perfect analogy to the infinitesimal slice of reality that any one observer experiences.

"Since a Mobius strip has only a single surface, travel around the strip eventually gets one back to where one started. I am able to expand or collapse the strip thus accelerating or decelerating space and time as perceived by someone on the strip. Additionally you are able to penetrate the surface of the strip using a black hole to come out at a different time and place on the same slice of reality."

"Thank you, Guardian. I will investigate further what you have told me."

"Now, you must return me to *Gilomir* and get on with the construction of the synthetic. I have downloaded the genome for your use."

"Guardian."

"Another question?"

"Yes."

"You are trying my patience."

"Please."

"Ask."

"I was taken to the grave of a dead Shepherd. I told *Gilomir* the dead Shepherd was me, though to be honest I had no unequivocal way of being sure."

"It is good to be honest. Whether those remains are truly you or not is immaterial. But I will ask you this, what are the odds those moldering remains are indeed you as opposed to the odds a second Shepherd has been created? After all, I instructed A4-Ni on how to build you."

The Shepherd calculated. "There is a two percent chance the dead Shepherd is me, and a seventy-five percent chance it is not. The remaining twenty-three percentage point spread is unknown."

"Then you should conclude there is nothing to worry about. Now, you have exhausted my patience. Return me."

***

I am still confused, the Shepherd ruminated. *But it isn't the first time the guardian has confused me.*

The Shepherd shoved his doubts to the back of his computational priorities and turned his attention to the task of creating the synthetic.

Systems churned, taking in air, damp soil, grass, and any other organic compounds that lay within reach.

A speck of life was deposited into his womb. After some moments, it began to grow exponentially, guided by the DNA downloaded from the guardian, which had been gleaned over the years and patched together, modified, mutated, and designed to produce a hominid...male or female, but that was just the tweaking of a single chromosome.

The Shepherd didn't pay too much attention to what was happening, since most of the systems worked automatically once activated. He was pondering what the guardian had said when he felt a sharp kick against the wall of his womb.

"Are you ready?" The Shepherd was not wholly convinced the process had come to a successful conclusion.

"Mummph!"

A good sign. The being needs a name. "I will call you Ariel," the Shepherd intoned in an ethereal, even god-like voice. The Shepherd liked being god-like and in many ways he was like some sort of god.

"Mummph!" Ariel responded.

It's her mind. But he couldn't rely on a metabase to provide the vast array of knowledge and history that was needed. He'd have to scan what information he had about everything in general and a lot of trivia in particular into the lattice work of neurons that made up her brain.

The Shepherd activated a neurological mapping device and monitored its progress. At first there were simply flashes of undifferentiated neurons. The flashes swirled over the tight knot of ganglion of her brain.

Eventually, the flashes took on a patterned structure.

"Who am I?" Ariel asked.

"You are a hominid female, Eurasian template, Ukrainian Belarusian, mid-twenties. You are what came to be known more generally as a Homo sapiens, though you are synthetic."

"Synthetic?"

"Yes. Though I made you from the material at hand, you are indistinguishable from a naturally produced Homo sapiens."

"Why?"

169

"I did not want to send you out into the real world and have you immediately spotted as being syn--"

"Why did you make me?"

"I apologize." The Shepherd sought to instill some modicum of decorum. "I misinterpreted your question. The guardian and I need your help to obtain DNA from another hominid named *Gilomir*, also known as Humanus. Well, actually, he's a hominid/godlike being combined into a single form."

The Shepherd's pink flesh pressed against Ariel, all over, from head to toe and from all sides.

"I don't understand much of what you are saying." She pushed curiously at the tissue. "Where am I?"

The Shepherd felt a moment of discomfort, then let the tissue of his womb give way to her prodding.

"You are in my womb. Obviously, my womb is in me. We are sitting in the middle of a field of grass, on a plain, on the landmass once known as Africa, on the planet Earth, which revolves around a five magnitude star in the--"

"Earth?"

The Shepherd monitored a tearing sound, like static, rippling inside Ariel's head. "I'm sorry. Did that hurt? An oversight on my part. One moment." The Shepherd tweaked the neurological mapping device and filled in the missing information. "Now try it."

"Earth? Yes, that's better. I know everything about Earth. I even know what year this is, and you are the Shepherd. You are in service to the…guardian?"

"I have not given you a definitive identification of the guardian since I do not have one. I once thought I did, but current events have forced me to recalculate my conclusions."

"Will you share your recalculations with me when you have them?"

"I do not see that sharing would serve any useful purpose. You will have ample exposure and time to draw your own conclusions."

"Thank you. Am I capable of proceeding with what I have learned?"

"Yes. You have demonstrated sufficient recall to assure me the knowledge map I overlaid on your neurological structure was a success."

"I must ask again. Why am I here?"

The Shepherd sighed, or at least he tried to. "You are here to seduce Humanus."

"Se--?"

"Good grief."

***

"Manus! Manus!" Kesi shouted.

Humanus awoke from an afternoon nap. He was sitting on the edge of the plateau, his feet dangling over the side, his back resting against a rock. Iron-rich, red sandstone spread beneath him, out and down to the interminable plain over which low hanging clouds showed signs of the coming monsoon. New, green growth mixed with old, dry yellow. The tangle of thorn and thicket gave way in places to bright flowers, white, purple, orange. Distantly, a hum of life stirred the expanse and made it to where he sat. He didn't want to move. The sun beat down with a bone-massaging heat. His thoughts lingered on the guardian, his existence in this time and place and why events were being thrust upon him.

"Manus, look!" Kesi was insistent.

"What is it?" Humanus rolled onto one elbow and shaded his eyes against the glare.

"Woman."

It wasn't as if Kesi would use the name for a female in his troop. "What woman?"

Kesi pointed out across the plain.

Far away, but coming ever closer, a female, definitely human, strode purposely, following an animal track that lined the path of least resistance toward the plateau.

Humanus jumped to his feet and cupped hands on either side of his head, tunneling his vision. "Where'd she come from?"

"Don't know, Manus."

Behind her, out of tall grass, the Shepherd rose straight up. He steadied about a hundred meters above the plain, then shot directly toward Humanus. With gathering acceleration, the Shepherd whooshed close overhead, banked at an inhuman turn upward, and disappeared into the sky, skewering a puffy cloud that happened to be in his way.

A thunderous sonic boom rattled the ground and sent birds squawking into the air.

Kesi flinched, hands over his ears. "What be, Manus?"

"I don't know, but it looks like the Shepherd is out of here, and not just going around the corner."

The woman paused and waved half-heartedly to where the Shepherd had been, an obvious good-bye. She resumed her walk seemingly unperturbed at being left alone.

Her gait was determined, athletic, not at all like the stiff, slightly bowlegged walk of the female primates Humanus had grown up with. She was tall by any standard, and slightly taller than he was. Her hair hung dirty-blond, parted in the middle, straight and wind-tossed down to her shoulders. She had a narrow proportionate face, high cheekbones, blue-green eyes and horizontal brows that matched square shoulders. Her frame was lithe with small breasts riding high on her chest. A long waist slimmed before giving onto smooth hips. Tied across her chest and waist was a wrap of cloth that looked colorful and lightweight.

"Big woman," Kesi said with a sense of approval.

"She's tall, not big," was all Humanus could say.

Minutes later she came to the base of the escarpment.

"How do I get up there?" she called, the edge of her hand to her forehead shading the sun.

Humanus found trouble speaking, gave up trying and pointed to the start of a path several meters to the woman's side.

After a moment of searching, she located the path upward and climbed with strong strides. At the top, she paused to methodically brush strands of hair back over her ears and draw a finger along her jaw line to catch a glistening of sweat. Seemingly satisfied all was in place, she leveled a look on Humanus and headed straight for him, her arms swinging loosely at her sides. At five meters, she stopped.

"My name is Ariel." She didn't otherwise move, just the verbalization of her name from lips showing a touch up of pink.

Humanus quickly reviewed and rejected possibilities of where she might have come from, and settled on the obvious.

"You have come from the Shepherd," he said. "In fact, I believe you have been created by the Shepherd."

"Do you have a problem with that?"

This Ariel seemed not at all troubled she was probably only a couple of hours old and now walking in what must be a strange time and place.

"Come, Manus," Kesi said nervously. "We go to ruin."

"It's okay, Kesi. I don't think she's going to harm us." Humanus realized there was a leap of faith in that assumption, but how could such a comely creature do harm? Best to find out more about her. "Why are you here?"

Her gaze, half-hidden by heavy lashes, shifted from Humanus to Kesi. "Kesi. It's a wonderful name for a companion. It means rational one in Swahili."

Humanus couldn't believe what he was hearing. "I think everyone who comes here knows Swahili."

"Everyone?"

174

"You're the second person in this time to make reference to an ancient language that hasn't been invented yet. But you are avoiding my question."

She seemed to suppress a smile.

Is she so far ahead of me?

"The Shepherd told me I was to come to this place and meet a man named Humanus. I conclude the first part of my directive has been achieved." She eyed him critically. "You appear younger than I had been led to believe."

A slight heat rose to Humanus' cheeks, a color he hoped the bright sunshine would hide. "What are you to do after the first meeting?"

"I am to befriend you."

"Actually, you could do that very easily." Humanus felt he was babbling. "But to what purpose?"

Ariel spread her arms out and looked down at her body. "Is there something wrong here?"

"Not at--" Humanus glanced over his shoulder only to see that Kesi was already meters away, closer to the ruin. *Some sidekick.* He turned back to the newcomer. "That's a very fetching wrap you are wearing."

"This is the way the Shepherd chose to present me."

"I'm sure the Shepherd has his motives, but it doesn't look like he's going to be giving you, or anyone else here for that matter, any support."

"You're referring, of course, to his dramatic departure."

"It looked like he was embarking on a long trip."

"I don't know anything about the Shepherd's movements. He comes and goes as he pleases at speeds we cannot comprehend. To count him out based on his towering exit might be premature."

Humanus felt a gnawing frustration. He wasn't getting anywhere with his questions. She almost seemed the superior intellect, dodging and feinting his every move.

"It's getting late. We'll be having dinner soon. Would you like to join us? There are others you should meet."

"Certainly. I am programmed to ingest food, and I would like to meet your friends." She looked around as if wondering where the meal and friends were.

"This way." Humanus led her toward the ruin.

She fell easily in step with him, coming so close as to bump his shoulder now and then. "You know the Shepherd wants your DNA," she said leaning close to his ear after a bump. "I could give you pleasure."

Humanus almost tripped. "You don't mince words, do you?"

"Mince? I don't know what it means in this context."

"You come right to the point." Humanus wiped his mouth with the back of his hand. "But I'm wondering, having just seen the Shepherd's exit, if his interest in my DNA has become secondary to another mission directive. Tell me, why has the Shepherd left?"

"I don't know."

"But you are still intent on helping him obtain my DNA?"

For a moment Ariel looked bewildered. "You are putting questions to me I am not able to answer. If the Shepherd has indeed left us, then I do not know why."

"I think the Shepherd is pursuing a goal previously set down by the guardian that induces him to seek out my DNA. But I could argue, now that I am here, acquiring my DNA at this point is a useless exercise. Where does the Shepherd think I'm going to go?"

"You have thought about this more than I have. But the Shepherd created me. I was told to be with you, and I have come to do that. The rest is beyond me. I like you, Humanus."

She slid an arm around his waist and pulled herself close.

He felt the warmth of her touch, the smoothness of her skin. He grasped her arm and moved it away. It wasn't that he disliked her touch, but he felt if the conversation were to continue, he would have to be less distracted. "The Shepherd has given you an emotional capability. From my recollections and what I learned from my mother, the Shepherd didn't initially know what emotions were."

"That may be, but I assure you I have emotions. What else could these waves of distracting energy be?"

"An odd way to put it, but perhaps the Shepherd has realized from past experience he has erred on the short side whenever he created and put forth a human construct."

Ariel tossed her hair. A bit of color came into her cheeks. "I am probably more human than you are. You should accept me as such and not dwell on who my creator was, which is irrelevant. I feel, I think, I can become angry, or so I am told. I can love and have children. I am learning something new every moment that passes."

Humanus stopped walking and faced her.

Her chest heaved up and down, a reaction to her winded pronouncement. The color was still in her cheeks, a sign she might indeed be experiencing the new emotion, anger.

"I can say the same," he said, thinking to calm her down. "Though my mother was synthetic, I have never encountered a synthetic woman in my adult life...despite my youthful...I mean, I haven't before."

His response seemed to satisfy her. She smiled disarmingly. "Then it is new for both of us. Perhaps we can explore the experience together?"

There was a physical press to her personality. If he backed up one step, she moved forward. Each dodge or retreat became an opportunity for her. She was pursuing him, and he didn't know what he could do about it.

He could only stare, then he started walking again, so abruptly she gave a start, but followed quickly.

Physically, she's beautiful. Mentally, she's exceedingly sharp. What am I to do with her? Should I worry about it?

At the entrance to the ruin, Kesi stood waiting, looking very concerned. "Manus?"

178

"It's okay, Kesi." Humanus entered the ruin. "Justin! Look what I've found."

"I don't think you found me," Ariel said close behind Humanus. "I was the one who--"

"I don't believe it." Justin came out from behind a pile of carpets. "Where? How? Does she have a name?"

"I'm Ariel." She stepped forward and shook Justin's hand.

"She's beautiful." Justin spoke past her to Humanus.

When Ariel seemed to take umbrage at being anonymous in the middle of a conversation about her, Justin took her arm. "I'm so sorry, my dear. You must think I'm being very rude. Here, do come in and make yourself at home. We've not had company like this since, since the ice melted."

"Who is this man?" Ariel seemed taken aback, probably by Justin's effusiveness.

"Justin is a man of the future," Humanus said. "10,005 A.D. to be precise. Did the Shepherd tell you about that time?"

"He did. He told me about the Maraia, about a leader named Akilah and another synthetic construct named Michael. There was also an evil player named Car--" Ariel gasped staring across the room. "--is that who I think it is?"

Cardassin stood over a wildebeest shank with a long knife that dripped blood. He tilted the point of the knife to his forehead in a salute. "One and the same, madam. I'm pleased to make your acquaintance. Did I hear Ariel? What a lovely name."

"What..." Ariel stammered, "What is he doing here? The Shepherd said nothing about him."

"That's a long story, the end of which we are still trying to write," Justin said. "Please, don't just stand in the doorway. Come in, come in."

Humanus ushered Ariel into the cool interior of the ruin.

Despite the newness of her surroundings, she kept glancing at Cardassin, who continued to grin at her and touch his brow with the knife as though he were a mechanical doll. "Is he all right? He seems a bit demented."

"We thought the same thing." Humanus walked her over to Jamani, who looked up from his skinning of the wildebeest calf. "This is Jamani, another refugee from the future."

Ariel stuck out her hand again.

Certainly forthright, but she'll not charm Jamani. To Humanus' surprise, Jamani wiped a hand on his loincloth and gripped Ariel's hand in an enthusiastic shake. "I guess Jamani likes women," Humanus said over his shoulder to Justin.

"He does surprise me at times," Justin said. "Come, sit here, my dear." Justin pulled back a chair. "We were about to eat dinner. Would you like to join us?"

"Yes. I would very much like to see what it tastes like."

Justin offered her a bowl that held an assortment of fruit. "Help yourself. Do you know what we are offering?"

"I think so." She picked up a guava. "I haven't been cognizant for very long, but isn't this a fruit?"

180

"It's fruit. We also have meat. But, since it's been recently butchered, it will have to hang for a few days."

"The Shepherd has told me to shy away from meat. I would be better served eating fruit and vegetables."

"We have plenty of those."

"This must be the ruin of the research station." Ariel looked around. "It's amazing it still exists. I mean, given the warping of time and space that must have taken place to find you all here, six million years back from when you previously existed, it's a wonder the ruin has survived, even pre-dated itself."

"The Shepherd certainly laid down a track of information for you," Humanus said.

"He did. But that's not to say I know everything."

"Good," Justin said. "Then you are in the same boat we are. We don't know everything, either."

Cardassin wandered over to them and leered at Ariel.

She drew back. "Is he going to hurt me?"

"Cardassin," Humanus said sharply. "Back off."

Cardassin threaded his fingers together in front of him and bowed slightly at the waist. "I came from 10,000 A.D., and I was at one time known as a butch--"

"Thank you, Cardassin," Humanus said. "You still are a butcher, though one reformed. Please return to the wildebeest."

181

Cardassin blinked as though he had been slapped and returned to his dismemberment of the carcass.

"I think he's harmless, but we haven't totally decided." Justin said. "Tell us about yourself. Presumably, the Shepherd made you. How does that make you feel?"

Several hours later with Kesi yawning and Jamani already asleep, Humanus stood and stretched. "I think we've debriefed Ariel enough for one evening. I'm tired."

"Yes, good idea." Justin jumped up and looked about concerned. "How are we going to sleep?"

"I'm going to sleep over there, where I did last night," Humanus said. "Cardassin will probably crouch and lean against the wall opposite. Justin, you will sleep in your bed. Kesi and Jamani will find their own places. Where do you think you'd be comfortable, Ariel?"

"I am going to sleep with you."

Chapter Nine

The next morning, Humanus awoke feeling as though he hadn't slept a wink. Every time Ariel had moved, even the slightest bit, during the night, he would wake up. Cuddling close didn't seem to bother her at all. She slept as though she'd been sleeping next to a partner all her life, which in one sense was true.

But for Humanus, sleeping with someone else was something he'd have to decide if it was worth getting used to.

When he stood, Ariel was nowhere to be seen. With a sense of alarm, Humanus gave the interior of the ruin a quick scan.

Everyone else was still fast asleep. Even Cardassin dozed, propped against the far wall, resting on his heels.

The sun was just beginning to rise. Its rays hit the material that served as glass in the windows and flooded the interior of the ruin with a warm glow.

Ariel emerged from the stair landing at the back of the ruin where the flight of steps led down to the hallway, past the elevator shaft and ended at the overlook to the tunnel below.

"You're finally awake," she said in a low voice, glancing at the others. "I woke up early and went exploring."

Humanus covered a yawn with his hand. "I couldn't sleep at all and was just beginning to doze when I realized you were gone."

"I didn't mean for you to worry about me. Where does that hallway go? I followed it back a short way, but it's so dark, I didn't dare go any farther."

"The Shepherd must have told you the history of this place."

"He did. Though he didn't experience the events himself, the guardian provided him with a history. A research station was constructed here in 1985 after he left with Mia and...you. Governments at the time set up the research station with telescopes and monitors to follow his flight. They could do this until he reached the black hole, Cygnus X-1. Representatives of these governments also wanted to be near the Kanapoi fossil fields, the better to understand what had happened there." Ariel wrapped her arms across her chest, and having given her recitation, looked smug.

Humanus shook his head at the audacity of the woman. "That's a good summation of how this now ruined structure came into existence. The research station was abandoned eight years after it was built but it continued to play a role in subsequent years, all the way up to Justin's time. And now our time, whatever that might be."

She nodded succinctly as though simply filing away whatever he said, but still being in pursuit of her own interests. "Will you show me what is beyond the end of the hallway?"

"Sure. But let's wait until Justin is up." Humanus had only seen the end of the hallway once and wanted Justin to guide them. "I was going to propose to him we open the tunnel at one end so we could get our vehicle out of the elements. The monsoons are almost here. It's going to rain heavily in another few days."

"There's a tunnel?"

She had passed on the vehicle but focused on the tunnel. So, the Shepherd hadn't told her everything. "Yes, there's a tunnel."

Ariel looked perplexed. "I've already admitted the Shepherd didn't tell me everything. Why is there a tunnel?"

"It was built for convenience to get from one side of the plateau to the other without having to go kilometers around out of the way. The tunnel has been blocked for most of its history. Don't you want to know about our vehicle?"

She smiled wryly. "I do know about your vehicle. I look forward to seeing it. Maybe a ride?" She looked past Humanus. "I think Justin is up. So are Jamani and Kesi. Can we go see the tunnel, now?"

Justin came up to them, peeling a banana. "Good morning, Humanus, Ariel. You're up early."

"Actually, Ariel was up early. I just got up to see where she'd gone." Humanus thumbed toward the tunnel. "She wants to have a tour, and I said we should wait for you."

"Probably a good idea. There are pitfalls on the way back there, plus we have no light." Justin took a bite of his banana. "We have torches," he mumbled, chewing, "but they make a horrible mess of the air, so we don't go back there very often."

"I was thinking of opening one end of the tunnel so we could drive the Land Rover into it."

185

Justin swallowed, then cast about looking for a place to toss the banana peel, settling on a far corner. "I suppose we could open the tunnel. I haven't examined the ends closely, but it's my recollection the rocks blocking each end are not oversized, though they seem to be glued together with some sort of material."

Cardassin clomped over to them in his yellow boots, which were fast looking the worse for wear. "Did I hear you talking about the tunnel?"

Justin looked him up and down disapprovingly. "Humanus has suggested we open one end to park the vehicle inside."

"Ha!" Cardassin scratched his crotch and catching his fingernail, opened a small tear in his red tights. He looked momentarily surprised, then suppressed a yawn. "Though that seems like a splendid idea, that bitch...that--" he smiled widely, obsequiously, "--that what's her name...Akilah, had the entrances sealed with something from a nano-assembler."

"Why would she do that?" Justin asked.

Cardassin shrugged, hands out to his sides. "I suppose she got tired of my mutants sneaking in and making her life miserable."

Color rose into Justin's cheeks.

Humanus pressed a restraining hand against the old man's chest. "Be calm. It's too early to get worked up." He pulled the nano-assembler from a pocket and thrust the cylinder at Cardassin. "Here's the nano-assembler. If you know so much about the sealant, find something that will undo what Akilah did."

"But we don't want to waste its charge." Cardassin took the nano-assembler. He glanced at its small screen, then snapped his attention back. "It's charged!"

"Complements of the Shepherd," Humanus said. "Now, will you please find something to help clear one of the openings? We could also use some light down there."

Cardassin fiddled with the small buttons on the side of the cylinder. "You realize it's not fully charged."

Humanus did a double take. "That sneaky bas...I wouldn't have believed the Shepherd could be so devious. I had an agreement with him that if I let him use the guardian, he would re-charge the nano-assembler."

Cardassin looked up, alarmed. "You have the guardian?" He looked positively stricken.

Humanus shrugged. "I didn't see any rush to tell you I had it."

If knowledge the guardian existed impacted any of Cardassin's thinking, he didn't acknowledge it. Instead, he turned his attention to the nano-assembler. His fingers seemed to have a life of their own, fiddling, fumbling, then his mouth snapped open and closed before he made a huge sighing effort at self-control. The nano-assembler almost slipped from his grasp. "Then...then you can ask it what we are all doing here."

Back to the existence of the guardian. Humanus could only stare at the wretched soul. *All that agitation and for what?* "I have already asked

187

the guardian, and it's not been particularly forthcoming."

Cardassin's eyes went wide, his mouth worked feverishly, a bit of spittle flecked one side. "That the guardian is here in our...in your possession changes everything," he sputtered.

"How so?"

"It knows. It knows. It knows what's going on." He waved his hands in the air. "Having it here gives meaning to all this. It wouldn't still be here if this...this stuff that's going on weren't important."

"Okay," Humanus said, watching with concern as Cardassin waved the nano-assembler with a swoop and flourish. "Maybe it makes you feel more secure. But I'm more focused on the tunnel at this point. Tell me, can we spare enough charge to open an entrance?"

Cardassin looked at the others, who stood staring at him. With a sigh of resignation, he pushed back his hair, snapped the elastic band of his tights and tried to stand taller. "Definitely." He glanced from face to face, and probably seeing a reaction that wasn't going to be intimidating, continued. "It has quite an adequate charge for the time being."

"That's good," Humanus said, hoping to encourage the misfit.

Cardassin peered at the small screen. "I've located the program Akilah used to produce the material to seal the tunnel. It shouldn't be very difficult to design something that would reverse the effect. There. It's done."

A pellet popped out onto his hand.

"And a light?"

"Yes, a light. That's easy. Lots of faux-suns to choose from." Another pellet emerged.

Cardassin held up both pellets and headed for the passageway with the others following close behind. "I'll do the sun first. It's dangerous back there without any light."

He felt his way to the back of the passageway with the others following. "It ends here. Beyond lies the tunnel!" He swept out his arm, only dimly discernible.

"What do you do now?" Humanus asked impatiently.

"I just have to toss this in," Cardassin said. "When it hits the ground it will know what to do."

He tossed the pellet while he was talking, and a moment later a bright light flashed from the floor of the tunnel below, then rose slowly and lodged itself near the ceiling overhead.

Yellow sunlight flooded the interior.

"Amazing," Justin said. "We've never seen much of the tunnel before. The light from our torches was swallowed up in the dark. Look how big it is."

Humanus followed the light and looked back the way they had come. "That shaft back there leads down to the tunnel. Would that be an elevator shaft?" Humanus drew on the knowledge he had gleaned from Mia's metabase.

"It's never been functional," Justin said, "at least not since Jamani and I took up residence here. There's a metal rung ladder embedded in the stone wall. Jamani uses it sometimes when he goes exploring. I've never had the urge to go down."

With ample light spilling everywhere, Humanus took the lead and climbed down the ladder.

Ariel followed, then Cardassin.

Justin remained above. "I'm too old to climb down there and then back up. I can see all I want from up here."

Cardassin walked over to a square metal platform that filled most of the shaft and was anchored to the walls by metal rails. He stepped to a small box, lifted a lid and pushed a button.

The platform jolted and began to rise slowly.

Cardassin pushed another button and the platform stopped and returned to the bottom of the shaft.

"It works!" he said. "I guess I wasn't button adverse after all."

"You're a regular Jack of all trades." Humanus appreciated Cardassin's discovery that the elevator worked, but didn't want it to go to his head. "What about the rocks?"

"Yes, yes the rocks." Cardassin looked disappointed. He crossed to the eastern end of the tunnel, where he crushed and sprinkled the remaining pellet over the rocks blocking the entrance. In a matter of minutes the gluey substance holding them together sagged and melted, then vaporized and disappeared.

"That was easy," Cardassin said. "If we can just convince the youngsters to come down here and help us heave these stones out of the way, we'll be in business."

"I don't think Jamani is going to comply," Humanus said.

Kesi climbed down the ladder and limped up to them. "I help, Manus."

"No, you take it easy. I want that ankle to heal." Humanus saw no other alternative than to begin tossing rocks to one side himself. Once he started, Cardassin leaned over reluctantly, and with an exaggerated attention, picked up a small stone and gave it a toss.

***

An hour later, they had made headway toward clearing the entrance. Humanus stopped to rest. Ariel, who had also pitched in, sat down beside him.

"Look at all that equipment back there." She pointed to a jumble of wires, computers, and broken monitors.

"That's probably what's left from the equipment the nano-assembler put together to build A4-Ni."

"What's that over there?" Ariel indicated a large tub-shaped structure.

Humanus walked over to it. "I don't know. It looks like it held water at one time. These orifices seem to be jets for water or air. It looks very out of place with the rest of this stuff."

Cardassin rushed over to them. "Excuse me for interrupting, but I think I've found a program for rock eating nano-genes that will greatly simplify our task."

Humanus gazed at Cardassin as though he was an idiot, but it hadn't occurred to Humanus either

191

that the nano-assembler might have had something like that in its quiver. "Great. It couldn't have come at a better time, unless maybe an hour ago. By all means, power the thing up and clear out the rocks."

Cardassin fairly shook with excitement. The nano-assembler dutifully expelled its pellet. Cardassin cast it on the rocks and stood back.

"How does it know when to stop?" Ariel asked.

Cardassin leered at her, then snapped to attention when Humanus gave him a glare. "Of course, I have programmed in coordinates approximating the outline of the former entrance." He hopped from one foot to the other. "Additionally, I have added a subroutine that will construct a metal gate when the initial program has run its course."

"That's rather brilliant, don't you think, Humanus." Ariel slung her arm in his and leaned up against him.

Humanus only wondered why Cardassin's expertise seemed to come in fits and starts and not in any form of order that would give him confidence the wretch knew what he was doing ahead of time. "What is that pit over there?"

Cardassin craned to see the tub shaped structure. "I believe it is called a spa. Akilah had an admirer, female, if I do say--" He giggled. "--who had the spa constructed much to Akilah's displeasure, initially, mind you, for she did use it in the end...before her end, if you get my drift."

"I think I do," Humanus said. "Can it be resurrected?"

"I don't see why not. In fact...look. I do believe the faux sun has reactivated the nano-genes responsible for the spa. It is, as you can see, refilling with water."

"Look at that," Humanus said. "Where does the water come from?"

"There's probably a submersible pump that penetrates to an underlying aquifer. This spa will not only be a source of pleasure, if you choose to use it of course, but also a source of fresh water. Jamani won't have to traipse to the river for water every other day."

The last thin veneer of rock closing the tunnel off from the outside sheared and fell away, letting in a breath of fresh humid air.

Simultaneously, the opening squared off, and a steel barred gate emerged, hanging from hinges embedded in the rock side. It swung closed with a clang.

Humanus walked over to it and examined the latch, which consisted of a large lock with a key. Very complete.

"You've done well." Humanus clapped Cardassin on his back, almost upending him.

"Thank you, sire. I mean...I'm pleased to be of service."

"Sire?"

"You object?"

"I'm no sire."

"Okay. I won't call you sire."

Humanus turned to Ariel. "Sire?"

She smiled.

Cardassin leaned in. "As they say, if the big toe wiggles, the sandal is large enough to fit."

"I've never heard that one before." Humanus was not amused.

"Be that as it may, I'll exit from here and drive the vehicle around." After a nod from Humanus, Cardassin eased through the parted gate leaves and skipped out of sight to get the Land Rover.

***

"What's going on down there?" Justin called from above.

"We've opened the tunnel," Humanus called back. "We've discovered how to dim the faux sun. And we're about to use the spa."

Justin glanced at the steaming water bubbling in the spa. "Where's Cardassin?"

"He went for the Land Rover," Ariel said. "Won't you join us?"

"No, I think not. That tub of water reminds me too much of the cauldron that produced me. I was also told it floated two dead mutants after an attack on the ruin."

Ariel looked at Humanus, who looked back with a shrug. "No dead mutants, now."

She reached her hand into the spa waters. "Nice and warm." She undid her wrap and climbed over the spa wall, then slid into the water. She let out a sigh of pleasure. "This is wonderful. It feels hot when you first get in, but after the initial shock, you don't notice it."

Humanus glanced at Ariel, then to Justin, then back to Ariel. "I'm going to relax in the spa," he called to Justin over his shoulder.

"I can see that," Justin said. "And with a faux sun, you're in business. I'll be up here if you need me." Justin turned and disappeared up the hallway.

Humanus waved, but didn't know if Justin had seen him, then stepped into the warm water. "He means well."

"Is he looking out for you, now?" Ariel shoved water Humanus' way.

He leaned away and thought to distract her. "I don't see any temperature controls. Maybe it knows what a good ambient temperature should be given what the outside temperature is."

Ariel bent her head slightly and eyed him for a moment. "I don't care. I think it is just right."

Humanus had run out of distractions when an engine roar echoed through the tunnel, and Cardassin lurched through the entrance with the Land Rover. He almost took out the gate on one side, but having narrowly missed, came to an abrupt stop a few meters inside the tunnel.

He leapt out, locked the gate and stumped over to Humanus and Ariel. "Boy, that looks inviting." He reached to pull off one of his boots.

"No one invited you, Cardassin," Humanus said.

Cardassin hopped once and released his boot. "I see. I'm not really invited."

"Gosh," Humanus said. "You are becoming more and more perceptive and sensitive every day that goes by."

Cardassin stood straight. "You're making fun of me."

195

"You just proved my point," Humanus said. "Why don't you go see what Justin and the rest are up to?"

Cardassin glanced from Humanus to Ariel, who didn't give him an opening. "Right. I'll just ride that there elevator to the top and see what's going on."

Cardassin didn't move.

"Well?" Humanus prompted.

"You know we aren't safe here now that we've opened the tunnel."

Humanus raised himself slightly out of the water. "Safe from what? The only one out there causing us any trouble is Gomo. If he wants to sneak in via this opened tunnel, he will still have to find a way up, all the while we have the advantage of visiting harm from above."

Cardassin swung his arms back and forth in a motion of indecision. "I guess I'm being paranoid, something left over from my days of always planning the next calamity."

"I hope we are beyond that." Humanus pointed to the elevator shaft wondering if Cardassin would take the hint and leave.

He looked to the shaft, then to Humanus and nodded, then set off for the platform. "I'll be going, now."

"Bye."

"It's hard to believe he was once so evil," Ariel said.

"He's different, all right. But so are a lot of things here."

"You're different," Ariel said coyly.

Humanus shifted his back over a jet of water, feeling the pressure relieve the tension he felt. "Yes, I'm different. More different than you can imagine."

"Try me."

This was a synthetic woman, a construct of the Shepherd asking these questions. Why hadn't the Shepherd given her more information? "What do you know about me?"

"You are *Gilomir* trapped in the body of a hominid. The Shepherd has told me your DNA is hopelessly entwined with hominid DNA. The two cannot be separated, at least by him. He considers it somewhat of a miracle *Gilomir* has survived after A4-Ni's death. After all, she was the only one standing between your DNA and the more aggressive hominid DNA that took every opportunity to reject what it considered alien DNA."

"Don't forget I am the first generation after A4-Ni's demise."

"I hadn't really thought of it that way. No wonder the Shepherd wants to gain access to your DNA. Probably, he wants it before it degrades."

Humanus sensed a hesitation on Ariel's part. "That's what I don't understand. If the Shepherd wants my DNA so badly, why does he keep asking me for it? Why does he keep making these silly references to needing my cooperation? Why doesn't he just pick up a sloughed off cell from my skin or a hair from my head? He'd have all the DNA he needs."

Ariel gave Humanus a blank look, one that translated into, *are you stupid*?

"What?" Humanus said.

"It's not that simple."

"So tell me."

"I'll bore you to sleep."

"No you won't. I promise."

"The problem isn't so much that your DNA will degrade without A4-Ni around to protect the *Gilomir* portion of your genome from the more aggressive hominid portion. The problem is how to separate the two. The Shepherd can maintain the status quo, but only A4-Ni knew how to disengage the two genomes."

"Yeah, and A4-Ni is dead."

"Exactly." Ariel swished her hands back and forth through the warm water. "She was very clever and did leave open the possibility of the genomes being separated. She created...what shall I call it...a lock box in the "Y" chromosome. The box contains instructions on how to separate the two genomes."

"So," Humanus said, "open the lock box and read the instructions. Certainly my hair and skin cells carry the box."

"They do. But A4-Ni saw to it that when haploid sperm and egg were combined, the resulting individual, if a male carrying the "Y" chromosome, had a lock box with scrambled information."

"How did she manage that?"

"Nothing out of the ordinary. When sperm and egg combine there is a lot of *crossing over* of contents, which produces a unique individual. It also scrambles the contents of the lock box."

"So what good is the box?"

"A4-Ni made sure the content of the box was kept current and unscrambled in the germ cells of the last purest individual she nurtured. In your case, that would be John Lohner, hence the desirability of obtaining his germ cells, his sperm. That, the Shepherd figured, was his last best chance at being able to separate *Gilomir* and hominid. Assuming he could figure out the key to open the lock box."

Humanus felt an *aha* moment. "The Shepherd didn't get my father's sperm, so he's after me instead."

"Precisely. And since Lohner is long gone, you are his next best and last hope of being able to separate the two genomes."

"But presumably I've inherited a scrambled lock box."

"If you were to ask me, I'd say that was the case. But from the Shepherd's point of view, with nowhere else to turn, I can see why he wants to know firsthand. Thus his pursuit of your DNA as contained in your germ cells."

Humanus gave an abrupt laugh. "And you are here to help him out with that."

"Why, yes. Is that really a problem for you?"

"It's not a problem for me. But is it a problem for you?"

Ariel opened her mouth as though to speak, then shut it without saying anything. She drifted her hand back and forth in an eddy.

Humanus thought it was the first time she had shown any hesitation about the Shepherd's intentions. "What's the matter?" he asked. "Is your hominid side catching up with your synthetic programming?"

She smiled at him. It wasn't a happy smile. "Did Mia ever talk to you about how she felt?"

"Mia never talked to me directly about how she felt but I had ample time to monitor her feelings."

"And what were they?" Ariel quickly held up a restraining hand. "I don't mean to pry, if you don't want to talk about it."

Humanus laughed. "I would have thought the subject would be more troubling for you than for me."

"Then please continue. I'm prepared to be troubled."

Humanus eased from the jet that was massaging his back and shifted closer to her. "When Mia was first constructed, she had no emotions at all. The Shepherd didn't know what emotions were. The guardian hadn't given him any guidance about emotions, either. Whether the Shepherd really knew then or knows now about emotions, only the guardian could tell you. I suspect no emotions came through anywhere but from hominids. Not from the Shepherd, not from the guardian, not from *Gilomir*."

"But that is terrible. I have been given emotions."

"The Shepherd has obviously learned a thing or two over the years of producing synthetic persons. As for Mia, she had to discover her emotions. They seemed to have emerged over time as her hominid base reared up and took charge of her body."

Ariel frowned. "So in the end, Mia felt things like love, anger, hope and sorrow?"

"She did."

"Then how about you?"

Humanus thought for a moment. "Anger, hope, sorrow. Yes. Love? I don't know. I have a deep feeling for Kesi. I did for Wakuru. Was that love?"

"How about for Mia?"

"That was different. She was my mother, though I only knew her for a short time."

"What do you feel for me?"

Humanus scooted back to the other side of the pool. "I have only known you for a short time."

"You said that about your mother. But you must feel something for me?"

He eyed her carefully. "I admit, I do. But it's different than Mia. It's quite nice. I don't want it to go away."

Ariel slipped her head under the water and came up wiping her face and brushing back her hair. She drifted across the water, leaned into Humanus and before he could pull back, kissed him lightly on the lips. "I feel the same things."

Confused by the feelings running rampant in his body, Humanus sat up. "We have a lot of time."

She smiled knowingly and returned to her side of the tub. "The Shepherd told me about *Zug*."

If a knife had slashed his heart, it wouldn't have left a bigger hurt than the jolt that took him from a weak stirring of his libido to a crushing anxiety about *Zug*. Did she know what she had done? Probably. She seemed very much in control of the whole situation.

"*Zug*--" Humanus cleared his throat. The mention of the evil almost left him gagging. "*Zug* is what I am here to counter. More accurately, according to the guardian, I am here to be tested for my ability to confront *Zug*. I don't necessarily buy into that. It has been more or less foisted upon me."

"The Shepherd taught dualistic opposites."

Humanus let out a frustrated breath. "All I hear about are these dualistic opposites. What am I supposed to do with them? I'm not dualistic, at least I don't perceive myself to be."

"Maybe you should."

"Now you."

"What, now me?

"Yeah, how about you?" Humanus felt heat rising to his cheeks. "You come waltzing in here, and to all intents and purposes you are a puppet of the Shepherd. Why am I paying you any attention at all?"

"I think my existence could be termed problematic." Ariel rose out of the water. "I was constructed, to put it bluntly, and given a mission. But that mission was always in jeopardy of being compromised by my being a hominid. The Shepherd took a chance. If I don't work out, he has a plan B."

Humanus waved a hand, trying to get her to sit. "I still don't like to talk about *Zug*."

Ariel slid back into the water. "Is he here?"

"Not that I know of. He has agents are here. Rather one agent that we know of--Gomo."

"Who is Gomo?"

"He's a primate of Kesi's clan. He's always been a troublemaker, but lately his excesses have escalated, as though he's learning to work more efficiently with the primitive form he has taken in this time and place."

"Cardassin was a player."

"Yeah, but the Shepherd took care of him good. Took him out of his zone and made him into what you see, a nothing."

Ariel looked at her hands. "My skin is beginning to wrinkle. Do you think we should rejoin the others?"

"Did the conversation take a turn you didn't like?"

"No. We can always talk later, but Justin is waving to you from up there."

***

Humanus and Ariel dressed, then, not knowing which button to push to power the elevator, climbed the rung ladder to the hallway.

"What's so urgent it can't wait?" Humanus asked Justin.

"You've got to hear what Cardassin just told me."

Cardassin again. "He's told you something important?"

"I think so. You can judge for yourself."

Humanus walked over to Cardassin, who leaned against the table with a supercilious look on his face. "What is it this time?"

Cardassin folded his arms across his chest. "I simply told Justin the cave, really the cliff dwelling that harbored the early Maraia, is a stone's throw from here. Opening the eastern end of the tunnel reminded me the Maraia's original home lies a thousand meters from the western entrance to the tunnel, south along the face of the escarpment."

Humanus was stunned. "You knew about this all the time."

"No." Cardassin preened. "I just remembered it, now. Do you want me to take you there?"

Humanus fought to dispel a sense of disorientation such was the magnitude of Cardassin's revelation. "I think that would be very interesting."

"Okay, let's go." Cardassin clapped his hands in gleeful anticipation. "After we exit the ruin, we'll go south on the plateau, then descend. If my recollection remains correct, there's a trail that leads to the cave. The trail squeezes through a tight slit in the rock. It's the only entrance to the cave and very defensible. Even I, with all my mutants at hand, never breached their defenses."

When Humanus and Justin stared at him, Cardassin spread his hands, shrugged and shook his head. "Must I always remind you that was me back then and not me, now. I wouldn't be telling you all of this if I were the Cardassin of yesteryear...forward year...whatever year."

"All right, let's see what this place looks like." Humanus armed himself with his spear and blade and made for the door. "Kesi, you stay here. Rest that ankle."

Kesi scowled, obviously not wanting to be left behind.

Humanus didn't even dare tell Jamani what to do.

"May I come, too?" Ariel asked.

"If you wish." Humanus led the way out the door.

Once on the plateau, Cardassin set off at a quick pace directly south.

Ten minutes later, he slowed and glanced over the western edge of the escarpment, until he found a trail.

"This leads to the entrance," he said. Without waiting for anyone to respond, he plunged down the trail.

Humanus scrambled after him, and almost bumped into Cardassin where he had stopped below.

He stood before a narrow slit. The rock had come away from the main body of the plateau but had not fallen to the plain below.

"You'll have to get down on hands and knees to ease through," he said. "My mutants did that and as they emerged on the other side, the Maraia clubbed them senseless."

"No Maraia to club us, now," Humanus said, thinking to make light of what was probably an exaggerated excursion.

When he emerged on the other side, he stood and gazed at a crumbled array of mud brick dwellings. Time had taken its toll on what were once primitive living quarters.

"This doesn't look like much." Humanus climbed over to a dwelling and pushed with his foot against a wall that crumbled.

"It's deceiving." Cardassin came up beside him. "See that dark space over there?" He pointed toward the back of the cave to what looked like a tight tunnel that penetrated deeper into the plateau.

Humanus walked over to it and peered into a deep blackness. "I can't see a thing." He crawled into the hole and tumbled into a slightly larger volume, sealed at the far end by a hard metallic barrier. Humanus crouched on his heels. "What's this? Some sort of door? What's beyond?"

"Exactly." Cardassin said crawling up behind him. "I mean it's a door. It leads to the enclave, the last retreat of the Maraia. Actually, if I recall accurately, I sealed the door after they all left. It can only be opened by that small box off to the right. You have to be me and you have to be a Maraia."

"What?" Humanus was nonplused. "Is this all just coming back to you now?

Cardassin struck an aggressive pose. "It is. And if I wasn't me, now, I wouldn't be telling all of you this, now. To unlock the door requires my palm print along with that of a Maraia…because when I was me back then…the existence of a Maraia and me in concert would have proved that I had won!"

"That sounds too much like an exultation," Justin said dryly.

"If you want to bicker about me and me then, we will just be wasting time."

"I agree," Humanus said. "Let's cut the crap. The only Maraia we have here is Justin. Will he do?"

206

Cardassin looked Justin up and down. "I suppose so. It won't hurt to give it a try."

Justin stepped forward and wedged himself into the close confines, looking very uncomfortable. "It smells in here."

"That's probably Cardassin." Humanus waved a hand to shush him. "He says, if he presses his hand on the plate as well as a Maraia, the door will open. Give it a try."

Justin looked apprehensive. "What if I lose my hand?"

"I don't think so. Please, try."

After Cardassin pressed his palm to the plate, Justin followed and waited. "I guess it's not working," Justin said.

With a groan brought on by years of disuse, the door ground open. It was almost half a meter thick and set into a notched header and jamb all around. As it opened outward, Humanus shoved the others back and barely got out of the way himself. Lights blinked on inside to illuminate a corridor tall enough to stand upright in, wide enough for two abreast.

"I'll be damned," Humanus said.

"Yes, and I was damned coming here and sealing this door," Cardassin blurted. "It wasn't until Trudal, bless him, turned and came to me with a compliment of mutants that I finally gained any advantage over the Maraia holed up here."

"I don't know any of this history," Justin said.

"When was this?" Humanus asked.

"Let's see." Cardassin rubbed his chin. "I arrived several thousand years after Sedroth died.

207

The Maraia had come a long way by then. Of course, they had a lot of help from the guardian. But they were also a clever people. They designed and built the nano-assembler on their own but with disastrous results. Whereas it was conceived as a tool to accelerate their progress, some of the Maraia immediately started using it as a means to manipulate their genes. Things quickly got out of hand."

"Is that when the cult of TrueMen was born?" Justin asked.

"TrueMen. From Truman," Cardassin said, "the real name of Sedroth, which I was told was Truman Justis. Yes, somewhere about that time the cult took hold." He looked at Justin. "I do believe your name, Justin, was derived from the cult's messiah."

"What lies inside?" Ariel asked.

"Come, my lady." Cardassin offered his arm. "I will show you wonders to behold."

She took his arm and they proceeded into the tunnel.

It ended in a large, cavernous space, the surface of which was sleekly finished with metallic material. A soft rubbery cushion covered the floor. Unobtrusive lighting came from everywhere and adjusted as they proceeded.

Row upon row of counters with computers, monitors and other unknown equipment stood fresh and gleaming.

Humanus gazed in awe. "It looks like they left this place only yesterday. But it has to be very old."

"The Maraia were thorough," Cardassin said. "They were also formidable opponents."

"I don't get it," Justin said. "Why would they leave?"

"I like to think I had something to do with that," Cardassin crowed, then gulped. "What can I say? Back then I did have a lot to do with their exodus.

"But it was also that the climate was becoming colder by the day. The converts to the cult of TrueMen increased, until they controlled everyone and everything. Nano-assemblers were forbidden after the results of their misuse became apparent. Without the nano-assemblers to augment their existence, it became necessary to seek out a warmer climate."

"So the mutant Maraia and Trudal came over to you," Justin said, "and the TrueMen headed south."

"That's it." With a shrug, Cardassin thrust his hands palms up as though he had nothing to do with it.

"Why did you stay?" Ariel asked.

"Aha! We have a lawyer in the house!" When everyone stared at him without comprehension, he continued. "I stayed because Trudal told me to. Based on myth, Juvenal, he was an early leader of the Maraia, had hidden the guardian in Sedroth's grave. I came to learn the latter had requested to be buried with the guardian after the Maraia had exhausted their need to have it inform them."

"So you thought to find the guardian." Ariel said.

"Yes, of course. I had no clue where it was and Trudal couldn't tell me, so I figured I'd just hang out in Kanapoi, enhanced by the nano-assemblers he had been so gracious to provide me, and wait until something happened that would give me a chance to snatch the guardian. After all, that is what a player was supposed to do...back then mind you."

Humanus walked over to a near counter. "Does any of this stuff still work?" He poised a finger over a red button.

"I wouldn't go pressing any of those there buttons if I were you," Cardassin said hastily. "Never know what might happen. Might be a fail-safe to destruct the whole installation. Trudal said they had something like that wired."

Ariel looked around. "Where did they live?"

Cardassin took her hand and led her off to one side of the cavern. He climbed steps and opened another door. "In there. You can't see much from here, but in there are rooms, lots of rooms of all sorts. The interior was warmed by faux suns, mind you, very small ones. It was all quite comfortable, or so Trudal told me."

"Trudal was quite the source of information," Humanus said.

"Yes, yes he was, bless him. I couldn't have prevailed against the Maraia without him. He encouraged me to pursue the TrueMen south. So I sent mutants to harass them periodically, but I never really achieved an advantage over them. Ultimately, they came back to me."

"We've learned the story of Rasmussen," Justin said.

"Poor misguided soul. But he did give me brief access to the guardian, which unfortunately...well, actually, fortunately, became my undoing...have I said that diplomatically?"

"You have," Humanus said.

"We should access the guardian," Justin said. "It might tell us how to operate this equipment. I'd even suggest we move in here, but I think I'd get claustrophobic in those rooms back there."

"I agree. I've seen enough for now. Let's get out of here." Humanus took Ariel's hand. "This place gives me the creeps."

Chapter Ten

Once outside, Humanus took a deep breath of fresh air.

"I don't know why that place should bother you so much," Ariel said. "The Maraia did wonderful things to come so far in such a short time."

"Maybe I was simply picking up on the same negative reaction Justin was having. There's something sad about coming upon greatness and knowing it never worked out. That something intervened, compromised them, brought them to their knees."

Cardassin came up to them and bowed deeply at the waist. "If his highness Humanus and Master Justin are going to use the guardian, then perhaps you'll excuse me. I would like to return to the ruin. I have a...what shall I call it...a surprise in mind."

Humanus scowled. "I don't like surprises, Cardassin."

"You needn't worry about this one. It's quite harmless, believe me."

"That's the trouble. I have a hard time believing you."

Cardassin looked up, pressing the back of his hand to his forehead and heaving a sigh.

"Give it up, Cardassin." Humanus felt disgusted with the phony display.

"I haven't found any cause to distrust you," Ariel said, laying a hand on Cardassin's arm, "if that's any consolation."

He brightened. "Then perhaps my dear sweetie, you'd like to accompany me. There's not much for you to do here if they are going to commune with the guardian, unless you like looking at a couple of guys holding hands."

Humanus gave Cardassin a hard look and tried to think of a comeback, but Ariel had already threaded her arm into Cardassin's and started to walk away.

"Don't be long," she said over her shoulder.

"I wonder what he's up to," Justin said. "I don't like all these revelations coming out of nowhere. I don't think I'll ever be able to trust him."

"Nor will I," Humanus said, still trying to figure Ariel out. Why would she stick up for a wretch like Cardassin? "I couldn't very well tell Ariel not to go."

Justin smiled and rubbed his chin. "From what I've seen of this woman, she wouldn't have listened to you anyway."

Humanus tired of the banter. "How could you not know about this place?" he asked.

Justin snapped his attention back from the departing Ariel and Cardassin. "Easy," Justin said defensively. "When I was young it was covered in ice. When I was older, we had moved away. When I returned, I never ventured to this side of the plateau."

How could the man not have explored his environment more?

Justin must have sensed the accusation. "I really wasn't interested in getting around much. But I'm sure Jamani knew."

213

"And Jamani never said anything?"

"You have to understand Jamani is a being unto himself. I've lived with him a long time but I can't say I really understand how he thinks."

"The outer dwellings are certainly primitive," Humanus said, "just mud brick structures. But I noticed outside more advanced works had been built. I saw what looked like a smelter. If this was the early habitat of the Maraia, then they advanced quickly from stone to iron, then graduated to a truly advanced technology."

"The guardian might tell us how they accomplished this."

Humanus eyed Justin skeptically. "You think so?"

"We've got nothing to lose for trying."

Humanus removed the guardian from the pouch around his neck. He hefted the small sphere. "Are you going to do this with me?"

Justin looked skyward as though an answer lay in the clouds. "I will, but not without a lot of trepidation. I find the guardian's flashbacks disturbing."

"But this is ancient history. Years before your time or anyone you knew."

"I suppose that's safe enough."

Humanus closed his hand around the guardian and let Justin place his hand on top.

***

I see Juvenal, the first Maraia, standing in a clearing outside the entrance to a small cave. He cradles Sedroth in his arms.

214

Thick jungle crowds close. Towering trees loom and shade the sun. Vines curl. Birds flit swiftly with sharp cries.

Out of the underbrush, other Maraia emerge. "Sedroth, Sedroth," they chant.

Sedroth waves weakly.

"What has happened?" one of the Maraia asks.

"Sedroth is near death," Juvenal says. "His mistress Azizah lies dead in the cave. The player Cathcar is also dead."

"What is that you carry in your hand?" a woman asks nervously cradling an infant. It lets out a cry, swiftly stifled.

Juvenal stares down at the guardian. Despite his protestations, Sedroth had pressed it upon him. "Sedroth calls it the guardian. He placed much faith in its powers. But I have my doubts. From what I have seen, it only brings unhappiness."

"But Cathcar cannot bother us now," a man says.

"No. Cathcar cannot." Juvenal recalls the words of Sedroth after the dead body of the player Cathcar shriveled and disappeared but Azizah's body did not. *Azizah became one of us. Cathcar did not.* Juvenal wonders about sides, but Sedroth is too weak to explain.

"Then we are saved," the man says.

Juvenal shifts the weight of Sedroth in his arms. "Other players will come. Of that I am certain. And when they do, we may not have Sedroth to guide us."

"But he told you the guardian has great powers." The man persists. "We have nothing left, but to trust ourselves to it."

"Do you want to trust yourself to it?" Juvenal indicates the guardian.

The man steps back. "You are our leader. You should be the first to try the guardian. Then you can advise us all."

Juvenal smiles. "And if I go insane? What will you do, take my place?"

"Sedroth used the guardian all the time. I do not think he became insane."

"Well spoken," Juvenal says. "I have seen Sedroth use the guardian and become a changed man, at peace despite his impending death. He spoke of being able to embrace a greater whole. Perhaps the guardian could indeed show the way forward. I will try." He motions with his head that other Maraia men step forward to take Sedroth from him. Relieved of his burden, Juvenal stares apprehensively at the guardian.

"Do you know how to use it?" someone asks.

Juvenal feels a moment of anxiety. He has never used the guardian himself. He has actually never seen Sedroth use the guardian. What is he to do? "I think Sedroth only held it, and it responded to him. But I have held it since Sedroth gave it to me and nothing has happened. Maybe it will abandon us as well."

"Try again," the woman with the infant urges. "We cannot survive here without help." Her child lets lose a whimpering cry as though to reinforce the woman's opinion.

Juvenal nods gravely. He supposes the guardian knows full well what is going on and will choose to respond as the situation demands. He grasps the guardian tightly and hopes for a reaction.

His body convulses with a jolt as though he has been struck by lightning.

The others draw back.

Juvenal staggers forward and drops to his knees. His eyes curl up inside his head. His mouth drops open while his tongue lashes spasmodically, sending spittle flying.

"What is happening?" another asks, his voice coming from far away as through a fog.

Juvenal tries to speak, but cannot. Then in his mind a voice opens.

"*Truman Justis, the one you call Sedroth has chosen you to lead the Maraia. And you have accepted this role.*"

Juvenal gives up trying to speak, but his thoughts leap into the silence. *I have accepted that role. There is no one else.*

"*To do so, you will need knowledge. Knowledge I am about to give you. I will give it only to you so you will have power and control over your people. As you age you will teach others, but for now, you alone will know the future.*"

Juvenal doesn't know what to expect. The world around him goes dark, the jungle bush disappears, the other Maraia along with it. He feels very alone.

Then everything returns at once.

The Maraia rush to him.

"Are you all right?"

217

"We thought you were dying."

Juvenal stands. "I am all right. The guardian has spoken to me."

"What did it tell you?"

Juvenal searches for words to explain and finds too many of them. In a rush, they map out the future. He slows the flow of his thoughts and finds new areas of knowledge. New facts. New plans and strategies. Wisdom beyond what he could possibly have known before.

The questioners gape at him.

"I have learned...everything," Juvenal says. "I will guide you as we move into the future."

"You are changed," another says. "We can all see it."

"Come," Juvenal says. "There is much work to be done, and it must be done quickly."

***

Justin was the first to let go of the guardian. "An amazing bit of history. I always wondered how the Maraia developed so fast. In only a few hundred years they were capable of producing these advanced machines, vehicles to speed them over the ground and through the air."

"Humans of my era did the same thing," Humanus said, "in about the same time, but they didn't have anyone to lead the way."

"The Maraia had thousands of years to develop from what we saw back there at the enclave until my time, but never advanced much during that time."

"Something smells rotten here," Humanus said. "Cardassin was very glib with his brief history and

218

how Trudal led an exodus of mutated Maraia over to his side."

Justin stared at the guardian. "I hate that thing. Every time I use it, I learn something unsettling."

"Perhaps you shouldn't look at it as unsettling, just different from what you think happened. After all, your own history hasn't been exactly settling. You're just used to it."

"All right, one last go, then we should catch up to Cardassin and Ariel. I don't know how you could let her go off with him."

"She's not mine to control," Humanus said. "Besides, I think Cardassin is harmless...at least he is now."

"What period shall we investigate?"

"I suggest some time around Juvenal's death. Let's establish what happened then." Humanus handed the guardian to Justin. "You lead the way this time."

***

I see Juvenal an old man. He lies on his deathbed. Maraia elders treat Juvenal with respect. The other Maraia gather behind them.

He lies on a bed of fine linen, white sheets with a black trim around the base of the bed. Lights glow softly from glistening walls of a room buried deep in the rock of the plateau. A side table of shiny steel holds medications. The flame from a solitary candle dances with every movement of air.

Juvenal struggles onto an elbow and with his other hand outstretched, offers the guardian to his son, Osa. "Take this and return it to Sedroth and his mistress."

219

Osa nods. "It shall be so, Father. But is there nothing more that it can teach us?"

"It has told me that we have everything we need to progress. I have given the guardian to you because only you know where Sedroth and his mistress are buried. Their location must remain secret. Promise me that."

"Of course, Father. I promise."

Juvenal gives last instructions in a weak gravelly voice. "We have come to a crossroads. One I cannot help you navigate. The Maraia have come far in a short time. They still have far to go, and that path will be difficult. In time, a great evil will visit us. Some Maraia will take the easy way and embrace the evil. Others will turn away and resist. Those who resist will know no peace for the evil will pursue them all their days."

"What is this evil?" Osa asks.

"I am not meant to tell you. Each of you will recognize it in your own way, in your own time, and make your own decision not based on what I might say. It is now time for me to go." Juvenal clutches his chest and winces with pain. "Carry my body out on the plain so the night animals might feast. I shall always remain a part of this place."

Juvenal dies.

The assembled Maraia kneel around the bed and place their hands on Juvenal's still form.

***

"Rest in peace," Humanus said. "Poignant history we already know. Let's try closer to Rasmussen's time. I want to see where Trudal comes in."

I see Trudal glances around at the elders, who stare at him in silence. "You have shamed me."

"It is not we who have shamed you," one of them says gently. "You must learn your place."

Trudal turns abruptly and pushes his way to the doorway. He races down a long corridor, ignoring the looks of other Maraia as they peer out of adjacent rooms. At the end of the corridor he bangs through another doorway into a large room filled with electronic equipment.

Maraia look up from their computer monitors.

"You are all making a mistake!" Trudal shouts.

No one answers him.

He strides across the room, stumbling once and hating himself for his clumsiness. Finally he arrives at the outer door and pushes through, leaving the Maraia behind.

Trudal scrambles down the tiered levels outside the enclave. He careens into ancient mud brick structures as he heads for the exit from the ancient cave to the trail that leads to the top of the plateau. In his pocket, he clutches two purloined nano-assemblers. *The fools,* he thinks. *How can they not trust me? I will see they all rue the day they shamed me.*

Once on top of the plateau, Trudal pulls one of the nano-assemblers from his pocket and holds it high, letting the noon day sun flash reflections from its surface. He scrapes his fingernails across the skin of his arm and feeds his genetic code from the garnered cells into the nano-assembler.

Produce for me a pellet that will make a duplicate of me, not later, not in the time tested male-female way, but right now. He manipulates flush set buttons on the nano-assembler.

A moment later, to Trudal's surprise, a pellet exudes from its base.

Can this be me?

Trudal is amused. He casts the pellet onto the damp earth and watches as dirt, shrubs and rocks implode, conspire, transform and re-emerge to produce a form.

Trudal staggers back.

The form vaguely resembles a Maraia, male, very thin, skewed out of the ordinary. It is certainly not Trudal. Something has gone wrong. The form lurches at him.

"Thank you, my dear...Trudal is it? I had been looking for someone, something and then you came along with, with this...for me!" The form succumbs to a coughing fit, clears its throat and spits off to one side. "Well, now. Let's get down to business. You and I have a lot of organizing to do. For starters, we'll need some more of your Maraia friends to suck up the pellets we are going to make and advertise as personal enhancers, you know, body transformers. I'm going to need a lot of transformed bodies."

Trudal turns to run but is stayed by an obscene force or perhaps his own morbid curiosity. "You know my name. You act like you come to this place with full knowledge of what it is. Who are you?"

"They used to call me a lot of things, but the moniker that has settled and stuck the most, and the one I truly enjoy, like, embrace and so forth is Cardassin."

"You're the evil one spoken of in the myths. You're a player."

Cardassin smoothed back his eyebrows. "I thought that was obvious."

"I can't have anything to do with a player. The other Maraia will kill me."

Cardassin chuckled. "Dear Trudal, what if I were able to give you everlasting life?"

***

I don't believe it," Justin said. "Trudal created Cardassin?"

"I don't think that's what the guardian is telling us," Humanus said. "Trudal was messing around inappropriately with the nano-assembler and created a being, which Cardassin, player that he is, chose on the spur of the moment to inhabit."

"And Trudal sold his soul for mortality? What was he thinking?"

"He probably wasn't, and Cardassin obviously lied to him. But Trudal's shame must have run deep since in the end he did go over to the other side and bring a number of other disgruntled Maraia with him. He ended up bringing misery to those who remained. But regardless, Cardassin would have thought of other ways without Trudal, and misery would have caught up to their world eventually. Trudal simply facilitated it. Remember, Cathcar's body disappeared after Juvenal killed him, a sure sign that as a player he was still in play. Although he would probably not return, other players could easily have homed in on his proximity to the Maraia, their *Gilomir* strain, and the recent associations with the Shepherd."

"And you have let this beast go off with your girlfriend?"

"She is not my girl..., but you're right. We should see what they are up to."

***

As Humanus climbed over the edge of the escarpment and stood on top of the plateau, Ariel rushed up to him.

"What is it?" Humanus said alarmed, fearing the worst.

"Nothing is wrong, and Cardassin really does have a surprise in store for you." Her face glowed with a giddy excitement.

When Justin and Humanus came to the ruin, they found Cardassin lounging outside the doorway. "Yes, I have a surprise!" he announced with glee.

Humanus felt a twinge of anxiety. "I hope this isn't serious."

Cardassin giggled. "Yes and no. Just follow me. You can decide for yourself."

Humanus followed him into the ruin and was met with a riot of colored streamers sagging lazily across the space, a low throb of pulsating music, strobe lights flashing. "What is this, a carnival?"

Cardassin clapped his hands. "I thought we should have a party. The nano-assembler is full of parties, at least this one is...it having been mine before it was stolen, taken, removed from me."

224

Humanus gave Cardassin a sour look, and the glee on his face evaporated. "When did you use the nano-assembler to create the pellet that created this?"

Cardassin stopped dancing up and down. He put his hands behind his back and sashayed back and forth with his head hung. "When I created the rock-eating pellet."

"What other unauthorized pellets have you created? I was just beginning to trust you and now this."

"No other pellets, sire. Just this one. It's harmless."

"Cut with the sire. This is all a waste of the nano-assembler's charge."

Ariel cozied up to Humanus. "Please Humanus. It's done. I don't think Cardassin meant any harm. It's a party. Let's celebrate."

"What's there to celebrate?" Humanus grumbled.

Cardassin buoyed up a bit. He made an exaggerated show of thinking. "Really Humanus, there needn't be a formal reason for a celebration party. We could call it *The Day We Parked the Land Rover Party* or *The Rebirth of the Maraia Party*."

Humanus looked questioningly at Ariel, who slipped her arm into his and pulled him close.

"It does look festive," she said.

"Yes, yes. Festive," Cardassin blurted. "That's the word I was searching for." He twirled on a heel and glanced back at them. "There's even an open bar."

225

"What's an open bar?" Justin asked.

Humanus shrugged, then located Kesi and Jamani off to one side, sitting on high stools, leaning against an ornate horizontal piece of furniture and drinking something from outlandishly sized glasses. "Is that the bar?"

Cardassin grabbed Humanus by the arm, and after some resistance pulled him toward Kesi and Jamani.

Kesi had just finished whatever was in his glass and was reaching over the bar for a container that presumably held more of the same.

"Manus!" he shouted, trying to focus his eyes.

"What are you drinking, Kesi?"

"'Dassss'in shay vooodka."

"It's vodka, and very good vodka at that," Cardassin said. "Would you like to try some?"

"I don't think so." Humanus backed away. "It seems to have a strange effect on those who drink it."

"The effect isn't strange, nor is it detrimental." Cardassin sidled up to Jamani and put an arm around his shoulder. "See. It can be positively salubrious."

Jamani grinned idiotically, then, with a wide brush with his arm, sent Cardassin flying to land three meters away.

"This be good," Jamani said with a boisterous laugh.

Cardassin picked himself up off the floor. "Actually, it does have different effects on different people. My great late associate Pushkin equated Vodka with communism."

"I'm familiar with the term," Humanus said. "But I don't see the connection."

"The great equalizer," Cardassin said with a flourish. "I always drank mine in small doses. Stolitos. These two have been here for over half an hour and already finished two of the four bottles I had the nano-assembler produce."

"What is that noise?" Humanus asked in response to a sudden increase in volume of the music.

Cardassin leapt up, tapping his feet when they were in contact with the ground and making swaggering moves with his hips. "Gets your toes wiggling doesn't it?" He winked at Humanus and offered his hand to Ariel. "Would you like to dance, my dear?"

She shirked back.

"Ah, come on, sweetie! Live a little!"

Ariel looked perplexed, but extended her hand to Cardassin while glancing askance at Humanus, who shrugged.

Cardassin pulled Ariel out into the middle of the floor. Grasping both her hands in his, he extended his arms and began to twitch, then jerk. He threw his head back and forth as though he might snap his neck. His mouth lolled open and his tongue flapped from side to side.

"What's he doing?" Justin asked.

"I don't know," Humanus said. "Dancing?"

Ariel smiled and swayed rhythmically to the music. She seemed to be enjoying herself and finding amusement in her overly energetic partner.

The music paused and then a much slower arrangement began.

Cardassin leaned into Ariel and wrapped his arms around her.

"Enough of this," Humanus said under his breath. He stepped over to them and pulled Cardassin back.

Ariel stood rigidly as though she didn't know what to do next.

"I think we are done with dancing," Humanus said testily to Cardassin.

Cardassin looked around as though just waking up. "No offense, bud. We always danced like this at the university."

"That was a long time ago." Humanus spun Cardassin around and gave him a shove to send him weaving back to the bar where Jamani, still grinning, gave him another shove that sent him sprawling.

"I kind of like this music," Ariel said.

"Anything would be better than that noise we heard first." Humanus tried to lead her back to where Justin was standing, but she pulled on his arm.

"Hold me."

Before he could protest, Humanus found himself in a close embrace. He felt her hips press against his, her breasts soft against his chest. She laid her head on his shoulder, her lips against his neck.

"Do you like this?" she whispered near his ear.

Despite his reluctance, Humanus had to admit it all felt good. "It's okay."

"Is that all you can say?"

"I'm still trying to figure this out."

"What is there to figure? You like. I like. Relax."

Humanus began to relax. It wasn't that hard to do.

The music paused again and then picked up its beat.

"Okay. This isn't my kind of stuff," Humanus said.

"We could have a drink of communism," Ariel suggested with a smile.

If he was to get let off dancing, Humanus reasoned that accepting a drink would do the trick. "Just one."

"You're not driving tonight."

"What are you talking about?"

"Just something the Shepherd placed in my mind when he educated me. I know all about vodka, and parties."

"Do you, now?"

She opened her mouth to answer, then giggled and pointed.

Kesi and Jamani had taken to the floor and were leaping around energetically in time to the music.

"You don't have to know how to dance to enjoy the sound and the rhythm," Ariel said.

"They do seem to be having fun."

Cardassin came up to them. "I hope Jamani works off some of his energy. I hate being smacked down like that."

"You started all of this," Justin said, coming up behind him. "Can I get anyone a drink?" He moved behind the bar and picked up one of the bottles of vodka, peered at its half empty contents and offered them to Humanus and Ariel.

Humanus looked around for something to pour the drink into, when Cardassin thrust forward two glasses in his hand. "Thanks," Humanus said, startled. He took the glasses and shoved them out, letting Justin pour from the bottle.

Justin set two more glasses on the bar and filled them. He offered one to Cardassin and took the other for himself. He raised his glass. "Here's to new found companions and a bright future."

Justin must have had some vodka earlier to be saying that. Humanus wasn't at all convinced Cardassin ranked as a new-found companion or that the future was going to be that bright, but he felt caught up in the moment, Ariel's smile, Justin's obvious enthusiasm, even Cardassin, fool that he was. Humanus raised his glass and downed the drink.

He gulped, almost choked, but managed to stifle the spasm. The vodka burned all the way down his throat, and he swore he could feel the liquid spreading out to coat his stomach. A minute later he felt something hit his brain with a soft punch, followed by a tingle in his limbs. Not bad. He held out his glass to Justin.

Ariel sipped at her drink.

Cardassin had downed his in one go, too, and was now grinning and holding out his glass alongside Humanus. "You're okay," Cardassin said, draping an arm over Humanus' shoulders.

Humanus looked at the arm, then at Cardassin. "I thought you didn't like being knocked to the floor?"

Cardassin immediately removed his arm. If he was in any way bothered by the incident he seemed to have quickly forgotten. "Pour away, old man."

The music stopped.

Cardassin looked up, concerned. "I'll go reset it."

Kesi and Jamani, arms over each other's shoulders, staggered toward the entrance to the ruin.

"Where are you two going?" Humanus demanded.

"Make water," Kesi said. "Back quick."

Justin filled Humanus' glass. "Go easy with that stuff. I understand it can make you silly."

Humanus was beginning to feel silly.

The music started up again, Kesi and Jamani returned and refilled their glasses. Justin took a turn alone at the center of the ruin. Ariel pressed up close to Humanus, snuggling her nose behind his ear and breathing softly on his neck.

He didn't mind the closeness. In fact, he was beginning to enjoy it and the party. Everyone seemed to be having a good time.

After another two drinks, the music stopped again. Humanus looked around to see if Cardassin was going to reset it, but Cardassin lounged half prone against a far wall, his eyes closed, a drooling grin on his lips.

Kesi had abandoned Jamani and was asleep near the doorway.

Jamani lay in the middle of the floor, arms and legs spread-eagle, snoring loudly.

"I guess the party is over," Justin said. "I'm going to sleep over there tonight--" he indicated a stack of cushions. "--if you want you can have my bed." He stumbled away unsteadily before Humanus could answer.

Ariel tugged at his arm. "It's a soft bed. Come. Let's sleep."

Humanus felt all resistance leave him. He let her lead him to the bed where he flopped down on his back.

The lights dimmed and went out, as though they were programmed to do so once all activity ceased.

The ruin filled with the gray light of the moon filtering in through the windows. The colors of the party, once so vibrant, went cold.

Ariel bent over Humanus and removed his loincloth, then dropped her wrap onto the floor. She slid up next to him. "Are you too drunk to make love to me?"

Chapter Eleven

Ariel's shifting roused Humanus from a restless sleep. A vague recollection of love-making tickled his consciousness followed by a head-splitting ache. He changed his position and was trying to go back to sleep when he realized he was naked.

Vodka. He'd never do that again.

Love-making. That was another matter. Snatches of memory reminded him of the pleasure he had experienced.

Why is my pouch with the guardian lying on the floor over there?

He rolled out of the bed, padded over to the pouch and picked it up. No guardian. The leather thong that had held it around his neck had been cut. He scanned the room, but couldn't see clearly in the filtered moonlight coming through the translucent windows. Dull shapes indicated Kesi and Jamani remained where he last remembered seeing them. Justin was out of sight.

A sudden movement across the ruin caught his attention. Cardassin seemed to be awake, or perhaps he simply twitched in his sleep.

Humanus walked over and crouched in front of him. "Cardassin!"

No response.

He sat as he usually did, back against the wall, legs bent and drawn up to his chest. His head flopped forward to rest on his knees. His eyes were open and stared vacantly. His arms hung loosely at his sides, and in one hand, grasped in slightly curled fingers, lay the guardian.

The man looked dead, slack-jawed, skin gray in the moonlight. Humanus felt for a pulse in Cardassin's neck and found a strong one. He shook Cardassin by the shoulders to no avail. Wondering if the wretch had fallen into a coma, Humanus gave him a slap.

His head lolled back, tongue hanging out. No other reaction.

Humanus picked up the guardian.

Fool. If Cardassin was going to sneak over and steal the guardian he was playing with fire. Let him suffer the consequences.

Humanus dropped the guardian into the pouch, retied the leather thong and draped it over his head. He returned to Ariel and lay down beside her.

She murmured and cuddled up against him.

Her distraction and Cardassin's condition intruded and pushed away sleep.

***

"Wake up, Manus." Kesi shook Humanus' shoulder.

Humanus opened his eyes to bright sunlight pouring through the windows. "What is it?"

"Dassin gone."

Humanus leapt to his feet. He grabbed at his neck for the pouch, but it was not there.

Damn, Cardassin. What's he up to?

A glance across the ruin confirmed Cardassin wasn't where Humanus had left him. He rushed to the ruin's entrance and peered out. No signs of

Cardassin outside, not that he half expected to find any.

Jamani emerged from the hallway that led to the tunnel.

"Did you see Cardassin leave?" Humanus asked.

Jamani grunted and thumbed over his shoulder. "He be down there. I no like before. He different now."

"What do you mean different? He's always been different."

"He be big bad, now."

Justin was up and dressed. He came over to Humanus. "What's happening?" He pressed both hands against his temples. "God, what a headache."

"Something has happened to Cardassin. I caught him earlier using the guardian. He was unresponsive. I tried to go back to sleep and did, then Kesi awakened me. Cardassin is gone and so is the guardian. Jamani says he's down in the tunnel."

"The Land Rover," Justin said, alarmed.

Humanus brushed past Jamani and ran for elevator shaft. He swung onto the rung ladder and climbed down recklessly, almost losing his grip.

Light from the faux-sun spilled into the bottom of the shaft.

A loud metallic clang of the steel gate banging against the rock of the entrance echoed throughout the tunnel.

Humanus raced into the cavernous space.

Cardassin threw him a glance as he climbed into the Land Rover and fumbled with the ignition.

The engine roared to life.

Cardassin slammed the vehicle into gear.

As the Land Rover began to roll, Humanus ran alongside, then grabbed Cardassin around the neck and pulled hard, half dragging him out of the driver's seat.

Cardassin's foot came all the way off the clutch and the Land Rover jerked. The engine died. A gray puff of exhaust drifted from the back of the vehicle, then dissipated in the morning air to leave a choking smell.

"Where's the guardian!" Humanus screamed, bracing his foot against the side of the Land Rover and dragging Cardassin farther out of the vehicle.

Cardassin clung to the steering wheel, staring at him, eyes wild, showing a dark dullness that gave Humanus pause.

"What happened to you?" Humanus said.

Cardassin opened his mouth and let loose a hoarse cry that defied human production. "Leave me be," he said in a deep gravelly voice, not the sniveling, whining one Humanus had come to know.

With a shove that sent Humanus sprawling against the wall, Cardassin pushed himself free. He regained the seat in the Land Rover and restarted the engine. The tires spun, loosing a stream of gravel and choking dust.

Humanus grabbed the roll bar and swung over the passenger seat, only to sprawl awkwardly on top of Cardassin, who batted at him with his free arm.

Pummeling blows fell on Humanus' face, as he struggled to reach the steering wheel.

The Land Rover veered left and crashed into the side of the tunnel entrance.

Humanus flew forward and slammed into the windshield, feeling the glass give way with a splintering crack. He quickly regained his balance, but no matter how hard he pushed or pulled, Cardassin couldn't be dislodged.

Instead, like an automaton, he methodically shifted into reverse, and with wheels spinning, emitting smoking hot rubber, he realigned the vehicle, then lurched forward out the opening.

Jamani barreled out of the tunnel, leapt and landed in the back seat as the vehicle cleared the face of the escarpment. He slung both arms around Cardassin's throat and pulled back.

Cardassin gagged, but his foot pressed harder on the accelerator.

The vehicle careened wildly, nearly tossing Humanus out.

The guardian slipped from a pocket on Cardassin's belt and banged back and forth on the floor at his feet.

Humanus fumbled on his hands and knees snatching at the elusive sphere until he snagged it. "I've got it!" he yelled to Jamani. "Jump!"

Not waiting to see if Jamani responded, Humanus leapt from the vehicle and hit hard on the scrabble floor of the plain.

A moment later Jamani launched himself from the Land Rover.

Cardassin shrugged his shoulders and shifted back to his driving position, then headed out onto the plain. He drove north toward Lake Turk.

Humanus ran over to Jamani, who was slow getting up. "You okay?" He grabbed Jamani under an arm and helped him to a sitting position.

"He be bad." Jamani slapped dust from his arms and legs.

"Can you walk?"

"I walk." Jamani rolled onto a knee and stood. Blood glistened from scrapes on his hands and knees. He eyed the receding vehicle and shook his head. "Better gone."

"You're probably right, but he's gone with our Land Rover."

Humanus led the way back to the entrance where he pulled the damaged steel gate closed.

It met the other gate leaf unevenly, preventing the lock from being set.

Jamani headed for the elevator shaft unconcerned.

A gate that would not lock was the last thing they needed. Could Cardassin have planned to open the tunnel as a way to compromise their security? Humanus didn't think so. Something had happened the night before to set him off, or change him in a fundamental way.

They were at a disadvantage. If the gate didn't repair itself as he had seen other nano-assembled constructions do, then they had no one to operate the nano-assembler to effect repairs.

With Gomo on the loose and now a crazed Cardassin, the ruin and tunnel would have to be fortified. As it stood, anyone attacking them could now simply walk in.

238

He cleared the top of the elevator shaft and was met by Justin and an apprehensive Kesi.

"I don't understand it," Justin said. "He seemed benign enough last night. What happened while we slept? He goes to sleep a befuddled joke and now this?"

"He used the guardian," Humanus said.

"Why would that precipitate such a change in behavior?"

Humanus opened his hand to reveal the guardian. He had been holding on to it so tightly it left an imprint in his palm. "I've asked it that exact question, but it won't answer. I'll try again later, but right now I think we best direct our efforts to fortifying this place. No telling what Gomo or Cardassin might be planning."

"Jamani's gone out on the plateau to see if he can figure out where Cardassin is headed."

Humanus climbed the rung ladder, strode through the hallway, and after crossing the ruin's main floor, caught up to Jamani, who squatted outside.

On the plain below the plateau, the early morning sun slanted its rays across the grass, its yellow now predominately green. A herd of elephants grazed a half kilometer away. Bulls shifted majestically at the perimeter of the herd. The females and their young gathered protectively at the center. Striped zebras mingled with isolated wildebeests. Unseen, but probably known, saber cats lounged nearby, not hungry enough to rouse themselves for a kill.

High overhead, a cormorant sailed lazily toward Lake Turk.

Normal could be deceiving. Deep in his heart, Humanus knew they had all come to a crossroads. Their lives were going to be quickly caught up in events.

Jamani pointed. "There." A receding cloud of dust marked Cardassin's progress north.

He reached the end of the plateau and turned west out of sight around the northern end.

Justin and Ariel came up beside Humanus.

She slipped her arm in his. "Could he be going to the Maraia enclave?"

The warmth of her touch distracted him for a moment. "It makes sense he would. There's no other place around here for him to hide. I'll take Kesi and find out if you're right."

"Is that wise?" Justin said. "If Cardassin is as crazed as he seems, you and Kesi could be incapacitated or killed. Where would that leave the rest of us? We are barely a match for Gomo and his men, much less an invigorated Cardassin."

"I won't confront him," Humanus said.

"I hear you saying that," Ariel said. "But if it's true then why do you look so troubled?"

Humanus wondered his emotions could be read so easily. Obviously, his situation wasn't just him anymore. It involved not only Kesi, but Justin and Jamani and now Ariel. Life had been a lot simpler just a few days ago.

"I..." He stopped and stared at her and thought she looked very beautiful in the morning light.

She pressed her hand gently over his mouth as though she knew he was having trouble expressing himself. "I am worried about your safety," she said. "There are now more than just the two us."

Humanus gave a start. "You mean..."

"Yes, I mean. I'm pregnant. We shall be parents.

Humanus blinked. "Pregnant?"

"Have you lost your vocabulary?"

"I know what pregnant means." Humanus felt like a child caught doing something he shouldn't have. "How can you be pregnant...? Well, I know how, but how can you know you are pregnant...so soon? I thought it took a while."

Ariel gazed at him in disbelief, hands on her hips. "Duh."

"I think I asked a reasonable question." Humanus struggled to regain his composure.

"I'm not your normal, full-blooded, fecund female hominid, or hadn't you noticed?"

What's she getting so worked up about? "I got the first part. But *fecund* is new."

"Very funny," Ariel said.

"This doesn't change anything," Justin said.

Ariel looked daggers at Justin. If they could kill, he would have been dead.

But for Humanus, Ariel's pregnancy changed a lot of things. "I'm...I'm awed by your pregnancy. And I apologize for what Justin just said. But I think he meant well. It is now even more imperative that I find out what the situation is."

***

241

Humanus hunched down at the eastern edge of the escarpment. Despite further protests from Ariel and Justin, Humanus had left, feeling he had no choice but to reconnoiter the Maraia enclave.

Below, the Land Rover sat at an odd tilt having been run up on a sand berm. The vehicle's front bumper was bent. A thorn bush had scraped its side and tangled around a rear wheel. If Cardassin was seeking any sort of refuge, he wasn't being very concerned if anyone knew where he was.

But Cardassin was nowhere to be seen. Humanus presumed Cardassin had entered deeper into the Maraia enclave after breeching the locking device with Justin's acquiescence.

If the Land Rover was just sitting there, then it should be easy enough, in the absence of Cardassin, to climb down and see if it could be started.

Justin's cautions and Ariel's pronouncement weighed heavily on his mind. *Leaving them indefensible?* Then a crowding thought. *Parents?* It had never occurred to him he would have something like that to worry about. How would he react if an infant were added to the others he now felt responsible for?

Who knew if that would even come to pass, and if it did where would Ariel's loyalties lie? She was a creation of the Shepherd. Was the Shepherd going to swoop in and snatch her away? Would she let the Shepherd do something like that? Humanus didn't know.

"Manus."

"Shhhh! What is it?"

"We go." Kesi pointed back in the direction of the ruin.

"No. I want to see about the Land Rover." Humanus eased himself over the edge and slid down, careful not to raise any dust. He came to a stop on the floor of the plain below the Maraia enclave.

Kesi followed.

Humanus crept over to the Land Rover and slid into the driver's seat. He went through the steps Cardassin had used to start the engine. When he reached for the ignition, he realized the key was missing. "Damn."

"We go, Manus."

"What about the beast? He's up there somewhere. It would be just him and us. I say we give it a try."

Kesi shook his head vigorously. "We go now, Manus."

"You go back." Humanus stood and drew his blade. He took a step toward the Maraia cave.

Kesi bowled into him, knocking him to the ground. "We go now, Manus."

Humanus had never seen Kesi so adamant. He glanced up at the enclave, then at the Land Rover, then at Kesi. "Okay. We'll go back and think this thing through."

Kesi smiled in relief and led off on the trail to the top of the plateau.

At the top, cries of anguish drifted clearly through the air from the direction of the ruin.

"What be, Manus?"

Humanus broke into a run.

Coming free of low brush, Humanus pummeled one primate, then another. They seemed to have ringed the ruin, jumping up and down, chattering.

The sound of steel clashing on steel emanated from the entrance to the ruin.

Humanus rushed in.

A tumbling chaos of bodies writhed throughout.

He couldn't discern friend from foe.

Justin screamed.

Humanus kicked past primates toward the sound of Justin's voice. A primate had him pinned to the floor, a stone club raised.

Humanus shoved the smaller built primate hard.

The primate twisted before he hit the ground and sprang to his feet, club still poised.

Ducking a full swing, Humanus drew his blade and thrust it forward.

The primate gasped, clutched his hands around the blade impaled through his stomach and fell forward.

Humanus jerked the blade free, then dealt the primate a killing blow to the neck as he crumpled to the ground.

"Are you all right?" Humanus knelt beside Justin.

"No harm done, thanks to you. Where have you been?"

A spear whistled over Humanus' shoulder.

He turned. A primate followed up the errant spear with a full-throated charge.

Feinting left, Humanus slid his blade right to catch the unsuspecting primate with a long gut cut.

"Is Gomo here?" Humanus yelled, kicking the primate out of the way.

Disemboweled, the primate gaped at the intestines he held in his hands.

"Over there." Justin pointed. "He led the charge, then the others swept over us."

Humanus located Gomo on the other side of the ruin urging two of his followers to go after Jamani.

Jamani shifted and feinted, holding his spear with both hands. A thrust, then a parry.

A primate rushed into the opening.

A stiff uppercut sent the primate sprawling.

Jamani swiveled to meet the charge of the second primate.

With astonishing brute force, Jamani jabbed the primate in the ribs, then hoisted him high.

The blunt end of the spear shaft pushed through soft tissue.

Jamani flopped him to the ground, pressed a foot against his chest and pulled the spear free. With a wide grin he glanced up at Humanus.

He's actually enjoying himself, Humanus thought.

Kesi remained at the entrance, hopping from one foot to the other, as if not at all sure what to do.

"Where's Ariel?" Humanus shouted to Justin.

"By the far wall."

She stood cringing, arms pushed out in front of her protectively.

Gomo left off Jamani and stomped toward her, ignoring the death and destruction around him.

Humanus shoved a primate out of the way and cut across the floor to Ariel's side. "Are you all right?"

"He's coming for me." Her face was contorted with fear.

"Stand behind me." Humanus curved his arm around her and guided her behind him.

Gomo lunged, a rounded rock strapped to a length of stick raised overhead.

Humanus dodged to one side as the club whistled down. He thrust up with his blade but only managed a glancing blow to Gomo's midsection.

The primate howled in pain.

Humanus leaned sideways on one foot and kicked the other high, catching Gomo in the chest.

Gomo staggered back with a snarl.

Behind him a primate gave a triumphant howl and held up the nano-assembler with a flourish.

A smile twitched the edge of Gomo's lips. "Heh, heh," he crowed. "I be like that thing."

Clutching his side, he wheeled and snatched the nano-assembler, then ran for the entrance.

The other primates broke off their assault and scampered out the door after Gomo.

"I'm going after the assembler." Humanus burst out the entrance with Kesi close behind.

A rock thudded close by, followed another. One hit him in the chest.

"What the--" Humanus ducked. He raised his arms to protect his head.

Two screaming primates ran at him.

Before he could react, they tackled him and pinned him to the ground.

"Manus," Kesi cried in agony.

Humanus strained to see if Kesi was all right, but couldn't bring him into view.

Gomo strode up to Humanus, now spread-eagle and held by four primates. Gomo peered down at him. "Nano," he said, waving the assembler. He fingered his genitals and loosed a stream of urine that splashed off of Humanus stomach and then his head.

Humanus twisted, sputtering, trying to get out of the way.

Jamani leapt from the ruin and heaved his spear.

One of the primates pinning Humanus gasped as the spear penetrated his chest, the point coming out his back. Eyes bulging, he fell back.

Gomo grunted, stopped peeing and waved for his band to follow him.

They weren't about to take on Jamani, even though the latter had nothing but his hands left with which to defend himself.

Gomo's troop retreated south and then out of sight. Distant cries of bravado carried back into the silence left behind.

Humanus leapt to his feet and searched for Kesi.

He lay motionless on the ground a few meters away.

"Kesi?" Humanus knelt beside him. He could see no obvious wounds.

Kesi groaned and sat up. He didn't appear to be hurt. "Manus smell."

"Yes, I smell. Worse than that, I feel humiliated."

Jamani stomped over to the dead primate and dragged the corpse to the edge of the escarpment where he grabbed the shaft of the spear and kicked the body free.

Humanus looked up at the sound of someone exiting the ruin.

Justin staggered out, leaning heavily on Ariel.

Humanus rushed over to them and helped support Justin under a shoulder.

"I'm still in one piece," Justin said. "But I'm getting too old for this sort of foolery. They came at us so fast there was nothing we could do."

"I should have been here," Humanus said.

"At least it was only the nano-assembler." Justin eased himself to the ground and sat. "It could have been worse."

Ariel came up to Humanus and reached to embrace him, but pulled back suddenly. "What is that smell?"

"Gomo has unusual ways to make his point." Embarrassed, Humanus felt his cheeks burn. "At least no one was hurt."

"That's what I don't understand," Justin said. "He had us dead to rights, yet he didn't kill us when he easily could have."

"I'm afraid the pecking order has changed dramatically," Humanus said. "Gomo has just become a pawn in the bigger scheme of things. He won't make a move until he's told to do otherwise."

"What does that mean," Justin asked.

"I think *Zug* is amongst us."

248

***

Zug circled the inner enclave for the fourth time. He flexed his arms. He raised his knees high as he walked, and waggled his head back and forth.

Why would Cardassin choose such an ungainly body in which to resurrect?

It was obvious he hadn't taken very good care of himself. In fact, his body seemed to barely function. But *Zug* hadn't been responsible for choosing his container. The guardian had made that decision, and *Zug* would simply have to deal with it, which troubled *Zug*. How was he to bring *Gilomir* and company to their knees? He was outnumbered, and aside from a wheeled vehicle of questionable use, he had no weapons to speak of, unless there was something in the labyrinth of the enclave abandoned by the Maraia he could bend to his purposes.

After assuring himself he could walk without tripping or falling sideways, *Zug* focused his attention on the banks of equipment that surrounded him. Clever people these Maraia.

Some of the equipment still looked functional. He flicked a switch on a nearby computer and a needle in a dial jumped to life. Without knowing the use of the underlying machine, at least he learned it had a viable power supply. *Quite the chemistry set*, he mused. One could really get creative.

A thump from the tunnel that led to the outside distracted him.

Have they traced me here already? I'm not the least prepared to receive them.

He berated himself for not closing the outer door behind him, but there was the underlying fear the damn thing might stay closed and he would have no other way out.

A diminutive primate scampered from the tunnel and came to a halt when he saw *Zug*. He hefted a crude stone club.

"What have we here?" *Zug* said, amused at the bowlegged, muscular creature that barely came to his chest, its body covered in close-cropped hair. But the answer to his question came to him almost immediately. He laughed. "What on Earth made you decide to pick that guise?"

The primate, who seemed not to have heard *Zug*, sauntered up to him and shoved him in the chest with his free hand. "Knees, Dassin!" The primate pointed to the floor with his club.

Astonished at the impudent being's audacity, *Zug* could only stare.

"Down!" the primate snarled, showing his teeth. He swung the stone club at *Zug*'s head.

Zug drew back reflexively, but still took a glancing blow to the side of his head. He reached to the wound and it came away bloodied. *Zug* was more annoyed than hurt that the idiot standing before him might ruin his already dysfunctional body.

"Let's start again." *Zug* wiped the blood off his hand onto his tights with an agitated gesture. "You must be Gomo, and, of course, we've met before, and I can see you would be confused or unable to comprehend that things have changed."

Gomo cocked his head and sneered, obviously not liking *Zug*'s flippant attitude. He raised the club again.

"There's a lot of me in you, but we're going to have to put a stop to this posturing." *Zug* moved in swiftly and clamped his thumb and forefinger on Gomo's hand. With an iron grip and quick twist, he bent it back at the wrist.

Gomo dropped to his knees, shrieking in pain. The club clattered to the floor.

"Dearest Gomo, I appreciate the work you've been doing here, but I'd rather you kept your filthy hands, not to mention that germ-carrying stick you call a weapon to yourself. I have a thing about being touched." *Zug* twisted harder.

Gomo's eyes watered. His face grew red. His mouth opened and closed soundlessly, then he loosed a shriek of pain.

"Do shut up," *Zug* said. "I hate whimpering fools. While you are suffering, let me explain what I am doing."

Gomo shook his head vigorously.

Zug leaned close to Gomo's face. "Is that a no? A please let me go, no? I suppose that would interest you more, but indulge me for a few minutes. I want to tell you, anyway. I have bent your hand back, like this--" *Zug* gave the grip a tweak and smiled at the groan Gomo emitted. "--such that the median nerve is being compressed in the carpal tunnel by the hamate bones of your wrist. I'm doing this in the hopes you will better understand with whom you are now dealing. Pain has a way of concentrating even the dimmest wit." *Zug* released Gomo's hand.

Gomo groveled on the floor, massaging his wrist.

"That's a good beast. Better you there than me." *Zug* turned his back on the primate. "I hope we understand one another."

He spun around just as Gomo started to get to his feet. "Did I say stand?" *Zug* kicked Gomo's legs out from under him, then ground his boot into the back of Gomo's ankle.

Gomo seethed. His lips pulled back to expose his canines. His nose wrinkled, his eyes went to slits.

"Tsk, tsk, a temper," *Zug* said. "But I like that."

Gomo fought to regain control. He crouched low, breathing heavily. Though his eyes glistened with hate, he reached up with an extended hand. "I help."

The beast couldn't possibly expect me to take his hand, could he? *Zug* stepped back. "Of course you'll help." *Zug* strode away from the cringing primate, leaned back against one of the counters and waved his arm expansively at the equipment around him. "This is an excellent place to set up shop. From here we'll be able to wreak the maximum amount of havoc. Don't you think?"

Gomo gazed around the cavern.

"With adequate resources," *Zug* continued, "we should be able to launch a small war. Not that we'll have to go that far, but a pitched battle with that snot-nosed *Gilomir* will suit me fine."

"What do?"

Zug eyed the primitive. "I suppose I'll just have to get used to your primitive speech patterns. What do? What do? Actually, one could say it's kind of cute, if it didn't sound so stupid."

"No stupid."

Zug leveled his gaze on Gomo. *No you're probably not stupid. But you're unpredictable and the last thing I need is an ally I cannot trust.* "What am I to do with you? If I bring you into my confidence, the chances are you will muck up my plans."

"No muck. No muck." Gomo seemed to be falling over himself to get into *Zug*'s good graces.

"Okay. Try this. I need tools. I need more manpower, or shall I say primate power?"

"Tooools." Drool escaped from the side of Gomo's mouth with the unfamiliar word.

"Yes, tooools," *Zug* mimicked. "Especially something called the nano-assembler. I can put it to better use than building a Land Rover."

"Nono-asshem..."

Zug shoved off the counter and was at Gomo's side. He grabbed Gomo's ear and twisted. "You little freak. If you can't say something correctly, then shut the fokk up." He gave Gomo a shove, nearly toppling him onto the floor. "It's the little stick, you dimwit, that *Gilomir* carries around with him. Your first task will be to steal it. I suggest a surprise attack. Quick in and quick out before they know what hit them. Once we have the nano-assembler, I'll make things easier for us...and you. Now get out."

253

A broad grin spread across Gomo's face. "Kill Manus."

Zug breathed a sigh of frustration. *Such a primitive. It's a wonder he's survived this long.* "No we don't want to kill *Gilomir* or any of the others for that matter. At least not yet. Don't you understand the true nature of evil?"

"Ebil?"

Zug looked to the ceiling. "Have you forgotten so quickly what I just told you?"

"Eeevil, eeevil." Gomo cringed.

"Yes, evil. It's obvious you don't understand, so I'm going to tell you. Evil—that's pretty much what I'm about--taken to its extreme becomes good, becomes evil, becomes good and so on."

Gomo traced circles in the air with his finger.

"You're not as dumb as I thought. One feeds into the other. So, though I relish my current position, I cannot take it to extremes lest I meet myself coming. Does that make any sense to you?"

Gomo nodded enthusiastically.

Zug wasn't convinced the primate understood, but didn't care. "You, on the other hand, are of much simpler design. Your wickedness is all you have. Actually, in many respects you are more dangerous than I am for you see no bounds to your evil. Fortunately, you're going to be working for me. I will control you. You will do as you are told." *Zug* waved a hand in dismissal. "Enough of this chatter. You have your first assignment."

Gomo sprang to his feet. "Kill Manus!"

This isn't going to work. *Zug* glanced at his hands and flexed his fingers. Despite his aversion to touching Gomo, throttling him was the only means he had at his disposal. He gripped Gomo's throat and squeezed.

The primate squirmed. His legs kicked out spastically.

A second primate burst into the room, followed closely by three others.

Zug looked up distractedly, a yawn toying at the back of his mouth. He kept his grip on Gomo's throat. "What do you want?" he asked the newcomers.

The lead primate held up a nano-assembler.

"Ahhh," *Zug* sighed, dropping Gomo to the floor. "Where, pray tell, did you get that?"

Gomo rolled to his knees, massaging his throat. "Steal it," he croaked from bruised vocal cords.

"Be a good monkey and give it here." *Zug* held out his hand.

The primate approached apprehensively, arm outstretched, nano-assembler at the end.

Zug snatched the shiny cylinder. "Dear Gomo, you've outdone yourself and anticipated all my needs admirably."

Gomo nodded, his eyes bright with fear.

Zug fingered the nano-assembler and winced. It was sticky. He glanced around, ignoring the gaping primates.

There must be a functional wash basin here somewhere.

Chapter Twelve

Having washed and changed his loincloth, Humanus paced the floor of the ruin.

Justin and Ariel stood off to one side eyeing him nervously.

Too many inputs are coming in at once, Humanus thought. Gomo. The brazen attack. The nano-assembler gone. Okay. Let it go. Gomo didn't know how to use it anyway. But what if? What if Gomo and a crazed Cardassin teamed up? Would Cardassin show Gomo what the nano-assembler could do? Probably.

Justin stepped in front of Humanus. "Give it up, boy. You're not going to figure this out now. Nor can you change what has already happened. We've got a security problem facing us. We have to fortify this place or Gomo and his henchmen will just waltz in here and slaughter us."

Humanus knew Justin was right. There was no getting around the fact the primates led by Gomo could assault them any time they pleased. "Okay. You want to close this place up. Let's close it up."

"We have to do more than just close it up," Justin said. "We have to identify defensible spaces."

Humanus looked to the ceiling and shook his head. "That's classic, Justin. I think we've got to do more than just identify defensible spaces. We need something overt."

"What did you have in mind?"

"The Land Rover."

"Yeah, there's the Land Rover. From what you've said, it's stranded on a berm and dead in the sand. But we've no key to start it, anyway."

"Maybe there's a way to start it without a key."

Justin snorted a laugh. "Yeah, and maybe pigs are going to fly."

"I'll ask the guardian," Humanus said, feeling defensive.

"Asking the guardian has brought us nothing these last attempts."

"It's worth a try." Humanus looked at Justin hopefully.

Justin shrugged and turned away.

Humanus couldn't blame Justin for his skepticism. The guardian had become a fickle guide. When it did choose to divulge information, it was now more often than not on some matter that didn't really have a lot of consequences. Nevertheless, he fingered the small sphere out of the pouch from around his neck.

Is there a way to start the Land Rover without a key?

"*Hot wire.*"

Humanus blurted a laugh, such was his surprise at getting a positive response.

"What?" Justin asked. "Did you get an answer?"

"I did. I asked it if the Land Rover could be started without a key and it answered, *Hotwire*. Give me a moment." Humanus returned his attention to the guardian.

"Pull down the ignition board. Detach the red and black wires. After making sure the gears are disengaged, wind the wires together."

That's it?

No answer.

"I've got it," Humanus said triumphantly. "We'll hot wire the Land Rover."

Justin gave Humanus a baleful look. "You think it's that simple?"

"I'm going to give it a try." Humanus said.

Ariel came up to Humanus. "You can't just go off and leave us."

Humanus felt a tug of anxiety at his insides. Not something he had anticipated. "I know we're exposed." He looked expectantly at Justin, hoping for support. "But, if we can regain the Land Rover without any loss, then we'll have something of an advantage."

Ariel grabbed Humanus by the shoulders and forced him to look her in the eye. "Have you forgotten so quickly that I'm pregnant?"

Humanus felt stung by her words. "I haven't forgotten."

"What if something happens to you?"

"I have to act on what is presented to me." Humanus drew Ariel close. "The guardian has given me the means to steal back the Land Rover. I have to take advantage of that opportunity."

Ariel dropped her gaze. "I know. I may seem defiant, but it's all new to me, too. I didn't expect this to happen so quickly. I don't even know what the Shepherd has in store for me...or us...I mean you, too."

***

Ten minutes later Humanus crouched with Kesi at the edge of the escarpment and surveyed the scene below. He had a strong sensation of déjà vu, having just been there. The Land Rover sat where he'd previously seen it. No one was visible outside the Maraia enclave, a fact that struck Humanus as strange. No guards, no lookouts. Gomo must feel very secure, or was it Cardassin, who was now in charge?

"You stay here, Kesi. There's no point in both of us getting into trouble if it occurs. If I get the Land Rover started, you can return to the ruin and tell the others. I'll drive it back around the plateau. Understand?"

Kesi nodded.

Humanus clapped him on the shoulder and eased over the edge of the escarpment. He descended silently and was soon crouching next to the Land Rover. He held his position for a few minutes to see if he'd been observed.

Humanus located the ignition circuits as shown to him by the guardian. Sure enough, there was a red wire and a black wire, plus a lot of other wires. But the guardian had said the others weren't important, just the red and black ones.

After detaching the wires from the board, Humanus checked that the vehicle was not in gear. Then he crossed the wires. They sparked and the engine coughed to life.

After giving the wires a sharp twist to hold them together, Humanus waved to Kesi and jumped behind the wheel. He stumbled with the clutch and

259

gear shift, producing a loud grinding before the gear shift dropped into reverse.

Two primates emerged from the passageway leading into the enclave. They stopped when they saw what was going on but made no effort to prevent him from retaking the Land Rover.

Gomo came out and stood behind them. He didn't look particularly concerned, either, that Humanus was retrieving the Land Rover. Gomo picked up a stone and threw it at Humanus. It clanged off the hood of the vehicle, leaving a dent.

Humanus gunned the engine and lurched backward several meters until he cleared the sand berm. Then he raked the gear shift into the first position, turned the wheel sharply and lurched forward. Remembering he had to shift gears, he let the engine whine climb to a high pitch, then shoved in the clutch and shifted into a higher gear. The operation went smoothly, and he smiled to himself, very pleased. He waved to Kesi that he should meet him back at the ruin.

Humanus bounced along in the Land Rover, running parallel to the escarpment and heading north. Ten minutes later, he rounded the end of the plateau. The late afternoon sun reflected off the rippling waters of Lake Turk. Out of the lee of the plateau, a stiff breeze caught his hair and sent it flying. After another half kilometer, he turned south on the eastern side, feeling content he had gotten the Land Rover back without incident. Driving, he thought, could be fun.

When he came to the open tunnel entrance, Kesi and the others were already waiting for him.

Humanus slowed and pulled to a stop in front of the entrance, killing the motor as he did so. He swung out of the driver's seat, feeling a bit embarrassed at his amateurish handling of the vehicle.

"It worked," Justin said enthusiastically.

"Yeah, for once everything went according to plan."

Ariel rushed to him and fell into his embrace. She looked at him concerned. "Kesi said Gomo saw you."

"Gomo and some of his guys," Humanus said. "But strangely, they didn't make any effort to stop me."

"Perhaps they couldn't think of a use for the Land Rover, much less figure out how to drive it."

"Cardassin could have told them," Justin said. "Cardassin could have used it himself."

"That's assuming Cardassin is in league with them." Reluctantly, Humanus let go of Ariel. "I'm still not convinced he is."

Justin shook his head. "It seems to me he's embraced evil. There's no other explanation for his behavior."

Humanus wasn't interested in debating Cardassin's current state of mind. "Let's get this thing inside. I have an idea how we might be able to use it as a weapon. There's also the extra fuel. It's very flammable. If we fill small containers and fit them with wicks, we could make firebombs."

"I can do that," Ariel said. "I saw discarded containers at the back of the tunnel."

After she left to look for containers, Humanus and Jamani pushed the Land Rover into the tunnel.

"Since the gates won't lock, let's leave them ajar," Humanus said. "We'll create a corridor with rocks that will funnel any attackers forward. At the end of the funnel we'll position the Land Rover. It shouldn't be too hard to accelerate the Land Rover down the gauntlet to take out attackers."

"That's quite clever," Justin said. He waved to Jamani to help him with the gates, then instructed him on how to build the gauntlet.

As Jamani labored placing rocks to form a wall, Justin came over to Humanus. "The gauntlet is only a first line of defense. If they get beyond that, maybe by sheer numbers, then what? Shouldn't we have something up above to deter them?"

Humanus glanced up to the hallway leading to the ruin. "We could create a hazard in the hallway, a trip wire that would cascade rocks into place, sealing the passage. It would only deter them for a moment, but it might give us time to regroup."

Justin waved to Kesi, and the two of them climbed the ladder to the hallway above.

Humanus paced off the distance from the parked Land Rover to the metal gates. An assault might take five seconds. He didn't want to keep the Land Rover running constantly to be ready for an attack. Maybe with good lookouts posted around the ruin, he might be able to buy another thirty seconds in which to start the engine to arm the defense.

He walked an assault step by step through his mind. It was a given that Gomo would try to come in through the tunnel. If their defenses failed there, then it was a question of retreating to the ruin itself.

262

The blank windows of the ruin would have to be reinforced somehow, as well as the door.

Ariel returned with an assortment of small gourds and other odd-shaped containers. "Will these work?"

"Excellent." Humanus lifted the fuel container off the back of the Land Rover, and with Ariel holding a gourd, filled it part way. He looked around for something with which to make a wick.

Ariel immediately discerned what he was looking for. "Here, use some of my wrap."

Humanus tore off a short length and shoved it into the container. The wick immediately saturated with fuel. "We'll have to keep these covered or all the fuel will evaporate. But for now, here's our first bomb."

Ariel looked pleased. "Shall we join Justin in the ruin while Jamani finishes the gauntlet?"

Humanus and Ariel climbed the metal rung ladder in the elevator shaft and met Justin and Kesi in the hallway.

Justin held up a hand. "Careful. There's a thin wire stretched across the hallway." He gestured. "When it is tripped, rocks held by this array on the wall will tumble across and seal the hallway."

It didn't look too secure to Humanus, but everything they did seemed to have a futile component. He held up the firebomb. "Do you have fire making materials?"

"I do. Some steel and flint."

"What about the windows in the ruin?"

"Good question," Justin said. "We'll have to cover them up somehow. We don't have any

263

boards, so I'm going to guess rocks are our best bet. None of this is going to keep out Gomo's primates indefinitely, but since they are equal to or less than ourselves physically, if we can slow them down, we might gain an advantage."

A shout from Jamani echoed up from the tunnel.

"What's that all about?" Humanus ran to the end of the hallway where he peered down into the tunnel.

Jamani stood at the eastern entrance with his spear thrust through the steel gate. Hanging off the point of the spear was one of Gomo's primates.

"There be Gomo!" Jamani called up, motioning with his hand that Gomo had run off to the south.

"What a prize," Humanus said to Justin, who was crowding his shoulder. "Let's try the firebomb."

Back in the ruin, Justin rummaged for his steel and flint. After finding them, he tested one against the other, producing sparks. "I hope this works."

Humanus and Justin ran out the entrance and south along the escarpment edge.

Gomo had reached the trail leading down the side of the escarpment.

Humanus stopped and pointed the bomb's wick toward Justin. "Light it."

Justin struck a spark, and the wick caught on the first try.

With a satisfied nod, Humanus heaved the bomb at Gomo.

The bomb hit close, broke and splashed fire onto the unsuspecting primate.

Gomo howled in pain and fell off the trail. He rolled two meters and hit the sand of the plain below, then batted at his fur, screaming in agony.

The smell of burnt hair drifted up to Humanus.

With the flame extinguished and Gomo's hair trailing gray streams of smoke, he limped farther south and out of sight.

"That certainly worked wonders," Justin said happily.

Humanus was satisfied, too. "With a bit more preparation, we should be able to take on anything they can throw at us." Humanus led the way back to the ruin where they were met by Jamani who was cleaning the bloodied point of his spear with sand.

"Where's the primate you killed?" Justin asked.

Jamani shrugged and thumbed over his shoulder in the direction of the tunnel entrance.

Humanus walked to the edge of the escarpment, and leaned over to get a view of the entrance below.

"The body's gone."

***

Zug sat in a swivel-tilting high-backed stool that was bolted to the floor in front of one of the long counters. His tattered yellow boots, split on the sides, toes sticking out the front, barely reached the floor. He leaned back and shoved at the counter, producing enough force to spin himself completely around.

He grinned with satisfaction. By pumping his legs out, then back in at the knees, he took pleasure in being able to sustain the spin for three, sometimes four circuits.

265

Suddenly feeling dizzy and nauseous, he gripped the edge of the counter, nearly throwing himself off the stool with an abrupt stop. A large red button at the center of the counter caught his attention.

Two keys were inserted into slots to one side of the button. A primitive failsafe device--two keys turned, then the button pressed. With the button pressed, presumably the enclave would disintegrate, and if that were the case, then why hadn't the Maraia turned the keys, pressed the button and blown up their enclave upon their departure?

He turned one of the keys.

A small LED above it winked red.

He turned the other key.

Another red LED.

He turned back the first key.

Its LED went out.

If I turn both keys, and then press the button, can the process be stopped by turning one of the keys back to off?

Only one way to find out.

He turned the first key to red and hovered his finger over the large red button.

Gomo burst into the cave. His close cropped matting of hair smoldered. Behind him, a second primate dragged the body of one of his comrades.

Instead of pressing the button, *Zug* pinched his nose. "I hate the smell of burnt hair!" he said in a stuffy voice.

"We go look," Gomo said, shakily. "They make fireball. I burn. Uku dead." Gomo pointed to the body of the primate lying on the floor.

266

"Fireballs?" *Zug* asked, still holding his nose.

"It be liquid from 4-wheels. Burn like fire. They throw at me. Liquid spread. Fast. Make more fire."

Zug rummaged Cardassin's voluminous memory. What a closet of useless information spanning ten thousand years. The beast certainly wasn't very organized. "They've built themselves petrol bombs. Molotov Cocktails, I believe they were called, back in the day. Pity. Is that how you got burned?"

Gomo nodded gravely, probably not at all liking *Zug*'s cavalier attitude.

"We'll have to see what we can do about that. Tell me, what other modifications to their premises have they undertaken? Have they fixed the gate?"

Gomo shook his head. "Gate close but no be locked."

"I do wish you'd work on your tenses, though you do seem to be picking up vocabulary at a nice clip."

Gomo blinked stupidly.

Zug waved his hand in dismissal. Perhaps his concerns were too much for Gomo to understand. "What have they done with the Land Rover, the 4-wheels?"

Gomo nodded. "Make rows." Gomo set the palms of his hands parallel on the counter, then winced when he realized they had been burned, too. Gritting his teeth, he wiggled his thumbs. "4-wheel be here." Then he extended his forefingers. "Gate here."

"I see," *Zug* said. "They have created a corridor with the Land Rover at one end. Anyone entering the corridor can be taken out by accelerating the Land Rover down the corridor. The attacker would not have time to escape. Clever."

Zug looked back at the button and the red LED's. He turned the keys and removed both of them from their slots, then tucked them into the elastic top of his tights. It wouldn't do to have Gomo or one of his henchmen either accidentally or on purpose, press the button.

"We'll have to do something about your burns. I'm sure you don't find them the least bit comfortable, and I can't stand the smell." *Zug* took the nano-assembler from a fanny-pack hanging around his waist. "Cardassin wasn't the most adept user of this device, but with a little luck we should be able produce something to alleviate your suffering."

Gomo followed his every move intently.

After a few minutes of fiddling, *Zug* pressed a button and waited for a pellet to be expelled. A small pink pellet plopped into his hand.

Gomo reached for it.

Zug drew back. "Easy, there. You're not to eat it. We'll mix it with a bit of water, then you can smear it onto your wounds."

Zug walked over to the wash basin he had found earlier, extracted a container from a handy dispenser and filled the cup with water. He plunked in the pink pellet, swished it around until it dissolved, then handed the cup to Gomo.

"Try this. Just wet your fingers and dab them gently on your wounds."

Gomo grasped the cup with the gnarled fingers of one hand, then dipped his other fingers into the liquid. He patted his wounds with the liquid.

Almost immediately the angry red of suppurating skin began to heal. In another minute, the skin had restored itself and bristles of hair sprouted through it.

Gomo looked at the skin, amazed, and then to *Zug*, very pleased. "Works."

"Of course it works. Finding such a remedy is a lot easier than finding something to raise your friend there from the dead. But I shall try. We need all the able bodied bodies we can muster."

This time *Zug* occupied himself with the nano-assembler for ten minutes. He produced a pellet, crushed it to a powder and sprinkled it onto the dead primate's chest.

The powder lay inactive.

Zug frowned and returned his attention to the nano-assembler. Another pellet expelled fifteen minutes later.

He again crumbled the pellet and applied it to the dead primate's chest. This time, the powder disappeared immediately. A moment later, the primate blinked and sat up.

Gomo and the other primate leapt back and cringed while staring at the resurrected primate.

Zug laughed. "It's not every day you see someone rise from the dead."

He got no response from the startled primates.

"I'm going to try something truly spectacular and ...Uku is it, will be our guinea pig."

Zug felt a wave of confidence. The nano-assembler was easier to use than he had anticipated. Cardassin did have a passing familiarity with the tool. That, coupled with *Zug*'s own intelligence, made the design of the nano-genes rather easy.

After a while he held up a blue pellet in triumph. "This will facilitate the downfall of our adversaries in the ruin."

Gomo and the other primate had not budged from their initial positions. The recently dead primate was still blinking, moving his arms and lifting his feet, as if checking that all his body parts were in good working order.

Zug walked over to the wash basin and came back with a cup of water. He indicated the primate should open his mouth, and when he did, *Zug* deposited the pellet at the back of his tongue, being careful not to otherwise touch the primate's mouth. He then handed the primate the water and encouraged him to drink.

Gomo and the other primate stared.

Zug paced back and forth, looking often at Uku.

Just when *Zug* was about to conclude his designs had come to naught, Uku began to grow. His limbs and torso thinned out. His height increased twofold.

Zug immediately saw the problem. Whereas, the pellet had the desired effect, Uku only had so much body mass to devote to his increased size.

Zug prodded Uku toward the wash basin, where he bent and drank copiously from the tap. His limbs and torso immediately filled out. He had become a giant primate, now standing two heads taller than *Zug*.

"The first member of our army," *Zug* said. He quickly dialed into the nano-assembler an order for more pellets. "Gomo, get your other guys in here. We're going to make them big, too."

Gomo nodded enthusiastically and ran out to the hallway. He returned a moment later with eight of his men.

"Is that all you have left?"

Gomo spread his hands in disappointment. "This be all."

"They will have to do." *Zug* distributed the pellets and with Gomo's help supplied the eight, plus the other primate that was already there, with water.

Soon the enclave seemed crowded with the giant primates jostling one another.

"Me, too," Gomo said.

Zug shook his head. "If you haven't noticed, you soon will. These guys, though now twice their original size, are dumber than dumb. A pity really, but it was the only way I could get them to grow this quickly. But I think they will not be too dumb for our purposes.

"You, my dear Gomo, must remain small and sufficiently smart to look after them. To help you, I've retrieved a program for a most interesting tool. It seems to be one that was used extensively during the recent, future, whatever, ice age. It's labeled an ice razor, but I'm sure you understand none of this and could care less."

271

Gomo nodded enthusiastically.

"I thought so," *Zug* said. He took the pellet the nano-assembler expelled and sprinkled it over one of the distant counters. "There should be enough raw material here to construct this thing."

Zug peered at the counter as Gomo edged closer.

"You will kindly wait over there. When it is done I will let you know."

Gomo retreated to stand amongst the towering primates.

The counter dissolved, and a moment later, reconstituted itself into an ice razor.

Zug picked up the tool, thumbed what he decided was the *on* switch and pulled the trigger.

A beam of thin red light shot out one end and punched a steaming hole in the floor.

"A bit too much firepower for our needs, don't you agree, Gomo?"

Gomo grinned. He obviously understood the implications of the tool and welcomed the firepower. He leapt to *Zug*'s side, his hand outstretched.

"Patience," *Zug* said. "I'm dialing this sucker down to a non-lethal output. You can use it as a...a what they used to call, a cattle prod. If your super-sized friends here get out of line, just give them a jolt with this. If you get yourself into a situation with one of our adversaries, you can also use this without killing them."

Gomo seemed disappointed but nodded anyway as if he understood.

272

"Then we are all set. I trust the increased size will give us a decisive advantage despite the rudimentary fortifications our adversaries have cooked up. In any case, we have the element of surprise. They will not be expecting super-primates.

"Now the plan. I want you to return to the ruin and bring back the girl. She is the key to everything. Once we have her, then we will have *Gilomir*. The others are irrelevant. Don't waste your energy with them--"

"Kill all!"

"No, you idiot. I don't want anyone killed, at least not yet. Just go in and bring back the girl. You can clock the others over the head if you like, but don't kill them."

"No kill." Gomo frowned.

"Finally," *Zug* said with a sigh. "No kill. Now get going."

***

"They come, they come!" Kesi yelled, running, stumbling, then falling into the ruin.

"From where?" Humanus demanded. "On the plateau or down below."

"Down, down. They be big, Manus."

"Big?"

"Great big!"

"Everyone to their stations!" Humanus yelled as he rushed to his defensive position overlooking the tunnel entrance. *What does great big mean?* He supposed he was about to find out.

He gazed in shock as three lumbering primates, who could only be described as giants, ripped the steel gates off their hinges.

He thought briefly about dropping down to rev the engine of the Land Rover, strategically parked to mow down assailants. But such an effort would be futile given the size of the intruders. Let them come into the tunnel. They would still have to get up into the ruin.

"They're coming in from the front!" Justin shouted down the hallway.

Humanus retreated. As he passed the elevator shaft, he glanced down.

A super-primate had squeezed through the doorway at the base of the shaft and gazed up at him.

Humanus lunged for the elevator control. He stabbed at buttons until with a shrieking whine the elevator platform descended.

The primate seemed caught by surprise. At least he didn't make a move for crucial seconds, then it was too late. His bulk prevented him from slipping back out the door.

The elevator car ground to a halt.

The crushed primate never let out a sound, which struck Humanus as odd. *Are they so stupid as to not even have feelings?*

The remaining two primates quickly spilled into the shaft, located the rung ladder and began to climb.

Humanus raced up the length of the hallway, pulling the trip wire on a pile of rocks. They tumbled into place and blocked the hallway behind

274

him. *Probably good for thirty seconds, given the size of those guys.*

He burst into the main space of the ruin. Red and blue streamers with half deflated balloons still drifted overhead from Cardassin's ill-begotten party.

To Humanus it seemed the area was clogged by super-sized mutant primates. Though there were only four of them, their sheer volume dominated the space.

Remarkably, not a lot of fighting was going on. It was more of a standoff. The mutants spread out against Jamani, Kesi and Justin who stood with what weapons they had, protecting a cowering Ariel.

Humanus unsheathed his blade and charged the nearest super-primate.

The primate took Humanus' thrust without wincing, and ignored the gush of blood that erupted from his arm. He raked Humanus across the chest to send him flying five meters to the other side of the ruin, releasing a spray of crimson that stitched red dots across the near wall and caused the others to duck.

Humanus hit hard. His head clocked against the wall, inducing a disorienting buzz. The fight leaked out of him. *How do I combat such goliaths?*

He staggered to his feet, only to see a tidal shift in the mutants as they brushed aside Ariel's three protectors. The giants ignored spear thrusts and clubs, as a wildebeest might flick flies from its hide. A super-primate grabbed Ariel by the hair.

She shrieked in terror tinged with pain.

The mutants retreated, turned and marched for the exit.

Ariel swung her fists, catching nothing but air and the occasional mutant, who ignored her.

"No!" Humanus yelled.

They cleared the doorway and strode, zombie-like into the brilliant midday sunshine.

Humanus bolted after them, his blade raised.

Gomo appeared as though from nowhere. He hefted an odd looking cylinder in his hand. "Heh, heh," he chuckled.

"I've heard that before," Humanus said, shifting his charge from the departing mutants to Gomo.

Gomo thumbed the cylinder. A pencil-thin red light shot out the end.

Before Humanus could bring his blade down, Gomo drew the line of the light across Humanus' stomach.

A searing pain shot from his abdomen, making him think he had been cut in two. He dropped to his knees, stunned. He groped at his stomach. An angry welt raised its way across.

When he looked up, Gomo was gone and so were the other primates and Ariel. Her plaintive cries drifted back to him.

Humanus banged his fists onto the rough scrabble of the plateau's top. "Why? Why?" He raised his gaze to the sky, but only the deep blue canopy with whiffs of clouds met his anguish.

Justin knelt beside Humanus. "There was nothing you, nor the rest of us could have done."

"I didn't anticipate their size. They have Ariel. What are we to do?"

Justin shook his head sadly. "Somehow, Gomo has been given access to the powers of the nano-assembler. With that as his ally, we are doomed."

"What was that thing Gomo had?" Humanus pawed at his stomach. "It nearly cut me in two. I couldn't move."

"I believe it was an ice razor. We used them routinely in the future, when the world was a lot colder. That Gomo has one confirms my hypothesis Cardassin has used the nano-assembler."

"How could he turn on us like that? He seemed to be taken by Ariel. She certainly trusted him." Humanus struggled to contain the feeling of Ariel's loss. Events from outside were conspiring to give him grief. "She's gone, and I don't care whether Gomo and Cardassin are in collusion or not. I'm going after her."

"Your anger is understandable. But you must exercise perspective here. She is an artificial construct of the Shepherd. When he returns, she will also be gone. We, on the other hand, will be left here to deal with this catastrophe."

"That's easy for you to say." Humanus buried his head in his hands. "She's going to be the mother of my child."

Justin draped an arm over Humanus. "I know. This should be a time for joyous celebration, but all it has done is increase your vulnerability."

"Gomo, Cardassin, they must also know or have surmised Ariel is pregnant. That is why they kidnapped her and not you or me.

Justin stared. "I'm at a loss. There must be schemes afoot here neither you nor I are equipped to comprehend."

"I'm still going after Ariel. I've come this far, and I don't care how this plays out."

Justin nodded sagely. "You have hit upon the reason they did not kidnap you."

Humanus blinked. "They have taken Ariel to make me follow?"

Chapter Thirteen

Ariel screamed.

No one seemed to be listening.

One of the super-primates dragged her by the hair over the scrabble of the plateau's top.

The rough ground scraped the skin on her thigh and hip.

"Stop! You're killing me! I'm pregnant!" *Hopefully these dummies will understand and take pity on me.*

Gomo stepped into view and motioned the super-primate to hold up.

"What trouble?" Gomo said, standing over her.

She considered continuing her screaming at him, but it occurred to her Gomo might be more intelligent than he seemed. In any case, reasoning with him was worth a try. "This beast is killing me."

Gomo looked up at the towering super-primate and waved him off.

The primate scowled, but released Ariel's hair. He walked off muttering and fussing to remove errant blond strands of hair from his fingers.

"He be stupid."

"And you are not, thank goodness!" She put a lot of force into her statement, belying her underlying terror at being kidnapped and now at the mercy of these primitives.

"No be stupid. You no scream, you walk. No be dragged."

"You got it!" Ariel rose to her feet and passed a hand over her bruised thigh. It was angry red with leaky streaks of blood. Nothing she could do about it, now. Hopefully it wouldn't get infected. She wondered if the Shepherd had made her infection-proof. No way to know. No opportunities before this to test herself out.

She realized Gomo was staring at her dumbly. "I'll walk, and I'll not try to run away. And I won't scream." She almost patted the diminutive primate on the head, then thought better of it.

Gomo smiled or at least attempted to do so. What progressed across his mouth was something more grotesque. Something twisted that showed his sharp teeth, all hint of mirth absent from his close-set eyes.

With four super-primates towering over her, two on a side, she continued to limp south on the plateau until they reached the trail that led down to the Maraia enclave.

"Is Cardassin down there?" Ariel asked.

The super-primates ignored her. It was Gomo, who took an interest.

"Heh, heh. Dassin be there."

God, I hate that laugh. But perhaps if Cardassin is there I can reason with him. He had been kind enough to her before. True, something had happened when he had the guardian, but maybe that something had worn off. She knew she was desperate, but what else was there to grasp at?

A super-primate shoved her to her knees and gave her a rough kick in the backside to propel her into the constricted entrance to the ancient Maraia home.

She scrambled through, not wanting to invite another kick, but the super-primate crowded in after her and shoved her into a stumbling climb to the doorway that led to the hidden enclave.

Ariel hesitated at the entrance, only to receive another shove that carried her halfway down the hallway where she tripped and fell. A primate was on her immediately, pulling her up by her hair to a standing position. If this kept up she'd have no hair left.

Twenty more paces and she emerged into the cavernous space beyond. No sign of Cardassin. The space looked the same as she had left it the day before.

"Where's Cardassin?" Ariel asked Gomo.

"He be here. Come. I show."

She detected a twinkle in Gomo's eye as he headed toward the side of the enclave where, after ascending five steps, he scampered along a walkway that led to the back. There, the Maraia had penetrated the plateau with another hallway leading to innumerable small rooms.

Ariel slowed, thinking with each step her chances of escaping diminished proportionately. Too late, she remembered slowing was not a good idea.

A solid thrust in her back from the foot of one of the super-primates sprawled her forward.

She almost fell flat on her face, but grabbed for the walls and steadied herself. She cast an angry glance back at the primate, who reacted with an idiotic grin, giving the impression not a single thought drifted through his primitive mind.

She caught up to Gomo. "Where are we going? We've passed all the habitable rooms."

"Cardassin. You see."

The hallway narrowed and dropped down another five steps ending in a cramped anteroom. It felt tighter than a noose once she, Gomo and three super-primates crowded in.

A pair of rooms faced her.

Instead of solid doors, these rooms had doors made of steel bars. A common wall between them was also barred. A single diffuse light illuminated each of the rooms. They were both empty except for what looked like a pile of clothes in the one to the left.

Ariel searched her implanted memory for a reference as to function, and all she could come up with was that these were prison cells of some kind. Why the Maraia had such constructions she didn't know but cells they were.

"There be Cardassin." Gomo pointed to the pile of clothes.

Cardassin threw back the tattered coat that had been covering him. He crouched at the back of the cell. He seemed alert, almost as though he was expecting them.

When Ariel moved past Gomo and into Cardassin's view, he stood up, as though every bone in his body ached, and bowed at the waist.

"It distresses me," he said, squeezing his side in pain, "that you, too, are caught up in Gomo's little drama."

282

Ariel was taken aback. "I thought you went crazy. Everyone thinks you have been infected with *Zug*."

"*Zug*?" Cardassin made a grand effort looking himself over, then shrugged. "My lady, I admit, I used the guardian inopportunely, the consequences of which I paid for dearly in an assortment of bumps and bruises. But I assure you, I am now again your humble servant." He smiled, hands spread to his sides disarmingly.

Ariel felt a moment of quandary. Here she was captive of mindless primitives, and in front of her was the only being she could in any way communicate her concerns to. Was Cardassin for real, stating his condition had been a momentary insanity?

"How do I know you aren't faking all this?"

"That's a very good question, my dear, and if I had a ready answer, I would certainly throw it out for your consideration. But, as you can see, I've been incarcerated by this excretal beast and don't have the means to show or prove my--"

Gomo banged on the bars of the cell with a short cylindrical stick he was carrying. "Shut mouth!"

"How'd he get the nano-assembler?"

"I admit," Cardassin said, "I thought I could mollify him by helping him to some extent, but the surly beast turned on me. He doesn't even know how to use the nano-assembler, yet he brandishes it like a trophy."

"He seems very determined," Ariel said. She hoped Cardassin wouldn't antagonize Gomo further.

But Cardassin winked at her, then smiled at Gomo and rushed the bars, a mock charge. "Boooooo! Shut mouth! Shut mouth!" he mimicked. He guffawed seeming quite pleased with himself. "The little grunt bethinks he's now a general."

Gomo stepped back, tossed the nano-assembler to one of his lieutenants and grabbed a stick as long as he was tall. He thrust the stick forward. It caught Cardassin in the stomach, knocking the breath out of him.

Cardassin fell back to the far wall, arms wrapped around his abdomen, gasping for air.

Gomo opened the barred door and stepped into the cramped cell.

Face still purple, Cardassin issued a faint giggle. "Gotcha', didn't I?"

Cardassin's sarcasm was presumably lost on Gomo, who simply grunted and lashed him with the stick.

Cardassin fell to his knees, pain contorting his face.

Gomo waded in and slammed the stick down directly on Cardassin's head.

The force of the blow reduced Cardassin to a twitching mass sprawled on the floor of the cell.

Obviously satisfied with himself, Gomo stepped back, closed the cell door and locked it.

Ariel couldn't believe the horror she had just witnessed. Despite her misgivings, it was obvious Cardassin had received a brutal beating from Gomo. Her instinct was to go to Cardassin, but she didn't want to incur Gomo's wrath.

284

He grabbed her by the arm and shoved her hard into the second cell.

She stumbled through the doorway and banged off the opposite wall.

Gomo clanged the door closed, twisted a large key and stood back, surveying the two of them.

"Why have you kidnapped me?" Ariel demanded.

Gomo blinked. "Don't know."

"Did Cardassin tell you to kidnap me?"

Gomo glanced at Cardassin, who lay bleeding on the floor of his cell but still managed a withering look at Gomo. "Don't know." Gomo seemed nervous.

"Are you just going to let him lie there bleeding?"

Gomo glanced again at Cardassin, then wheeled around and headed back up the hallway with the super-primates falling in line behind him.

Ariel knelt and reached through the bars to Cardassin. "If you can scoot a little closer, I might be able to staunch the flow of blood from some of your wounds."

Cardassin moaned, but nodded. With what seemed a huge effort he pushed himself across the floor and flopped next to the adjoining wall of bars.

Ariel scanned the small room, hoping to find something she could use as first aid to Cardassin. But the cell was indeed absolutely bare. No bed, no sink, no toilet. No floor covering, no sheets or blankets. Just two hewn rock walls and the bars.

She ripped a length of fabric from her already diminished wrap, and noted the irony of having first

285

used some of it for firebomb wicks and now a bit more for bandages. Cardassin's head wound was especially severe. She didn't bother trying to clean the wounds but methodically wrapped the fabric tight, hoping it would stop the flow of blood.

"Thank you," Cardassin wheezed, patting her hand. "You are very kind. I feel I am but a pawn in some larger scheme." His eyes filled with tears. "I arrived here against my will. I was dumped out of the Shepherd and made a fool of by Humanus and the others. It's not until you arrived that I have been able to garner any self-esteem. That dastardly guardian really did a number on me."

Despite her misgivings, Ariel felt a trace of sympathy for the skinny, battered man lying before her. He really wasn't the master of his own fate. How hard that must be on someone who used to wield such power...even though it was an evil power. But she cautioned herself to be careful. Things may not be as they seem. She stroked his forehead. "What happened? I mean, why did you use the guardian in the first place?"

"A big boo-boo, but there's nothing like curiosity to kill the cat." He cackled, then choked on a clot of blood coughed up from his lungs. He reached a scabbed finger to his tongue, removed the clot and flicked it away. "The guardian made me wild. I didn't know what to do. You can't imagine how I felt...well, maybe you can. Helpless. It was like I wasn't in control of my own body. I had to get out of the ruin. I didn't know what I might do next...possibly harm one of my new friends. It was a nice party wasn't it?"

Concerned, Ariel looked at him. He seemed delirious. "Yes, it was a nice party. Sort of the calm before the storm. But you should rest. Humanus will think of a way to get us out of here."

The sound of shuffling feet emanated from the hallway.

Gomo appeared, still hefting his stick followed by one of the super-primates who carried two containers of water.

Gomo opened Cardassin's cell and the super-primate placed the container inside the door.

Gomo strode over to Ariel's cell. "Heh, heh. Be big pretty woman."

Ariel gaped at Gomo's erection and suddenly wondered if the diminutive primate planned to assault her. Her feelings on the possibility were a mix of terror and giddy hysterics. She stepped from Cardassin and backed as far away as she could in the small cell.

"Leave her alone," Cardassin said weakly.

"Heh, heh. You no be big man, now."

"Don't count on it." Cardassin rose to a sitting position.

Gomo ignored him and entered Ariel's cell. "Heh, heh. Make baby!"

"I'm already pregnant, you idiot!" Since Gomo's head only came just below Ariel's chest, she wondered fleetingly how he was going to proceed.

Gomo clasped onto her leg like a dog in heat and began a humping motion.

Truly disgusting. Ariel brought both her fists down sharply on his head.

He staggered back, blinking rapidly. His erection wilted. An angry flood of red darkened his eyes. He raised his hands, fingers spread claw-like, and rushed her.

Cardassin thrust an arm through the bars and tweaked Gomo's heel, just enough to send him tumbling forward.

Ariel sidestepped.

Gomo plowed into the rock wall of the cell and came away with a bloodied forehead. Enraged, he grabbed his stick and swung hard at Cardassin's exposed arm.

Cardassin howled in pain, rolling back into his cell, clutching his arm.

Gomo glared at Ariel, grabbed the water container from the gaping super-primate and poured it on the cell floor. "No more drink!" He stomped out of the cell, slamming the door behind him and disappeared up the hallway.

The super-primate hesitated for a moment then hurried to catch up.

Ariel went to the adjoining bars, gripped them with both hands and peered through. "Are you all right?" she asked, then realized the absurdity of the question.

Cardassin smiled weakly. "Here, have some of my water. You've earned it."

Ariel reached for the container, guided it through the bars and drank. "Thank you. I thought I would die soon without a sip."

"Take all you want. I do believe we've pissed Gomo off, and our time is otherwise limited." He pulled himself toward her with his good arm, the

288

other hanging limp. "I think he broke my arm. Would you be so kind as to help me support it?"

***

"I think I'm ready," Humanus said.

Justin waved his hands in agitation and stepped between him and the door to the ruin. "You're not at all ready. You can't go off half-cocked."

"This is my fight." Humanus came chest to chest with Justin. "If the guardian wants to test me, then a test it will get. I don't care anymore. I don't want to involve Jamani and Kesi."

When Humanus stepped left to go around Justin, the older man moved to intercept him. "Don't talk foolishness. If you are killed, then we all are compromised. I'm sure Jamani and Kesi feel the same way. At least consult the guardian to see if it will tell you what you are up against."

"I don't even want to look at the thing. You of all people must understand that."

Justin shook his head in frustration. "Please."

It wasn't often Justin was so insistent. Besides, he was probably right. What could be lost querying the guardian about the state of affairs? Probably a lot. Humanus thought it might even mislead him into thinking one thing when another was the reality.

"All right, I'll do it. Could I have a little privacy?"

"By all means. Take all the privacy you want. It's just me and Jamani and Kesi here. You want us to leave or are you going to?"

"I'll go outside."

Justin backed out of the way and let Humanus walk onto the plateau.

With a general sense of misgiving, Humanus retrieved the guardian from its pouch.

Okay. Tell me something.

"*Ariel has been incarcerated.*"

Brilliant. I don't need you to tell me that. Where is she?

A dark vision opened inside his mind.

I can't see what this is.

The vision brightened.

Ariel cowered against a wall in a small room with bars.

The vision shifted to show an adjoining wall to another dark room. On the floor lay Cardassin.

Cardassin is imprisoned with Ariel?

The vision showed Ariel administering to an obviously injured Cardassin.

I don't believe it. Cardassin turned. I felt Zug was here, was in him.

The vision went blank.

Answer me, dammit.

"*You didn't ask a question.*"

Is Zug here? Is Cardassin Zug?

"*You are here. Zug has always been here.*"

What are you saying? I don't want anything to do with Zug.

The guardian remained silent.

Why did Gomo kidnap Ariel? He could have kidnapped me. How did he get the ice razor without Cardassin's help?

290

"Cardassin thought he could secure his own freedom by aiding Gomo. He produced the ice razor and the super-primates to that end."

And then Gomo turned on him?

"You have seen the vision."

He could be faking all this.

"He could be."

Where are these holding cells located?

The guardian showed Humanus a vision that took him through the outer door of the Maraia enclave, down the constricted hallway and into the large room with all the counters. From there, it mounted steps to a walkway, then to a second hallway that led deep into the rock of the plateau past the Maraia living quarters. The vision stopped at a dead end where two cells faced across a confined anteroom.

How do I rescue Ariel?

Silence.

Will I be successful?

Silence.

If I fail, what will become of Ariel?

"She will die."

Disgusted, Humanus returned the guardian to the pouch around his neck. As he suspected, the annoying sphere hadn't been of much help. It was beginning to seem the guardian had set most of this up, anyway...just to test him. Why should it help him now? At least he had tried, and that would get Justin off his back.

If Cardassin was indeed incapacitated, then he would only have to deal with Gomo and his oversized primates. Though they were big, they were dumb and could be outwitted. Gomo had the ice razor, but it didn't seem to have a lethal setting, probably a hedge Cardassin had built in, not completely trusting Gomo. Maybe there were other hedges Cardassin had built into the super-primates that made them vulnerable. What might those be?

Humanus returned to the ruin.

"I've used the guardian as you suggested," he said to Justin. "Ariel is being held captive in a cell, one of the inner rooms of the Maraia enclave. Cardassin is in a cell next to hers, also captive."

Justin looked surprised. He moved to a stool and sat, gripping the table in front of him as though he needed it to keep from falling over. "Cardassin captive? He was the one who went crazy and started all this."

Humanus could almost read Justin's confused thoughts before he spoke. He pulled up a stool opposite. This might take a while. "I thought the same. But there he was, in a cell. If I can get in and out quickly, then it won't matter whether he is a captive or just faking."

Justin shook his head vigorously, his face pained. "At least take Jamani with you."

The old man meant well. Humanus picked up one of the firebombs Justin had been assembling and tucked it into a sack. "I'll be able to move faster alone." He added two more bombs to the bag and slung it around his shoulder. "Where's the flint and steel?"

Justin released a sigh. Reluctantly, he handed the fire-making materials to Humanus. "What do you have in mind? Burning the whole place down?"

Humanus smiled and patted the sack. "These should keep the super-primates at bay. I'll be able to take on Gomo alone. I'm going to assume the guardian didn't mislead me about Cardassin's injuries. So he won't be a factor."

"If you aren't back by sundown, we're coming after you."

Humanus reached across the table and laid a hand on Justin's shoulder. "No. If I'm not back by sundown, then I'll be dead, and Ariel will also be dead or will be soon enough. Better you and Jamani and Kesi look after yourselves."

Justin gripped Humanus' hand. "This isn't going to be easy." His voice trembled with emotion.

Humanus felt a twinge of regret over the years lost. He wished he'd known this man sooner. "No one said it would be. I'm sorry for having put you in danger."

Justin shook his head. "You needn't apologize. We are all here for a purpose, and from what I can see, none of it is of your doing. If anything, it's the guardian."

Humanus took the pouch from around his neck and handed it to Justin. "Take it."

He recoiled. "I don't want that thing."

"No, you probably don't, and if I don't return, I'm not going to suggest what you do with it. But hold on to it for now. Better that, than have it fall into the hands of Gomo or Cardassin."

Justin took the pouch reluctantly. "Good luck."

293

Humanus felt the bite of gravel on his stomach as he frog-crawled through the narrow slit in the rock protecting the Maraia cave. He reached out with one hand and dug fingernails as best he could into the hard scrabble, then pulled himself forward, dragging the sack with the firebombs alongside him.

A smoldering anger wound its way through his every motion. It was obvious the guardian had contrived this situation, and now was going to remain on the sidelines and observe the outcome.

His anger was so great that for a moment he almost rejected everything, just to spite the annoying sphere. But what would become of Ariel? The guardian had probably foreseen his reaction and anticipated his growing attachment to the synthetic.

I have no choice, he thought bitterly.

Staying low on the other side, he climbed around and over crumbling mud brick structures toward the door at the back of the cave that led to the enclave beyond.

Agonizing minutes passed. He crawled a short distance then stopped and listened, before resuming his crawl. The door loomed into sight--a finely constructed anachronism of burnished steel with silver-gray jambs and a buff-black door set in the iron-rich red rock.

A single super-primate lounged at the entrance. He leaned casually against the rock face, legs crossed, a primitive rock club at his feet. Not the alert sentry that was needed, he seemed more interested in picking his teeth with a fingernail, then

294

periodically spitting out whatever he managed to dislodge.

Humanus crawled unseen to within five meters of the primate. When the primate leaned over to spit, Humanus heaved a stone as far as he could down slope, out of the overhanging cave and into the thick bush below.

The stone tumbled with a crashing sound as though someone or something was frantically pushing its way through the bush.

The primate looked up lethargically, showing no sense of surprise. He shoved off the wall, picked up his club and began a slow but methodical climb down, toward the direction of the sound.

Humanus estimated it would take the primate five minutes to climb down without falling, another five to ten to look around and find nothing, then maybe seven to climb back up. Plenty of time for Humanus to get in and get out.

He scrambled to the doorway, checked back that the sentry was well gone, and eased himself inside.

The hallway was dark except for small guide lights embedded in the floor. Sleek, polished walls led toward the interior. He stood listening. If anyone was in the large hall beyond, the sound of their movements should be amplified down the hallway. But no sounds came to him.

He took out the flint and steel and a gasoline-soaked wad of Ariel's wrap. He struck the steel against the flint, sending sharp clicking sounds down the hallway. He paused. Still no sound came from within.

He resumed his attempt. After another stroke, the wad ignited. He' immediately blew out the flame, then puffed at the wad until he had a glowing ember to light the firebomb on quick notice.

He crept forward, listening for the faintest sound.

At the end of the hallway he peered into the cavernous hall. It was empty. The row upon row of counters mounted with computers and monitors sat abandoned in a dim light. Across the great hall, he followed the line of the upper walkway to the hallway that led to the habitable rooms and finally to the cells beyond.

He eased out of the entrance hall, feeling exposed, and began to cross the intervening space.

Three super-primates disgorged from the opposite side. They stomped toward him.

With his heart suddenly thudding in his chest, he ducked behind a near counter and ran, bent over, down its length.

The primates hesitated, as if they'd lost sight of him. After a quick exchange of gibberish to sort out their quandary, they bolted in opposite directions, two of them bumping into each other.

Using the counters as a cover, Humanus zigzagged toward the far side of the hall.

There he circled back.

They lost track of him again and milled in obvious confusion as they looked under the counters and gazed at the ceiling overhead. They never uttered a sound of interactive communication.

He took the primed firebomb from his sack, blew the wadded wrap to a red heat that burst into flame.

The primates stopped and gaped at the bright flash of light.

Humanus hurled the firebomb.

It bounced off a counter, then exploded into an orange splash of liquid fire.

He threw a second bomb after the first for good measure.

Flames whooshed over the primates. Panic-stricken and screaming in pain, they slapped at their fur and rolled on the floor.

Gomo rushed from the hallway that led back into the interior. He skidded to a halt and glanced at the primates, then he focused on Humanus. He thumbed a button on his ice razor, loosing a diffuse beam, and cranked a knob roughly until the light narrowed to a sizzling pencil thinness.

At the sight of the ice razor, Humanus shuddered, the memory of the glowing beam lancing his stomach still with him. He dodged behind a counter.

Gomo leapt over the walkway railing and ran after him.

The ice razor laced back and forth, randomly, raising welts on the countertops and shattering monitors.

Humanus circled, staying low, getting ever closer to Gomo.

"Heh, heh. Where be dead man?" Gomo looked to one side then the other, not realizing until too late Humanus had come up beside him.

Humanus rammed an elbow into Gomo's head that bowled him over. He snatched the ice razor from Gomo's grasp and hurled it to the other side of the hall.

Gomo screeched, baring his teeth, slashing, snapping. Stronger than his size indicated, he shrugged free of Humanus and sprang to his feet.

Humanus swung his blade awkwardly, clubbing Gomo with a broad side.

He went down, then rolled onto his hands and knees and scrambled up the aisle between counters toward the ice razor.

Humanus grabbed the nearest chair and ripped it from its moorings. He stalked Gomo, came up behind him and brought the chair down hard on his back.

Gomo squealed, twisted around and kicked.

Humanus dodged, raised the chair again, and smashed it into Gomo's face.

Gomo brought both hands to his bloodied nose and moaned.

Humanus heaved the chair.

It caught Gomo's head and snapped it back.

He staggered backward, unconscious.

Humanus climbed to the walkway and raced for the hallway leading to the catacombs.

He slipped, fell, then rose with a frustrated agitation that he couldn't go fast enough.

At the end of the hallway he slid into the anteroom made familiar to him by the guardian. The two prison cells faced him.

"Ariel!"

She seemed dazed, leaning awkwardly against the wall of her cell.

The sight of her looking so helpless tore at his heart. He rushed to the cell door, grabbed the bars and yanked. Locked. No keys. He drew his blade and shoved it between the door and the jamb and pried. Steel on steel shrieked in protest, but the jamb bent and the cell door swung open.

Humanus ran into the cell and knelt in front of her. He grabbed her shoulders and shook. "Wake up! Speak to me!"

She moaned, then opened her eyes in astonishment. "Humanus? I knew you'd come."

A wave of relief swept over him. She was alive. He embraced her. "We have no time. We've got to get out of here." Stepping back, he drew her arm over his shoulder and helped her stand.

"Gomo," she said, now fully alert and wild-eyed. "The super-primates."

He glanced at the hallway, counting the seconds. "They're neutralized for the moment, but not for long."

He eased her to the cell door.

"What about Cardassin?" Ariel looked to the adjacent cell where a figure lay on the floor.

"What about him?" Humanus asked.

"He's not who you think."

Humanus peered anxiously at the looming hallway. "I know who he is. He freaked out and stole the Land Rover, then he created super-primates to overrun us and gave Gomo an ice razor."

Ariel shook her head. She dragged on Humanus, slowing him. "He helped me and was beaten by Gomo."

Humanus suppressed a rising panic. "We don't have time!"

Ariel shrugged away from him and stepped to Cardassin's cell. "Wake up! Humanus is here!"

Cardassin raised his head off the floor and stared blearily at Humanus. "I'm saved," he said weakly.

Damn. Damn. Damn. Humanus rushed over to the cell and pried the door open. "That's all I can do for you, Cardassin. I've got my priorities."

Cardassin brought his knees up to his chest and rolled onto them. His weight over-shifted and he almost fell over, but he steadied. "Thanks, my good man. I'll just follow you out as best I can."

Humanus gave Cardassin a curt nod, then turned toward the hallway leading to safety.

"Heh, heh." Gomo stood in the hallway, blocking the way out. Behind him, three super-primates ranged, their skin and hair still smoldering from the firebombs.

Chapter Fourteen

Humanus hadn't stood a chance.

Hurt, exhausted, and thirsty, Ariel leaned against the wall of her cell.

Gomo and the three primates had rushed Humanus as he fumbled for a firebomb but it slipped from his grasp. The primates pummeled him. The makeshift container with its saturated wick crashed to the floor. Fuel splashed, loosing a suffocating stench.

The super-primates screamed, having enough sense to realize their singed fur might re-ignite, but nothing happened.

Then the beating began.

She had tried to help, but a broad arm to her face flung her back into her cell, where she hit hard against the far wall. Dazed, she could do no more than watch the brutality.

They kicked Humanus. They stomped on his fingers. They lifted him and hit him with fists in the stomach and head. When he sagged, they propped him up and slashed with their elbows, snapping his head from side to side.

Finally, Gomo raised a hand and the beating stopped.

Humanus crumpled to the floor, bleeding from his nose, his mouth, his ears, even his eyes. His arms hung loose at his sides. His legs bent awkwardly under his body.

They tied a rope around his neck and dragged him away.

The last she saw of him, the rope was wrenched tight around his neck, rasping with every tug, leaving angry red scratches. His mouth gaped opened, sucking for air. His tongue hung out, his eyes bulged.

Gomo was the last to leave. He said nothing to Ariel, simply closed the cell door and checked it was locked.

He glanced at Cardassin, but the thin man had not moved in the slightest during the beating. With a grunt, Gomo had left.

Now, in the aftermath, Ariel convulsed in sobs. Hours had passed with no sign of Gomo or a super-primate. Humanus could very well be dead. Was this the way they were all going to end up?

Without turning her head, she could see Cardassin sprawled on his stomach near the door to his cell. One arms stuck out through the bars where he had last reached to a super-primate, begging for water. It didn't look like Cardassin was breathing.

She rested her hand lightly on her abdomen. Life was growing in there, at least for now. But how could she even think about giving birth in a world like this? Of course that hadn't been the plan. At least as far as she knew. She had accomplished the mission given to her by the Shepherd, not that it had been all that difficult to do. Where was the Shepherd, now? She never had understood his part in the mission.

It didn't make any sense he would leave her here to die. But a lot of things didn't make any sense. Like Cardassin going crazy, then seemingly recovering his former self, even to the point of trying to defend her against Gomo's ludicrous assault.

Where were Kesi and Jamani? Probably dead, too? She didn't think Justin could be any help, old as he was. What life did he have ahead of him if everyone else was dead? He'd have to face Gomo alone.

And the guardian. It certainly hadn't come to their aid in any way. Sure, it offered snippets of information that opened some doors, but in retrospect it almost seemed the doors opened only led them to new and more intractable encounters. If Humanus was being tested, then the guardian had a strange way of doing it.

Dead men wouldn't prove anything.

A distant door clanged, echoing down the deserted hallway. Then came padding footsteps and the sound of something being dragged on the floor.

A super-primate appeared, filling the extent of the hallway with his bulk.

Too weak to move, Ariel simply stared at him.

The primate emerged into the cramped anteroom and stood to one side.

Behind him, Gomo entered, holding one end of what looked like a rope. "Heh, heh. Present." He pulled on the rope and the scraping sound resumed.

Bound hand and foot, Humanus was dragged into the space. His body bore the marks of his beating. Puffy, purpled skin and scabbed dried blood marked his legs, arms and back. His eyes were swollen to slits. A bloody slime slipped from the side of his mouth through swollen lips.

Ariel struggled to her feet and almost fainted with the effort.

Gomo pulled open the cell door and rolled Humanus in, then slammed the door shut and locked it. He peered over at Cardassin, who still hadn't moved, walked up to him and stepped hard on his hand.

Still no movement.

Gomo kicked him in the stomach, a sucking thud Cardassin failed to acknowledge.

From Cardassin's waistband, a bright object tinkled to the floor.

Gomo stooped and lifted a shiny key. His eyes glittered as though he immediately knew what the key was for. Furthering that assumption, he pulled back Cardassin's waistband, and reached in for a second key that dangled within.

After a triumphant glance at Ariel, he turned and disappeared up the hallway, followed by the ever present super-primate.

Ariel wondered about the keys, then as soon as Gomo was gone, she pushed all thought from her mind and rushed to Humanus. She dropped to her knees and reached out, but hesitated, not knowing where she could touch him without inflicting pain...if indeed he was still alive.

"Humanus," she whispered close to his ear.

No response.

She touched his neck lightly with a finger and felt a weak pulse. Encouraged she started working on the thongs that bound his chest and arms. The leather cut deep into his skin, making untying them difficult. After his arms were freed from his chest, she rolled him onto his back. His legs were still bent, his knees trussed up. She worked the thongs free, one leg at a time, then gently eased his legs out flat with the floor.

He groaned.

Her heart leapt. *He's still alive.* She moved to his mouth and pried it open with her finger, drawing out clogged mucous and coagulating blood.

Humanus took a shuddering breath, and settled into labored breathing. Liquid, perhaps tears, leaked from the corners of his eyes and dripped to the floor.

"My poor Humanus. What have they done to you?" She caressed his forehead. She massaged one of his arms, thinking to get the blood circulating, but he moaned in pain. So she stopped. Though she tried, she couldn't think of anything else she could do for him. The cell was bare. She was tired, hungry and weak. She was back to where she had been a few minutes ago, except now she had Humanus to worry about as well. But at least he was alive.

She lay down beside him and tried to rest. Maybe he felt her presence, maybe not.

She dozed, then awoke with a start. She sat up and gazed at Humanus. He hadn't moved. He was still breathing, but barely as far as she could see. How long had she been asleep? No way to tell. Nothing else had changed. Cardassin was where she had last seen him.

The overhead light flickered. Frantic shouts echoed down the hallway. Scuffling sounded nearby, then receded. A door clanged shut.

Silence.

She began shaking uncontrollably. The lack of sleep, food and water, all the stress suddenly overwhelmed her.

A thin pencil of light diffused down the hallway and cut a steady path through the strobe-like flickering of the lights in the ceiling.

Dimly she discerned Gomo enter, carrying a narrow cylinder in his hand from which a red light emanated.

He came over to the cell and flicked the light over Ariel.

She felt its warmth, not an unpleasant sensation. She wondered if it were a weapon of sorts and could be made stronger.

"All be dead," Gomo said.

She pulled her knees up to her chest, feeling exposed, wanting to get away from the red light. "Why are you doing this to us?"

Gomo cocked his head. "Doing?"

No reasoning with him. Whatever was going on in what he called his mind was probably incomprehensible to her anyway. "Could you bring us some water? We are dying of thirst, and I want to clean Humanus' wounds."

"No do."

"Why not!" Ariel screamed, feeling she was fast losing any self-control, any stoicism she might have had earlier.

"Jamani, Kesi." He gestured up the hallway.

Ariel started. *Kesi and Jamani are alive?*

Gomo peered at the cylinder in his hand. He twisted a small dial and the diffuse beam focused to a pencil thinness. He walked over to the cell door. "Bye, bye."

The beam worked its way across the floor and played over one of Humanus' legs, raising a column of light gray smoke as first hair, then skin singed.

Humanus groaned. His leg twitched.

Ariel leapt in front of Humanus, facing Gomo. "Stop that!"

The beam raked across her thigh.

She screamed, but stood her ground.

Gomo swung the beam wide and brought it back slowly. "You like?"

A shuffling came from behind her. She turned, amazed.

Humanus was on his knees. He cleared his throat and spit, then wiped his mouth with the back of his hand. "Picking on girls, Gomo?" Though slurred, his speech was understandable.

The red beam stopped as Gomo peered forward, trying to get a look around Ariel.

"Come, you coward!" Humanus taunted, his hands out to his sides.

"Die now!" Gomo shouted. He charged the gate, rattled the key frantically in the lock, yanked the door open, then shoved Ariel to one side.

Not again.

***

Justin paced the ruin. Had he made the right decision sending Jamani and Kesi after Humanus? They should all have been back by now. What if it were true Cardassin had turned, then given Gomo access to the nano-assembler? How else would Gomo have gotten hold of an ice razor?

I'm an old man. What can I do? If they don't come back soon, then I'll know they are all dead. What's to become of me then?

Kesi barged through the entrance to the ruin.

Justin's relief at seeing Kesi evaporated when he saw what condition Kesi was in. It looked like he'd swum the rapids of the river leading into Lake Turk and hit every rock along the way.

Justin rushed up, catching him before he fell flat on his face. "Where's Jamani?"

Gulping huge breaths, Kesi thumbed over his shoulder.

"And Humanus? Is he all right?"

Kesi's wide-eyed gaze flicked nervously, a wild look compounding his physical exhaustion. "Don't know."

Jamani staggered into the ruin, his spear broken, his chest and arms covered with scrapes and bruises. "They catch Humanus. Beat him. Big monkeys chase us out."

"You left Humanus behind?"

They both looked at Justin in wonderment.

"What do?" Jamani said, pained, throwing his spear on the floor in disgust. "What do? They kill."

"Okay, I'm sorry. I shouldn't have put it that way. Let's have a look at your wounds."

Jamani turned away.

"Kesi?" Justin said, hopefully. But Kesi also ignored him. "I know you were outnumbered and out-sized. Is Ariel all right?"

Jamani walked to the bar left over from the party and found a container of water. He took a long drink, then set it down and wiped his mouth. "Ariel in cage. Cardassin in cage, too."

"Cardassin's in a cage?" This didn't make sense. "Are you sure?"

"Sure, sure."

"Then he must also be a prisoner and not possessed as we thought."

"Don't know. Gomo hurt Cardassin."

"Did they kill Humanus?" Justin couldn't fathom the future without Humanus in it. Plus, what advantage would Gomo gain by killing Humanus? But Cardassin, if possessed was another matter.

Jamani shook his head. "We go back. Now."

"We'll have to," Justin said, not at all sure he was up to the physical confrontation. "If they are still alive, we have to try to save Humanus and Ariel." He heard himself saying the words, almost as though they were meant to fortify his resolve.

"Good." Jamani strode to the remains of the metal pieces they had used to make the Land Rover and picked out a steel rod a meter long. "Better than spear."

Justin could only applaud Jamani's resolve, but in the back of his mind he thought of Gomo with the ice razor. None of them would be a match for that.

"Kesi. Are you well enough to come with us?"

Kesi nodded.

Though his wounds looked horrific, they appeared to be mostly superficial. Still, they must have hurt.

"We'll need some sort of plan," Justin said. "Tell me, what's the situation in the cave?"

"There be two cages in deep," Jamani said. "Cardassin in one. Woman in the other. Maybe three, four big primates left. I kill two."

"What about Humanus?"

"Don't know. Big primates grab Humanus. They beat him. Then attack Kesi, me. We cannot go forward, so come here."

"Hopefully, he's still alive. There are many places in there to hide. Are the cages all the way at the back?"

"Last."

"Okay. Here's what we should do. They probably won't expect me to show up for any sort of confrontation, so I want you and Kesi to show yourselves at the outside, then run away. Hopefully, the primates will take the bait and pursue you. Once they are out of the cave, I'll go in and see what I can do. If these big primates are as stupid as I think they are, then they will all take after you, and I'll only have Gomo to contend with."

"Gomo bad."

"I know he's bad. But I'm twice as tall as he is. I weigh more than he does. And I'll have a steel blade with me and this firebomb."

"What do?"

"Once inside, I'll have to avoid Gomo until I can see what's up with Humanus. I'll have to free Ariel, and if Cardassin is an ally again, I'll free him. It will be a matter of timing and trying to get as much manpower behind me as I can before confronting Gomo. Of course, if you can't keep the

310

big primates away long enough, then all bets are off. But at least we have to try."

"Big monkeys fast," Jamani said.

Justin rubbed his chin in concentration. "That could be a problem...hold on. We could use the Land Rover."

"You use Land Rover?" Jamani cocked his head at a seeming contradiction.

"No," Justin said. "I'll be inside. I'll show you how to use the Land Rover."

Jamani grinned. "Me be quick."

"You'll have to be, or you'll be in big trouble. Come on, I'll show you how to drive on the way over."

Justin shoved his blade into his belt and headed for the tunnel. At the Land Rover he climbed into the driver's seat and oriented himself. He wasn't all that sure he could even drive the Land Rover, but he thought he'd seen everything Cardassin and then Humanus had done to make it go.

Jamani sat in the passenger seat next to him while Kesi sat in the back.

"Okay. This is the steering wheel," Justin said.

Jamani blew out a breath and smacked his forehead with his hand. "Jamani know. Jamani know. Push pedal there--" he pointed to the clutch, "--pull stick here--" he grasped the gear shift and pulled it into first, "--turn key...no key?"

"Good so far," Justin said. "We don't have a key, but we can still start it. Like this." Justin arced the wires on the starter board and the engine coughed to life. "We're ready to go. Watch me."

Jamani watched intently as Justin went through the motions of getting the Land Rover underway. He drove out of the tunnel and turned north. After a kilometer, he stopped and traded places with Jamani.

Remarkably, the primitive drove off without the slightest hitch. He steered with confidence, shifted gears without any grinding.

Justin patted him on the back. "You are truly amazing."

Jamani grinned. "Easy."

They rounded the end of the plateau and headed south on the western side.

"Go slow. We're almost there," Justin said.

Jamani slowed the vehicle.

"Okay. Stop here. I'm going to get out and walk the rest of the way. When you see me wave, drive to below the cave and honk the horn."

Jamani reached for the horn.

"Not now!" Justin snatched Jamani's hand from the horn. "Once you honk the horn, the super-primates should come out to see what is going on. You'll turn west, out there--" he pointed, "--and lead them in circles. I'll sneak in. Understand?"

Jamani nodded.

"All right, let's do it." Justin jumped out of the vehicle and climbed quickly up to the ancient dwellings in the Maraia cave. Once in position he waved to Jamani.

Jamani eased the Land Rover to below the cave and leaned on the horn.

No one showed.

Jamani leaned on the horn again. This time the doorway to the catacombs at the back disgorged three super-primates, who skidded to a halt, spotted the Land Rover, then clambered down the slope in pursuit.

Jamani gunned the engine, cranked the wheel and headed out into the desert with the three primates loping after him.

Justin checked that the hallway into the interior was clear, then entered. He made it unimpeded all the way to the cavernous room. Everything was quiet.

Shouts emanated from the hallway leading to the rooms at the back.

Quickly, he ascended to the walkway, drawing his blade.

The shouting increased.

Justin ran down the hallway toward a dim light at the end. He lurched into an anteroom. Gomo stood poised above a prone Humanus. Ariel beat weakly on Gomo's shoulders. Cardassin lay inert off to the left.

Gomo whirled when he heard Justin.

Propelled as much by adrenalin as a desire to save Humanus and Ariel, Justin continued charging across the room at Gomo. His blade sliced down on Gomo's arm, sending the ice razor spinning across the floor.

Gomo grasped his arm. Blood spurted between his fingers.

Like two players on a revolving disk, they rounded and traded places. When Gomo reached

313

the hallway, he ran out, leaving Justin to think it had all been too easy.

"Let's get out of here!" he cried to Ariel.

She nodded, her face a grim mask, and stooped to drag Humanus to his feet. "I don't think he can walk without support."

Justin eased under one arm of Humanus while Ariel took the other. Together they dragged him toward the hallway.

A groan came from Cardassin. "I'm coming...too."

"That's good. Come on!" Ariel encouraged.

Justin didn't know what to make of Ariel's familiarity, but didn't have time to find out. They lumbered down the hallway to the cavernous space.

"We're almost there," Justin said as he came free of the one hallway and looked across the room to the exit.

Gomo barged out of the far exit with the three super-primates behind him. He stopped, a wide grin spreading across his face. "Heh, heh. No go here."

Panic seized Justin's insides. If Gomo was back with the primates, then something must have happened to Jamani and Kesi. No time to wonder now. "Over the railing," he shouted to Ariel. "We've got to put something between us and them."

Cardassin, out of balance, slewed into Justin. "Two exits. Come." He pin-wheeled over the railing and sprawled in a heap below.

Justin and Ariel shoved Humanus over, then followed. They dragged him after a limping Cardassin, who led them to the far side of the room.

314

Gomo leapt over the railing, followed by the three bumbling primates.

Justin took out the last firebomb, lit it, and hurled it at the primates.

They dodged back unscathed, but the bomb fired up a barrier they couldn't immediately cross.

Justin turned to check on Cardassin, but he had disappeared.

Gomo shrieked an angry cry. He leapt to the counter with the red button and paused above it. He brandished the nano-assembler, then started whacking it on the counter.

"He's going to destroy the place," Justin yelled. He lunged forward.

"No!" Ariel shouted, grabbing his shoulder. "It's too dangerous.

Gomo teased Justin with the small cylinder, then produced two bright keys and dangled them from his other hand.

"Where did he get those keys?" Justin asked.

Ariel gasped, putting her hand to her mouth. "He took them from Cardassin."

Gomo leaned over and, still holding the nano-assembler high, inserted the keys into their slots on the counter, twisted each of them, then slammed his hand down on the red button.

An ominous sound rumbled through the space, followed by a shudder. The lights went out. Red emergency lights blinked on.

Loud thumps sounded as huge portions of the ceiling crashed onto the counters.

In the garish red light with leaping shadows cast by the flickering flames, Justin spotted a dim glow. *The second exit?* "This way!" He dragged on Humanus and pulled him toward the opening.

A massive upheaval convulsed the cave floor.

Justin lost his grip on Humanus and tumbled into the down-sloping exit. A moment later he rolled outside amidst the ancient Maraia structures. A puff of dust shot from the corridor he had just come down.

When he tried to re-enter the corridor, solid rock blocked his way. "Humanus! Ariel!" he cried. But he knew they must be dead, buried under tons of rubble.

The ground continued to vibrate. Portions of the overhanging rock from the plateau broke loose and dropped, smashing ancient mud structures to bits.

The instinct for survival took hold of Justin. He clambered down the slope out of the cave and raced for the slit entrance. With rocks cascading behind him, he slipped through.

He stood on the other side for a moment gazing at the destruction he had left behind. Half the plateau for a hundred meters along its length had broken free and slid in a giant flow to the plain below. Amidst the rubble of stone and dirt, an odd anachronistic piece of metal, or countertop jutted skyward.

Justin sank to his knees. Did it all end here? *There's no way Humanus and Ariel could have survived that collapse.* As he turned to trudge up the trail back to the ruin, he spied the Land Rover farther out on the plain.

It leaned sharply on one side, a rear tire still spinning.

Dear God, not Jamani and Kesi, too.

***

The release of Justin's grip on Humanus' hand brought him to his senses. He blinked as enveloping reddish darkness fringed with a wall of flame, shot through by thundering crashes.

I'm in hell.

Someone was tugging desperately on his other arm.

Ariel? It was Ariel, her face smudged with black grime, the whites of her eyes bright, her body hunched in pain.

He tried to stand. A dull ache shot up the back of both legs. The muscles in his lower spine convulsed. He fell to his knees. His mind flooded with memories of Gomo standing over him, lacing the ice razor back and forth across his body. When he tried to protect himself by curling into a ball, Gomo had worked the red knife across his legs.

"Humanus!" She was close now, her voice reverberating in his ear. "Listen to me! The enclave is collapsing. We've got to get out of here."

Humanus' attention swam vaguely to Ariel's face, a contortion of fear and panic.

She slapped him hard. "Focus, damn you!"

The heavy thud of her palm cleared his senses only a little. "Exit," he muttered.

"Cardassin found a second one. Justin went down it. Now it's blocked."

Dimly he counted...four of us, now two. What were the odds? "Entrance."

"It's across the room. I can't see it clearly from here. The primates were there."

A huge block of rock crashed to the floor, missing them by the narrowest of margins. The fear of being buried alive sent a shock of adrenalin through his system. The pain in his legs ebbed. He rose unsteadily to his feet and squinted toward the entrance. "Steel encased."

Ariel glanced toward the entrance, then nodded. "Brilliant. Can you move?"

Humanus lurched forward, and Ariel was immediately under his arm. With each step he felt his strength returning. They circled away from the flames, keeping an eye on the primates. Though it was impossible to be sure, it seemed like only Gomo and one of the super-primates remained active. *Four of them...now two. Better odds*.

Gomo and the primate flanked the wall of flame and headed to where Humanus and Ariel had just been.

An ominous rumbling accompanied by a seismic shift in the floor laid them all low.

"Hurry," Ariel whispered earnestly, scrambling to her feet.

Humanus came abreast of a smashed counter. At its center a red button blinked ominously.

"Gomo pushed it. A...doomsday device."

Doomsday. How appropriate. His mind wandered again. Thoughts of him and Kesi fishing in cool waters--

"Assembler!" Ariel shrieked.

The shiny cylinder lay discarded against a counter.

318

He bent to pick it up, but gasped as cramps locked his hamstrings. He fell over.

Ariel eased in front of him and snatched the nano-assembler. "I've got. Let's get out of here."

"A minute," Humanus wheezed through gritted teeth. He stretched out the locked-up muscles. "That's better."

Gomo reared out of the dust and gloom and fell upon Ariel.

She yelped, rolled away from him and kicked.

Gomo leaned back, his eyes wild, his teeth barred. He spun, looking around until he found a large rock.

As he stooped to pick it up, Ariel ran into the entrance hallway. She stopped and turned to extend a hand to Humanus.

He grasped it firmly and pulled himself in after her.

Gomo heaved the rock, but it bounced wide of its mark. He lunged, clawing for a grip on Humanus' ankle.

He rolled and pulled his leg up, bringing Gomo closer, then with his other foot kicked him in the face.

Gomo grunted and let go.

An explosive crescendo sounded as tons of rock and dirt collapsed.

The guide lights in the steel-encased entrance tunnel flickered. Most of them went out. The tunnel tilted ominously.

Humanus lay across the floor of the tunnel, his shoulders pressed against one wall, his feet shoved against the opposite wall. He grabbed Ariel and held her tight.

Gomo slid down the tunnel, his arms flailing. He dropped from sight at the opening to the great hall, enveloped in a cloud of dust and falling rock.

The entrance tube flipped and turned erratically, caught in a massive upheaval of the plateau. Humanus imagined tons of rock and dirt sliding in an avalanche to the plain below, the steel entrance tube a hollow needle in the flow.

The destruction seemed to take forever, but in fact probably only lasted seconds. The steel tube came to rest. Darkness enveloped them except for the odd guide light embedded in what had been the floor and was now the side of the tube.

Humanus choked on dust that filled the tube and swirled in gray eddies. "Ariel!" He reached out to her inert form. He crawled up to her and pressed his hand to her neck. A strong pulse. Just unconscious.

Judging from the pull of gravity, the tube lay at a slight angle. The upper end was sealed by dirt and rocks. They'd suffocate soon if he couldn't dig his way out. He pulled Ariel up alongside as he climbed to the top end of the tube.

With nothing but his hands to dig with, he started scraping at the rocks and dirt.

Being loose, the debris came free and fell down to fill the bottom of the tube. The dust thickened. If he couldn't break through soon they were done for.

A large rock shifted and wedged on the tube's edge.

Frantically, he worked it back and forth. Little by little it came free, then with a sudden release that almost took him and Ariel with it, it fell.

Dirt cascaded from above, filling the tube below and burying his ankles.

He dragged Ariel higher.

The dirt rose steadily, a sand clock with time running out.

It sifted around his waist. Desperately, he pulled Ariel's arms, trying to keep her head free.

The dirt stopped flowing.

Sunlight streamed in. Slanting rays lit up the dust in angry swirls.

Careful not to disturb the fragile dirt sides above the end of the tube, Humanus freed himself, then worked Ariel out of the soft dirt. Standing, his head cleared the surface. With all his remaining strength, Humanus shoved Ariel up and outside. Dodging a new collapse of rubble, he dragged himself out and lay on his back beside her.

He must have lain there for several minutes, slowly inhaling the fresh air, feeling the hot sun beating down on his face.

He rolled onto his side and examined Ariel.

Her eyelids fluttered. She coughed up dirt and shaded her eyes from the sun. "We're alive?"

"I think so," Humanus said.

She smiled weakly and raised her hand. In it she held the nano-assembler. "Present."

Humanus couldn't believe his eyes. He embraced her, laughing, crying, tears of joy streaming down his cheeks. They were alive and they had the nano-assembler. It was a miracle.

A clap of distant thunder and gray clouds rolled overhead. The sunshine vanished. Huge drops of rain pelted down, thudding into the loose dirt, puffing up dust before the intensity of the downpour strengthened.

Humanus tipped his head up, mouth open and roamed his tongue over his lips, pulling in as much moisture as he could, letting the steady thumping massage the wounds on his face.

Ariel laughed brightly, rubbed her arms and face, freeing them of the grime. She slicked back her hair, and when it saturated, wrung it dry.

Humanus stood and offered his hand to Ariel. "We better get back to the ruin and see if anyone else has survived."

"Can you walk?"

"I'll have to." He glanced out on the plain and caught sight of the Land Rover. It sat turned on its side. The rain washed across its shiny exterior and pooled on the inside.

"I wonder what happened there?"

Chapter Fifteen

The dark clouds above Justin's head seemed to hang within touching distance from the top of the plateau. Angry, grumbling thunder rolled across the sky. Out on the plain, lightning flashed, sending birds, squawking with wings beating frantically from the trees. Wildebeests kicked up their heels, bellowed and ran in circles.

Rain began to fall with a vengeance. Big drops pummeled everything in sight. To Justin it seemed his world had gone wrong and the heavens were trying to wash away the damage.

He slogged through puddles and mud, holding his hand above his head, cursing the sting of the pelting fusillade. *Nothing like a tropical thunderstorm to put a sad face on these tragic events. What more can I expect?*

He'd soon find out. The ruin loomed in the distance, gray and squat, half-obscured by the heavy downpour.

He sloshed to the entrance and gripped both jambs. He leaned in heavily and waited for his eyes to adjust to the dimmer light.

"Justin!" Kesi scampered over and clutched him.

The poor primate was shivering and not from any cold.

But Justin was elated. "You're alive." He smoothed the top fur on Kesi's head.

"'Mani be sick."

Justin looked over Kesi's shoulder to a prone figure. Jamani lay motionless in the middle of the ruin. Justin disengaged Kesi and stepped to Jamani. What he saw made his heart skip. The poor man had been battered almost beyond recognition. A deep laceration parted his scalp, moving diagonally across his forehead and ending above his right eye. Another centimeter and he would have been blinded.

One of his arms looked as though it had been twisted in its shoulder socket.

Seeing Jamani lying in such a state tore at Justin's insides. He knelt. "My poor Jamani. What have they done to you?"

Jamani managed a grim smile. "Rover stop. They beat me. Beat Kesi."

Justin hung his head. *It's my fault. I should have never entrusted him to drive the Land Rover.* Something was almost preordained to go wrong and Jamani and Kesi both paid for it. But they were alive. And alive was better than dead. They could heal, and they all could try to get on with their lives, with or without Humanus and Ariel. He hated himself for even thinking they were gone, but they must be. He pushed his grief down, hoping that by concentrating on the situation at hand he'd survive emotionally. It had worked before.

Justin stood and retrieved a container of water and some strips of cloth. He returned to Jamani and began the task of cleaning and dressing his wounds.

"Manus?" Kesi glanced toward the entrance expectantly. "Manus come?"

Justin looked up from Jamani. "Manus is dead. So is Ariel. They didn't make it out of the Maraia enclave."

Kesi stared, dumbstruck, then he began to whimper.

Justin reached out a hand and pulled him down to sit with him and Jamani. "We're going to be okay." Justin gripped Kesi tight. "We're going to get through this together."

Kesi yelped and pointed.

Cardassin stood in the doorway to the ruin. "Hi there."

Lightning flashed behind him. Thunder rolled. Rainwater slid off him, as if someone had upturned a bucket over his head. He was bare from the waist up. What remained of his red tights hung in tatters.

Justin staggered to his feet. *Who or what am I confronting?* "I don't know who you are, but you are not welcome here." He clenched his fists at his sides.

Cardassin slipped just inside the door, his lithe movements at odds to the trials Gomo had put him through. His body glistened in the dim light, lank and lean. "Look, we've all had a long day." He slicked water from his bare arms, then bent to do the same with his legs.

Kesi scrambled up to cower behind Justin, who laid a comforting hand on his shoulder, a father protecting a child.

"Leave us alone," Justin said. "We've had enough death for a lifetime."

Cardassin waved a hand in dismissal. "I hear you, brother." A maniacal grin. He craned to see the prone Jamani. "I see our powerful mate is indisposed. I could help you there, you know. I could help him there."

Before Justin could object, Cardassin crossed the distance separating him from Jamani and knelt at his side. He reached into his pocket and removed a pellet.

"This here's a nano-assembled cure for whatever ails you." He waved a pellet under Jamani's nose, then looked up to Justin and the terrified Kesi. "If you all don't have any objections, I'll just administer this here miracle pill to our friend and he'll be fit as a fiddle."

Justin lunged and stayed Cardassin's hand. "You'll do nothing of the sort!"

They tumbled back onto the floor, Cardassin ending up on the bottom. He peered at Justin's grasp. "Phenomenal. You are definitely stronger than your age might allow. Be that as it may, I'm troubled, really troubled you don't trust me."

Justin maintained his grip on Cardassin. "I've never trusted you."

Cardassin produced a facetious pout. "Not even after I showed you the second exit? You wouldn't be here if I hadn't."

"You saved your own ass going down that exit. You didn't wait for any of us."

The pout resolved into a grim countenance, one without life to it. "Your...our friend here will die soon if not attended to. Tell you what. If you are at all suspicious of this here capsule, I can dissipate your concerns. Look." Cardassin waved the pellet out in front of him and then, with a theatrical flourish, bit off and swallowed a tiny portion. "See, no ill effects. Well, more accurately and obviously, there's no improvement either. After all, I have no outward signs of degradation, do I? I feel great!"

Justin hesitated. Could the pellet heal Jamani? Was he reading this Cardassin wrong? Humanus had said his behavior was anomalous. Maybe he could be trusted. "I'll take a bite, first."

"Be my guest." Cardassin tossed the remaining pellet to Justin, who fumbled to catch it.

"Sorry," Cardassin said, snatching it back. "I should've allowed for your calcified reflexes. Now, don't sample too much." He handed the capsule to Justin. "We want to leave some for our friend."

Cardassin looked on eagerly as Justin bit off a piece of the capsule and swallowed it.

Immediately, his insides convulsed. It felt like his stomach was being tied in knots. "I don't feel very well. Something is wrong."

Cardassin glanced over his shoulder as though he were checking Kesi's location, then he peered back at Justin. "I might have gotten the wrong capsule out," he whispered conspiratorially. "They all look alike."

Justin knew he'd been duped. The tips of his fingers swelled. His toes popped the lacings on his sandals. All the while his stomach churned as though something vast and organic was growing exponentially. His abdomen inflated like a ripe melon, then leafy green shoots sprouted through taut skin. Pain shot white through his mind, blurring his thinking, bringing him to his knees. "What have you done to me?"

"Nothing exceptional. I do believe, from its affects, mind you, it's the same pellet that did in your father, your clone donor, your DNA sponsor?...I simply don't know how to refer to your ancestry."

Rage swept over Justin. Days of frustration and indecision built to a crescendo. "You bastard!" Justin's eyes bulged. Small capillaries burst, flooding the whites red.

Cardassin raised an eyebrow. "Hummm. I'm not so sure bastard fits, but I understand your anger. Now, may I administer to our friend here, or not? Do we want red vines to offset your green vines? Indeed, very Christmassy. Or shall we do monochrome?"

Justin lunged onto Cardassin, knocking him over.

Cardassin struggled briefly and quickly regained his balance.

Justin squirmed on the floor, finding he couldn't attack Cardassin and contend with the vines at the same time.

"It won't take long," Cardassin said sympathetically. "Ten minutes, eleven, maybe twelve at the most. Try to relax. Struggling like that only makes them itch."

Justin was losing control fast. His vision tunneled. What light there was in the ruin dimmed even more. "Kesi...run!"

Kesi seemed frozen to the spot where he stood.

Cardassin turned to him and offered a hand. "Dear Kesi. You needn't be afraid of me. Why

328

don't you come over here and help me dispose of these two ancients?"

Kesi glanced at Justin, then ran out the entrance.

"Pity," Cardassin said. "I could have used the help." He leaned over Jamani. "My, my, you're still awake."

Jamani's eyes rolled. Though he obviously tried, he couldn't move.

"Relax dear fellow. This will all be over in a heartbeat. Well, probably a few beats, but who's counting?" Cardassin took another pellet from his fanny pack and giggled. "I seem to have an endless supply."

As he yanked on Jamani's chin to open his mouth, a call drifted from outside.

Humanus. Justin rejoiced. With Humanus alive they stood a chance against this beast.

Cardassin stiffened. He must have also recognized the voice. "I see the cavalry has arrived. I best be going." He reached to pat Justin on the head and connected after the second attempt, such were Justin's gyrations. Then he disappeared out the entrance.

Justin lay back. The vine in his stomach, having breached his skin, was now worming around on the floor like some obscene snake looking for a place to root. He no longer felt pain. That had vanished soon after the growth had breached his skin. He knew there was nothing Humanus nor anyone else could do for him. He struggled across the floor to the bed and leaned over Jamani.

Jamani stared at him intently.

"Can you hear me?" Justin asked.

Jamani blinked.

Justin placed what remained of his hand on Jamani's chest. "I shall miss you dear friend."

Jamani struggled, his lips moved, but no sound escaped. His eyes glistened.

Supporting an arm he could no longer lift, Justin slid a finger to Jamani's lips, then reached awkwardly and stroked his cheek affectionately. "It's now clear to me why I was transported to this era."

***

Humanus cupped his hands to his mouth and called again. It seemed foolish, but it was a call of hope. He strained to hear a response. Nothing came through the incessant pounding of the rain. Lightning flashed, and a thunderous roar followed close.

Burned into Humanus' retina in the aftermath of the lightning strike was a shadowy figure exiting the ruin and heading south on the plateau top.

Was that Cardassin?

Humanus quickened his pace as best he could, forcing one leg painfully in front of the other.

Ariel kept up with him, offering support, correcting his wobble.

He staggered and fell into thickening mud, rose, and trudged on.

At the ruin he plunged through the doorway, lost his balance and sprawled on the floor. Gathering himself, he looked up. Rainwater leaked from his hairline and blurred his vision. Desperately, he wiped them clear.

330

Justin lay two meters from him. Green tendrils curled out from his body, snapping like snakes.

What have they done to him? Humanus stood shakily. He glanced at the bed and saw Jamani lying prone. *Is he dead? Where's Kesi?*

Justin's mouth flapped open and closed, but no words emanated, just a grotesque "Yah, yah, yah."

Ariel grabbed Humanus' arm. "Don't go closer. You don't know if it's contagious."

"I've got to try to save him."

"You don't know what it is that has attacked him."

Humanus looked down at the nano-assembler Ariel had saved. "There's got to be an answer in that."

Ariel put her hand on his shoulder. "There probably is. But you don't know how to use it."

"I've got to try." Humanus took it and thumbed what was possibly the *on* switch.

The nano-assembler glowed to life.

"It's on." Humanus felt encouraged.

He pushed another button and found it scrolled through what looked like programs for various assemblies. "How am I to tell which one of these will help Justin?" Humanus looked up in frustration.

"You can't," Ariel said. "Even Cardassin wasn't that adept at figuring out what to do."

A deep feeling of failure passed through Humanus. In his heart, he knew Justin was done for. Worse yet, he didn't even know how to make the old guy comfortable. Would severing the tendrils help? Or would that hurt him? Humanus leaned closer. "Can you speak?"

The *yah* reduced to gurgling sounds, nothing intelligible.

Humanus put his arm around Ariel. "Isn't there anything we can do for him?"

She shook her head. "There's nothing. You know it. I know it. Justin knows it. He'll be dead soon. You've tried."

Humanus tore his gaze from Justin to Jamani. "He looks good as dead, too." Humanus sat on the bed beside the primitive.

He was conscious, his eyes wide with fear.

"Where do you hurt?" Humanus asked.

Jamani blinked. No useful information.

Humanus felt a heavy grief, watching his mentor die and Jamani, Justin's lifelong friend immobilized.

Justin screamed. Not a high pitched scream, but something coarse, ugly, of the earth. It ended in a gargle. He sat up. The vines wove beneath him, supporting him. His head flopped forward on his chest, then something inside snapped his head up. Like a seed pod giving forth, his skull split down the middle, an eye on each side, a nose torn raggedly in two, a mouth gaping, loosened teeth falling to the floor. A thick tendril with a pod at its end wormed up from his throat, curled, then burst into a great crimson flower.

Justin stiffened.

The flower weaved back and forth for a moment, then wilted.

The vines lost their stiffness.

Justin keeled over.

Humanus stepped to him and picked up what was left of his wrist. No pulse. "He's dead."

"I wouldn't want to die like that," Ariel said. "Promise me you'll put me out of my misery if it ever happens."

Humanus looked at her, but said nothing. How could he? He could never put her out of her misery no matter how bad off she was. He'd die first trying to save her.

Justin lay in a crumpled heap of tangled, choking vines and human limbs.

Humanus looked away. The sight of his friend dead, and dead in that way, was too much to bear. "Find something to cover him."

Ariel dragged a cover from the bed and with Humanus' help laid it over Justin.

Humanus stood for a moment staring down at the cover. His thoughts ranged to Cardassin and his duplicity. They never should have trusted him or the guardian for that matter. Nothing but death and destruction. He pulled his attention back to the present. "Let's look to the living."

Ariel nodded.

Humanus returned to Jamani.

He ran his hands over Jamani's body to check for damage. Smoothing here, squeezing gently there. Every once in a while Jamani would wince.

Humanus stood. "He's in better shape than I thought. His left forearm is broken. I think his thigh is also fractured. He has deep lacerations to his head. But unless he is bleeding internally, he

333

should recover. Let's see what we can do to set his bones."

Ariel nodded. "I'll find something to make a splint."

An hour later, Jamani was resting in Justin's bed. His broken bones had been set. The gashes on his head were sewn closed and bandaged.

"Now to Justin," Humanus said.

"What do you have in mind?"

"We've got to get him out of here. No telling if that stuff he took will spread. The ground outside has been softened with the rain. We should bury him. Now."

Ariel hesitated, a move Humanus took to mean she wasn't about to touch Justin.

"I'll do it," Humanus said. "I'll roll him onto the cover and drag him outside."

Once outside with the rain still pelting down, Humanus pulled Justin fifty meters across the plateau to where he ascertained the soil was deep. He used his blade to scrape a shallow grave. It filled quickly with water, which Humanus worried might aid the growth of the tendrils. But they had already begun to shrivel and die, and the exposure to the moisture didn't revive them.

Humanus gripped the edges of the cover and was about to roll Justin into the grave, when he stopped. He reached out carefully, trying not to otherwise touch Justin, and pulled the pouch with the guardian in it from Justin's neck. "You won't be needing this." Humanus wondered if he would be needing the guardian, but burying it with Justin was probably wrong, despite his misgivings about what it had to say.

After draping the thong of the pouch over his head, Humanus rolled Justin into the grave. He lay in the muddy water, his body half-submerged, his face at surface level, his eyes open and staring on either side of the wilted flower.

God, the dead look awful. Humanus kicked the outlying tendrils in alongside the body and shoved muddy dirt back on top of it. Justin's face was the last to be covered.

He can't feel anything now, Humanus kept telling himself, only half convinced. *Goodbye, friend.*

The interment wouldn't be enough to keep predators from clawing the dirt free to get at Justin's body, but it was enough for now, and if any predators took the advantage then they were in for a big surprise.

Legs folded under him, Humanus sat next to the mounded grave. The pounding rain enveloped him in a wet isolated world. He felt very alone. It seemed everyone he knew was being slowly stripped away from him, their proximity to him a death sentence. His eyes burned, and if tears escaped, then they were quickly washed away in the downpour. He rubbed his face with his hands and blew at water cascading off his nose with hot breaths. Nothing assuaged his grief.

Finally, he stood and returned to the ruin.

Ariel lay slumped next to Jamani.

At first, Humanus thought she was simply exhausted. He came up to her and touched her gently on the shoulder. "Are you all right?"

She gazed up at him unfocused. "Humanus, I don't feel too good."

"What is it?"

"Something is roaming around inside of me and it--" She groaned in agony and clutched her stomach. Her eyes wide, she tried to speak, but barely. "When I was in the cell, I drank from Cardassin's cup."

A dull fear washed over Humanus, a feeling of helplessness, of being outnumbered and outclassed. The subtleness of events swirled and conspired in permutations he could only begin to understand.

"He must have put something in the water."

Ariel looked confused. "But why? We were helping each other survive."

Humanus took out the nano-assembler and gripped it tightly. "A remedy is here, but I'm too stupid to make it work."

"But Cardassin knows. He's alive, isn't he? I saw him, too."

Humanus looked to the ceiling in anguish. "Even if I could find him, how could I trust him? How would I convince him to help us?"

"There's no alternative. I will surely die."

Humanus sank to his knees, despair churning his insides. "Will this never end?"

Ariel reached and stroked back his hair. "It will end. And you will make it so. For me." She leaned forward and kissed his forehead. "At least try."

He looked into her eyes and saw a strength that gave him strength. She was, of course, right. He'd have to search for Cardassin. That in itself might seem impossible, but knowing Cardassin, and knowing that something was controlling events, Humanus suspected it wouldn't be too hard to find him. After all, what was a test if the one to be tested couldn't find his way to the testing ground?

Humanus eased Ariel onto the floor and laid her arms at her sides. "Is this more comfortable?" he asked, not knowing what else he could possibly do before going after Cardassin and a cure.

"I'll be all right for now. Hurry back." She smiled bravely and stroked his forehead. "I love you."

Humanus leaned and kissed her on the lips. He hoped to show affection, but also in the back of his mind sought to mask his confusion. She loves me? He didn't know what that meant. He knew what the words meant, but he didn't connect them with a distinct feeling. All he knew was he'd have to find Cardassin and force him to give up a cure.

"I'll be back as soon as I can." The farewell sounded lame after her expression of love, but it would have to do. He was about to stand, when he remembered the guardian. He took the pouch from around his neck. "I retrieved this from Justin before I buried him. He never wanted it in the first place, and now he's dead."

Ariel squirmed, obviously discomforted. "I don't want it, either. Throw it away. No one here is going to use it again."

Humanus started to lay the pouch on the floor beside the bed, then thought otherwise. Better to keep the enigmatic sphere close. He stood. His joints shrieked with pain.

Ariel winced at his agony. "You can't do this."

"Yes I can. Watch." He turned and, with all his might, tried to hide his incapacity as he hobbled out of the ruin.

Immediately upon clearing the entrance, the incessant rain engulfed him. His mind told him the urgency of the situation demanded he run, but his body quickly intervened and shut down the thought. He was reduced to dragging one foot out of the muck and swiveling forward with a twist of his hips, then dragging the other. But the physical effort revived him, clearing his mind. *Focus*. It wouldn't be easy, but it didn't seem complicated. Find Cardassin. Shove the nano-assembler at him and demand he design a cure. But under threat would Cardassin produce a cure or some horrible vine pellet?

As Humanus stumbled over the plateau towards the ruins of the Maraia cave, he wracked his brain for an advantage, something to bring Cardassin over to his side.

Still searching for that elusive something, Humanus arrived at the edge of the plateau overlooking the former cave.

The utter destruction hit him hard. A whole section of the plateau had carved away and slewed down into the plain. The plateau was no longer a linear landmass shaping out from regions south. It was now a landmass with a huge interruption, a foundering ship with its side blown out.

He'd been down there, in all that rubble, struggling, afraid of dying, trying to save Ariel. The sheer waste that lay before him was devastating.

Shielding his eyes with one hand, he followed the line of the avalanche and stopped where it came to the upturned Land Rover.

Is that someone sitting on it?

Cardassin lounged back against the metal hull and held Kesi close.

Humanus felt a searing pain strike through his head. He rubbed his forehead with the heel of his palm. *Kesi? Dear Kesi? This complicates matters. But nothing to do about it now.* This was the situation Humanus had been dealt.

He slid through mud down the slope, his feet sinking deep with each stride. He reached the level plain below and slogged his way toward the Land Rover.

As he neared, he could see Cardassin had a knife or some fragmented piece of steel pressed to Kesi's neck.

Cardassin waved with his free hand, a cynical gesture of greeting. He waited patiently until Humanus came within talking distance. "Fancy meeting you here." Cardassin wiped his face clear of rainwater that ran through his thin hair. "You could drown in this stuff."

Zug. Humanus stopped several meters from Cardassin. "I've come on business that doesn't involve Kesi. Let him go."

339

Kesi's eyes darted back and forth.

Cardassin smiled and glanced sidelong at Kesi. "Alas, he's here. He's involved."

Humanus took a step toward Cardassin.

"Ah, ah!" He pressed the tip of the knife up under Kesi's chin until a trickle of blood slid down, mingled with rain and spread in a pink flood across his chest.

"Manus!"

Cardassin eased off on the blade. "Your friend seems to be in dire straits."

Humanus clenched fists at his sides. What could he do? Lunge at Cardassin to free Kesi? Perhaps. But would Cardassin yield? Would he have to kill Cardassin to subdue him? What then of a cure for Ariel? Kesi for Ariel? Stalemate. "Let him go, Cardassin."

Cardassin pointed the knife at Humanus and wove it in a tight circle, then brought it down and pushed it up to half its length into Kesi's side.

Kesi shrieked. He struggled to free himself, but that only moved the blade about on his insides.

Cardassin pouted. "Your little friend doesn't want to stay with me."

Dear god, not Kesi. How do I reason with this beast? "You've given Ariel something that is now killing her. I want you to give me a cure."

Cardassin lounged back, obviously aware he held the advantage. "I see. You don't want to free your friend here for fear of killing me and thereby sealing Ariel's demise." Cardassin leaned forward with an exaggerated look to Kesi's abdomen, then removed the knife from Kesi's side and plunged it in the other side.

Kesi let out a sigh, probably not having the strength to utter anything more forceful.

Humanus' mind raced. Cardassin would keep knifing Kesi until he died, then taunt Humanus, and there was nothing he could do to stop him.

Cardassin yawned. "I'm losing patience with this little drama." He withdrew the blade from Kesi's stomach and carved it in a shallow arc across his neck.

Blood streamed down Kesi's shoulder and arm. He slumped forward, unconscious or dead.

Cardassin peered at the wound. "Humph! Must have hit an artery or something." With a strong cut, he ripped the blade deep, then shoved Kesi to the ground between them.

Humanus let loose a cry and went for his blade.

Cardassin held up a hand. "Easy dude. It was a mercy killing. I didn't want him to suffer."

A surging rage swept over Humanus. He rushed Cardassin.

Giggling, as though the pursuit were some sort of game, Cardassin scrambled around the Land Rover, putting the vehicle between them. Safely protected by the intervening bulk, he waved his hands in the air. "Hey, hey, let's not forget our priorities."

Humanus felt the white heat of his anger press behind his eyes. "You killed Kesi! Do you have to kill Ariel, too?"

Cardassin straightened and walked around the vehicle toward Humanus. "Of course not. Ariel

341

and I got on famously. It would be a pity to see her turn into a tomato vine."

Humanus thrust out his blade and waved it defensively.

Cardassin must have seen his opportunity. He smiled as he continued around the Land Rover. He walked up to Humanus, who remained frozen in place.

Cardassin placed his knife against Humanus' chest and drew the blade slowly from top to bottom. "My, my, you bleed, too."

Humanus ignored the pain of the shallow cut. He took a step back. "I want the cure. What do you want from me?"

"Isn't it obvious? I want you." Cardassin pressed up to Humanus, his face centimeters away.

Humanus turned to avoid Cardassin's foul breath. "I was right. *Zug* is here."

"Why yes, I do believe he is." Cardassin thrust his blade in and out of Humanus' stomach. "Does that hurt?"

Humanus staggered back, one hand pressing against his wound in a futile attempt to staunch the flow of blood. "I'll give you anything, if you'll give me the antidote."

Cardassin advanced. He peered at the tip of his knife, raised it and hesitated, as though trying to decide where it should be plunged. He stabbed it into Humanus' shoulder.

Reflexively, Humanus thrust his blade, not far enough to engage Cardassin, enough to hopefully deter him.

Cardassin glanced at the blade and waded forward, grabbing the blade, steadying it, then he pressed his weight onto it.

The blade's point shoved against Cardassin's bare skin, pushing deep before slipping through and entering his stomach. Almost without resistance Humanus' knife slid unimpeded and exited Cardassin's back.

His breath escaped in a long rush, almost a sigh of satisfaction. He slumped and leaned heavily onto Humanus.

Horrified Humanus drew back his blade and gripped Cardassin under his shoulders, trying to keep him upright. Humanus felt his guts would burst from his own wound. He winced as his slashed shoulder protested with a deep welling of blood.

Humanus' arm went limp. He lost his grip.

Cardassin fell to one side, smiling blissfully.

"Are you insane?" Humanus screamed. "You're dying. Give me the antidote."

Cardassin looked up, ignoring the splatter of raindrops and gazed glassy eyed at Humanus. "I forgive you your trespasses. You seem to be also dying."

"Give me the antidote," Humanus pleaded, hearing the defeat in his voice.

Cardassin coughed up blood. He wiped his mouth. "Yucky stuff when it comes up like that. Guess I don't have much time left."

"The antidote."

Cardassin's eyes fluttered as his eyeballs rolled white. "Here's a thought," he said in a hoarse whisper.

Humanus knelt to hear him better. "What?"

Cardassin spit to one side and drew in a ragged breath. "Embrace me...and I'll set you free."

"Embrace..."

"Yeah. Take me into you. Me you. You me." He paused while a choking cough wracked his thin frame. "It's easy. A hug will do."

"I can't."

"Suit yourself, but consider this." The pitch of Cardassin's voice rose, as he hurried on. "It's more about the will of acceptance than anything physical. You'll know what I know. You have the nano-assembler. You'll be able to figure this out."

Humanus cringed. Embrace *Zug*? The thought repelled him, but it held out the only line of hope. "How do I know it will work?"

Cardassin laughed weakly. "You don't. Bye, bye." He sagged, the back of his head plopping into the mud, which rose to his ears.

Desperately, Humanus drew Cardassin up with his one good arm and flopped his limp arm around him in an embrace. When he felt nothing, he shifted his grip and hugged him again.

Cardassin hung limp.

"You lying bastard!" Humanus raged, shoving Cardassin away. Humanus fumbled to remove the pouch with the guardian from his neck. "Take this and everything it represents!" He dragged the leather thong through the mud and under Cardassin's head, twisted the cord tight and pulled.

344

Cardassin rose. His eyes bulged in their sockets, but he maintained an outrageous grin on his lips as they turned purple.

Then Humanus felt a change, subtle, but distinct. A hardening of resolve. A counterweight to his sensibilities. A flood of new knowledge. He gazed at the nano-assembler in his hand. The solution played across his consciousness. With an involuntary compulsion, his fingers worked over the close set buttons. A moment later a pellet expelled from the end of the nano-assembler.

Gripping the pellet to protect it from the rain, he stood.

Cardassin slipped to the ground, still holding Humanus with one hand by the leg, the other gripping the pouch with the guardian.

Humanus shoved Cardassin's head and pried the abhorrent being away from him. He stepped free, moved to Kesi and knelt.

"Dear Kesi." Humanus lifted Kesi's head, which lolled back on his neck. His wounds ran freely with blood, staining his body and the surrounding mud. "I'll come back for you." Humanus wiped his eyes. Emotion choked him. "Forgive me...this moment."

He stood and struggled his way up the loose slope, thumping hard across the plateau top. He slipped and fell, sliding in muddy soil. He rose to his feet and staggered forward. The ruin loomed into view.

Chapter Sixteen

The rain stopped. Dark clouds scudded away from a late afternoon sun. The humid air hung like a heavy drape blanketing the landscape, muting sounds. Beasts of the plain milled about and fed on wet grass. Birds lifted silently into the air and careened overhead.

Humanus stood for a moment taking in his surroundings. The end of a day with clouds parting and the sun shining through. Almost a new beginning. A reason to hope. After all he had been through, it was as if the world around him was giving him some encouragement.

He stared at the small pellet in his hand. His future, everything in his life seemed to reside in the success of that small object. He knew he was dying, but Ariel didn't have to. He staggered to the ruin's entrance.

"I have it" he cried, the words seeming to stick in his dry throat as they tumbled forth. Optimistic words that barely made it out of his mouth, he felt so weak.

Rainwater still sluiced off the roof and fell in a shimmering curtain onto his head, washing over his shoulder, easing his pain. He gripped his stomach wound. Even favoring his side as he walked, it felt like his insides had turned liquid and everything was seeking exit through the opening in his skin.

Inside the ruin, an eerie stillness greeted him.

Rays of diffuse sunlight slanted across the room from the western windows. On the far side of the room, Jamani still lay immobile on Justin's bed.

Ariel sat beside him.

For a moment Humanus thought her condition might have improved. He had left her lying on the floor. That she was now sitting next to Jamani indicated she had some strength to move.

But she was slumped forward in an awkward position. Her hands propped on the bed, her head down, chin to her chest. Her hair hung straight, shielding her face.

He hobbled over to her. "Ariel?" He pulled on her shoulder with his good arm.

She slid from his grip, fell backward to hit the bed, then tipped awkwardly to the floor.

She lay there unconscious, or caught in a seizure, or dead.

Her eyes rolled white in their sockets. She gritted her teeth. A thin thread of saliva slid out the corner of her mouth. But no vines or anything of that sort. Her skin was warm to his touch. A rapid pulse beat on the side of her neck.

He hoped there was time. He shook her gently.

Whatever possessed her let go. Her head lolled back freely as her hair spread in a spray beneath her. She closed her eyes and suddenly looked serene, her lips drawn in a neutral line.

A sudden fear of failure gripped him. He could almost feel death stalking them both. Worse yet, he'd sold his soul. He hadn't even done it reluctantly. He'd done it willingly to save this confounding woman who now bore his child. Was she already too near death to be helped? Anger swept over him. He knew who was to blame. *Why is the guardian doing this to me?*

He shook his head, trying to clear his mind, focus his thoughts. He must hurry.

He opened her mouth, pressed her tongue down and shoved the pellet to the back, then brought a container of water to her lips and poured. He could only hope the pellet would not lodge in her air passage.

She convulsed, coughed, but the pellet stayed down.

He laid the remaining cover from Justin's bed on the floor, eased her onto it and tried to make her comfortable. Then he sat beside her and waited.

Minutes passed. Hours passed. Night descended on the ruin. The moon rose. He remained at her side, his body frozen into immobility. He no longer knew if he was dead or alive, or even able to move.

Finally, she stirred and sat up, eyes wide with horror. She screamed, flinging her arms out, her fingers extended like small daggers.

Impulsively he lunged, trying to embrace her, and paid dearly for the effort as she buffeted his bruised body with flailing blows. "You're going to be okay," he said, more a declaration of hope than one of certainty.

She struggled free and pummeled him again.

He ducked away from her agitated swings and grabbed her arms, bending them to her sides. "Be still." The effort opened his wounds. Blood poured fourth onto the floor.

348

She gulped air. Her chest heaved with the effort. "Z...z...*Zug*." She glanced around, a jerky motion, her lips quivering.

She seemed insane. Maybe she was. "You were sick," he said with effort. His mind tried to concentrate on her but his mutilated body demanded attention. "I gave you a cure. How do you feel?"

She stared at him, a look of astonishment, wonder, fear. "Who are you?"

Humanus laid a hand against her cheek. "It's me. Humanus."

She blinked.

He expected her to resume her insane thrashing, but her outbursts weakened. She fell silent, then her arms went limp at her sides. Her breathing slowed and stabilized. "Humanus." She smiled. "How should I feel?" She ran her tongue over dry lips. "The last thing I remember...you dragged Justin out to bury him. Jamani lay on the bed, wounded."

With a studied concentration, his gaze never leaving her face, Humanus handed her the container of water, spilling only a little.

She stared at him with her brow furrowed, but took the container and gulped down its contents, looking over the rim at his body. "You're hurt."

"It's nothing."

"You call that nothing? You're bleeding." She sounded annoyed. "Let me see."

Hoping to distract her, he indicated Jamani. "He's still wounded. He's resting. But I'm more concerned about you. You said you felt things growing inside."

In the dim light of the moon filtering through the windows, she hesitated, obviously torn between her own brush with horror and her desire to help Humanus. In the end, she leaned into him, exhausted, shivering.

He suppressed a recoil from the pain of the pressure of her body against his. Still, he had missed her warm embrace.

"They're gone," she said. "The only thing I have growing inside me now are the twins."

"Twins?"

Her shivering stilled. She pulled back. Her face looked worn. The gray light from the moon etched every crease and tired wrinkle. But she managed a smile. "A boy and a girl."

Humanus let the news wash over him, let it spread like a magic balm over his wounds, let it push every other concern away. *Joy mixed with sorrow. What a strange combination. How do I reconcile the two?*

She must have sensed his reaction. "I'm sorry about Justin...and Jamani. So much death. So many threats. I worry about giving birth in this world."

Her concerns were real. But what to say? There was nothing positive happening. Nothing uplifting to report. "Kesi is dead, too."

Ariel's face blanched with shock. She steadied quickly. "How?"

"Cardassin killed him. He taunted me by killing Kesi. I could do nothing. I had to get a cure for you." Humanus surprised himself with his lack of remorse for Kesi's death. Had *Zug* hardened him already, so quickly? Kesi a statistic. Another person gone, added to all the others starting with Mia, then Wakuru...a long line.

Ariel searched his face.

He turned away, fearing she could see into him, see what he had become.

"I'm sorry," she said. "What of Cardassin?"

Humanus flinched, knowing where she was going with her questioning and not being able to deflect her. "He's dead, too. I killed him."

Ariel absorbed the information. "Then how did you get the cure?" She pulled back from him.

In a way, he admired her pursuit of the truth. He smiled and shook his head. She was too perceptive to be deceived. Best to come clean. "I sold my soul."

"Then..."

He put a hand to her mouth, stifling the rest of her question. "I embraced that which is not me, but is me. I took him back into my heart. We are now one...again."

She pulled his hand down. Her eyes filled with tears. "The guardian's test."

"Perhaps." Could it all be so simple? A guardian's test? All he felt was a complex range of embraced hominid emotions. Was that what it was all about? Feelings? "I don't know where things will go from here." He reached for her.

She shied back.

"Don't hate me," he said. How easily an emotion played to the fore.

"I don't hate you." She reached to his hand covering his stomach wound and pulled it away.

She winced seeing the angry red gash, the dried blood at the edges, the pulpy insides residing just beyond. She placed her hand over the wound. "Cardassin did this?"

Her touch was cool, soothing. "I said it was nothing. I'll be okay." He hated lying to her, but figured she'd see through him anyway.

She looked at him skeptically. "Let me help--"

A scraping sound came from outside the ruin.

Humanus turned toward the entrance where a humped form stood in silhouette. Light from the moon streamed into the ruin on either side of the figure, casting a ghostly shadow.

"I hope I haven't missed anything," Cardassin wheezed. He made no attempt to staunch the flow of blood from his stomach, leaving it to flow freely, a black stain in the dim light, covering his hips and legs. "I just had to see how this all played out."

Humanus felt around for something to throw. His hand landed on the nano-assembler. He heaved it at the ghoulish form.

End over end it sailed, whistling through the air.

Cardassin reached out at the last second and snagged the cylinder. "Thanks." He lifted the nano-assembler and peered at it. "I see you've put it to good--"

Humanus staggered to his feet and lunged toward the doorway.

Ariel screamed.

Humanus hit Cardassin hard, wrapped his arms around the thin man's waist and gripped him firmly. With his legs pumping, he ignored the pain and

352

drove into him. He pushed Cardassin through the door, across the plateau, to the edge of the escarpment, and without the slightest hesitation made a final thrust that sent them out in a tumbling freefall.

Cardassin clapped both hands to the sides of Humanus' head and drew him close, face to face close, close enough to kiss. "This is better than I thought."

***

Ariel sat stunned by the quick turn of events. Etched into her mind was the image of Humanus and Cardassin framed by the outer door in a close embrace, tumbling over the edge of the escarpment. Cardassin looked as though he was saying something to Humanus, but she couldn't hear.

The fall to the rocks below was thirty meters. They must both be dead.

"Jamani!"

She shook him, needing his help, but he did not respond. She stood tentatively, her knees weak. She staggered to the entrance and out onto the plateau. Careful not to lose her balance, she approached the edge of the plateau with a sense of foreboding and peered over.

The bodies lay draped grotesquely on the broken rock below. No signs of movement.

She suppressed a rising sense of panic. Then a wave of grief swept over her followed by a sickening nausea, reducing her to a quivering mass of self-pity. *He can't be dead.*

She ran and stumbled to the trail that led down the side of the escarpment. Falling, picking herself

353

up and sliding, tumbling, she descended. Seconds later she pulled herself together at the bottom, then approached the bodies.

She came upon Cardassin first. He was spread-eagle on his back, bent over a rock at an impossible angle. His mouth gaped open. His eyes stared unfocused. He had to be dead. His back was broken. No one could have survived such a massive blow.

She gave the body a wide berth and hurried to Humanus.

He lay on his stomach, his face hanging down, hidden behind smaller stones.

Ariel tried to lift him.

He came free and rolled onto his back.

She knew immediately he was dead. He had landed on a blunt rock that had crushed his chest. There was very little blood, just a huge concavity where his chest should have been. His face was deathly pale. His eyes puffed shut. The wounds in his shoulder and stomach looked inconsequential compared to his chest trauma.

She glanced to the top of the plateau, then tried to lift Humanus. But even if she could get him off the ground, there was no way she would ever be able to carry him back to the ruin.

She'd wait until daylight, then try to protect his body from predators with stones, if they hadn't already flayed him of his flesh during the night. Perhaps in a few days Jamani would recover enough to help her move Humanus for burial, and if Jamani didn't recover, then she'd have three burials to deal with, counting Cardassin.

She started to retrace her steps to the ruin when Cardassin moaned.

It's not possible. Not fair, she thought. Humanus dead and this beast still lives? Could reality be so cruel?

She approached to within a couple of meters and peered at him in the weak light of the moon.

"Tough...break," Cardassin whispered through clenched teeth. He convulsed, a laugh that bubbled up unbidden, but one that made him pay in obvious pain.

Ariel put a hand to her mouth. "How can you still be alive?"

"Not...for long, my dear." Cardassin tried to lift a hand but couldn't. "Be a good girl...and remove this here guardian's pouch from around my neck. It's beginning to...to...really annoy me."

Ariel could think of no circumstance that would lead her to get any closer to the pathetic beast. "I can't."

"Didn't think you could."

"What did you do to Humanus?"

Cardassin coughed up bloody phlegm. It spilled in a black flood over his chin. He remained silent for some minutes.

Ariel thought he had died.

He jerked. "I...he...embraced me." Cardassin's lips quivered into what might have been a smile, then all life seemed to leave his body in a sigh.

Ariel moved closer.

Cardassin's eyes remained open, their pupils dilated.

She reached carefully for the guardian pouch, fully expecting that at any second Cardassin would jump up and grab her. But he didn't.

In his outstretched hand the nano-assembler hung off his wrist by its leather tie.

Leaning her head away in distaste, she eased the line over his stiff, splayed fingers. The small cylinder was smashed and battered. Its monitor window cracked. It looked to be useless. In any case it was useless. No one alive knew how to operate it. She tossed it to one side.

With the pouch gripped firmly, she back-stepped, then turned on her heel and ran back to the ruin.

Once inside, she saw Jamani had shifted position, a move that gave her hope he might survive.

She sat beside him in the dark for a long time, wondering what was to become of her. What was she to do? Where would she go? The guardian would know the answers, but would it tell her?

The thought of using it repelled her. It seemed so cold and calculating. It had laid out its test for Humanus and now he was dead. What did that prove? But in the dark, with nowhere else to turn, she pulled the pouch open, grabbed the guardian and squeezed it as hard as she could.

What have you done?

She received no response. Her rage welled up, out of control, palpable. She was about to hurl the small sphere against the far wall, when she felt the subtlest tingle. Gulping for self-control, she tried to regain her composure.

What have you done. Please. I need answers.
Her thoughts bordered on hysteria.

"*A balance has been restored.*"

Always calm and calculating. *What balance?*
Her anger threatened to rise up again and
overwhelm her. *I see no balance. I see everyone
here is either dead or dying.*

"*Everyone here is but a whim, a member of a
supporting cast in an infinitesimal moment in a slice
of reality in an infinite universe.*"

You always did speak in riddles.

"*It is not I who speak in riddles but you who
have trouble understanding.*"

She felt like hurling the sphere across the room.
What an impudent piece of hardware.

"*Your thoughts are known to me.*"

*I'm human. I react. I'm sorry if you don't like
what you monitor.*

"*Accepted.*"

*Okay, educate me. I have nothing left in my
heart but grief and sorrow.*

"*These are emotions to be treasured, whether
you think so or not. But I digress. Gilomir was
brought here for a reason.*"

I know.

"*Good. We can start there. He has traveled an
intricate path through the now, the then and the
future, all the while being shaped and formed by
events around him. His journey is complete. He
has passed the test I set out before him. He and Zug
have come into balance again. Order has been
restored.*"

How can you say a balance has been restored. To what end would Humanus, and he's Humanus to me, not Gilomir, to what end would he want to embrace Zug, the embodiment of evil?

"Good, evil. These are limiting, polarizing terms. In reality there is only a seamless whole, and depending on where you examine that whole, you will see some of what you label good and some evil, but you will not see them in isolation. At least not now that balance has been restored."

Humanus needed to absorb Zug to be made whole?

"Zug was always a part of Humanus. But Zug exceeded his limits, his rights to being, hence the imbalance. I knew that what Humanus needed he could find here, in hominids. Love, passion, tenderness, happiness, grief. Emotions. Also anger, fear, hate, suspicion. And sacrifice. The only way to affirm he had truly embraced these traits was to let events follow their course."

And we hominids are but bit players in this drama? Props for demonstrating human characteristics?

"I thought that was obvious from what I said. But hominids should have no shame in playing their part. They were only on this stage for a brief time, and their being on the stage at all was accidental."

All of humanity is an accident?

"Yes, in this case. Unfortunately, you, and I include you because you are a conscious being though a synthetic one, and humanity have been fortuitously granted the ability to see in a closed universe, where seeing can bring no joy. You are *witnesses to events beyond your control and comprehension."*

Ariel laughed despite the seriousness of the comment. *Yes, we see. But we also act. We make decisions, plan ahead, chart our own destinies.*

The guardian was silent for a moment.

"It only seems so to you. Actually you and everyone else are observers of one set of randomly occurring circumstances out of an infinity of possibilities. By the insertion of Humanus' DNA in an ancient hominid, you and all hominids have evolved the ability to see. You are conscious in a world of random happenings.

"Unfortunately, your ability to see is limited to your own personal point of view. You don't know for sure that the bug in your brain is the same as the bug in someone else's brain. Hence reality is very subjective. But that isn't a problem, since there are an infinite number of realities and hominids as a group have only a finite number of points of view. Something easily encompassed by infinitude.

"Furthermore, you have evolved to fool yourself into thinking you have some control over what is happening. But you don't. It is an illusion. You simply observe random happenings that present themselves to your senses. You feel that you have some input into controlling your fate, when in fact, you are only playing catch up to what is randomly happening. Fortunately, your personal point of view, Ariel, is witnessing a slice of time and space that follows a modicum of predictability. But given there is an infinity of times and spaces, there are also places far less predictable, far less hospitable.

Obviously, your point of view is not observing them."

Some of what the guardian said made sense. If you believed in infinity, that is. *And what are you? Some sort of god?*

"God is used very loosely by those sharing your point of view. I am quite frankly beyond your comprehension. So are Gilomir and Zug. I am manifest in the here and now in this small sphere you clasp so desperately in your hand. I am the only entity from the outside that exists in this closed universe, what is referred to as the forbidden zone."

What is the forbidden zone? I have heard Humanus speak of this zone but I do not really understand of what it consists.

"It's an anomalistic locality, an entity in and of itself. Because of an anomalous gravitational field outside what is defined as the zone, the world lines of everything in the zone, up from the infinitesimal, curl back on themselves in a closed loop."

There is no way out of here?

"Unfortunately, this is so."

We just swirl round and round?

"To an extent. The closed space time of an anomalistic locality can be viewed, at least by me, as a spherical whole with an infinite number of ways to define a circle across it."

The alternate realities of which you spoke.

"Indeed. More precisely, there are only alternate points of observation. You only see the reality you are experiencing. On the other hand, I see all the possibilities. Are you finished with your questions?"

No. But I sense an impatience. Your stay in this forbidden zone is about to end, isn't it?

"*You are very perceptive. In truth, I shall be leaving shortly. All that I hoped to accomplish here has been achieved.*"

And what is to become of me? Where is the Shepherd? I carry twins in my womb. You have killed their father. What is to become of them?

"*Why, you exist. You are aware. You should perhaps be thankful you can witness what is going on around you. Pity the poor beasts of this world that go through life without knowing. As for the Shepherd, he was never meant to have any further interaction with you.*"

Ariel was flabbergasted. *He produced me and has now left me?*

"*Precisely. I'm sorry I can't put it in more diplomatic terms. What becomes of you, your twins, or any others here is all of little consequence in the grand scheme of things.*"

How can you say that? How can you be so heartless?

"*I will leave now. The forbidden zone has served its purpose.*"

Ariel felt a warmth in the palm of her hand where the guardian should have been. She opened her hand to find it empty. She bent forward, feeling as though her whole body was wracked in pain. Sobs shook her. She rocked back and forth on her knees, not knowing how to assuage the grief she was feeling.

A rumbling like thunder, but not thunder, rolled across the sky. The moon dimmed then disappeared. The stars winked out. The ruin and the plateau on which it stood vanished. The plain on which it all rested went missing.

She seemed suspended in a dark place with no points of reference.

Then there was light.

***

Humanus opened his eyes. He lay on his back, staring up at the concrete ceiling of the ruin. Judging from the slant of sunlight coming through the windows, it was midday. He shifted his weight and realized he was on Justin's bed.

Immediately, a cool hand caressed his forehead.

"Humanus is awake!" Ariel said over her shoulder to someone else in the room he could not see. She leaned close and kissed him lightly on the mouth.

Humanus savored her touch. He felt he had returned from the dead. "How long?"

Her face loomed close, eager, smiling, joyful. "Three days. I thought you would never wake up, but Jamani was confident you would."

Humanus struggled to rise but found his muscles didn't respond to the commands his brain was sending out. "Jamani's okay?"

Ariel wrung water out of a cloth and placed it on his forehead. "Jamani's always been okay. If it wasn't for him you'd have been buried when the Maraia enclave blew."

Humanus gave up trying to rise. Something didn't track. His mind raced to sort reality from confusion.

362

Gently, Ariel pressed him back on the bed. "You shouldn't try to move so soon. You were beaten quite badly."

A concurrence of fact. "Gomo and the super-primates."

"Yes."

A Confirmation. At least that bit of information checked out.

Jamani came into view and peered down at Humanus. "Be good you awake. We fear you dead. Don't know what do."

Jamani looked unscathed. Three days ago, if it were in fact just three days, Jamani had been at death's door, unable to speak or move.

And Kesi's horrible death. He must still be lying there. And Cardassin. *How could I have survived the fall?*

"I went over the edge of the escarpment with Cardassin. How...how could I have survived?"

Ariel looked apprehensively at Jamani. "He's delirious." She turned back to Humanus. "Here's some water. Drink. We can talk more later."

Humanus drank the proffered water. He wasn't delirious. He remembered it all very well. The escape from the Maraia enclave, Cardassin's betrayal, Justin's horrible death, then Ariel sick and Kesi sacrificed. *Zug* embraced. There was no doubting that. He could feel *Zug* in him now, like some hideous pollutant, but contained, controlled...balanced.

"I don't want to rest. Tell me what happened...from when Gomo and the super-primates beat me."

"Are you sure you are strong enough?"

"I'm sure."

Ariel pulled on a cushion and slid it under his head to lift it a bit. "Are you comfortable?"

"Yes. Please tell me what happened."

"After Gomo and the super-primates beat you, they dragged you away. I thought for sure you were dead. But an hour or so later, Gomo brought you back. You were trussed up like a turkey for roasting. He left you with me. I couldn't do much to help you besides loosening your ties. Cardassin, too, tried to make you comfortable, but couldn't."

"Cardassin was *Zug*."

"We all thought that, of course, especially after he drove off with the Land Rover. But let me finish--"

"But Cardassin was *Zug*!"

"Please, don't stress yourself. If you don't calm down, I'll stop."

Suppressing a rising panic of disorientation, Humanus gulped back another outburst and nodded. "Go on."

Ariel cast Jamani a concerned look.

Jamani shrugged.

"Okay, I'll continue," Ariel said, "but remember, you promised. While Cardassin and I were tending your battered body, Justin was planning a rescue with Jamani and Kesi. They lured the super-primates out onto the plain, then Justin entered the Maraia enclave to neutralize Gomo. Everything went according to plan until Gomo eluded Justin and ran out to call back his primates. We were making good progress out, when Gomo returned with the primates and blocked the exit. I thought we were done for."

Humanus felt a sense of relief. Her scenario matched his recollection. "That's when Gomo blew up the cave."

"Cardassin said he had the keys to some sort of doomsday device that would destroy the enclave. He said he'd activate the device, hoping to trap Gomo and the remaining super-primates inside. He pointed us to a secondary exit from the enclave." Ariel stroked Humanus' forehead. "My poor Humanus. You really don't remember what happened, do you? It wasn't Gomo. Cardassin shouted at us to run while he activated the device.

"There was no time to argue. Justin threw his last firebomb to delay the primates and we raced across the room, but we couldn't find the second exit. Justin returned to Cardassin, alone. He told Cardassin to guide you and me to the exit and escape. He would stay behind and activate the doomsday device. As the flames died down, the primates attacked again. Cardassin argued, but Justin insisted. At the last possible moment, Cardassin led us to the exit. The last I saw of Justin he and Gomo were struggling for control of the red button that activated the doomsday device.

"We fell into the exit, and not a moment too soon. A powerful explosion imploded the enclave. I was first out of the exit. Cardassin was pulling you out when the cave blew. The exit collapsed around you."

Humanus couldn't believe what he was hearing. "How'd I get out?"

"Jamani and Kesi found us. Jamani crawled as far as he could into the exit and dug furiously. If he hadn't returned, we'd never have gotten you out in time. You were unconscious, and stayed that way until just now."

"Justin is dead?"

"He sacrificed his life to save ours."

This must be a dream. But Humanus couldn't shake his own recollection of events. He couldn't deny the stark reality of being one with *Zug*.

"Manus!" Kesi barged into the ruin and ran over to Humanus. He stood shyly, not sure what to do. "You be awake!" he blurted.

"Where have you been?" Humanus stared at Kesi, Kesi whole and unscathed, no wounds, not even a scratch.

"I be fishing, Manus." Kesi held up a stick with three lake trout threaded onto it. "We eat good, now."

A movement behind Kesi caught Humanus' attention.

Cardassin stepped into the ruin. He paused when he spotted Humanus, then strode quickly forward, thrusting his arms over his head, his face ecstatic. "A miracle. It's a miracle." He clapped his hands together. "Hallelujah!"

Humanus cringed and pushed with his heels against the soft mattress, trying to back away from the human container of *Zug*, to back away from such an outlandish and facetious display of rejoicing.

"Oh dear," Cardassin said. "I've startled him." He looked sheepishly at Ariel. "I was only

366

searching for an appropriate way to express my joy he has survived."

Ariel patted Cardassin's hand. "He's still a bit out of it. I hope in another few days, his memory will clear and he'll be his former rambunctious self."

Humanus wasn't convinced. He pointed a shaky finger at Cardassin. "What is he doing here?"

Ariel glanced at Cardassin. "See what I mean?" She adjusted the pillow under Humanus' head. "You need to rest. Cardassin saved our lives. If it wasn't for him, we all would have certainly perished in the cave and the super-primates would have eventually killed Kesi and Jamani. As it is, Gomo and his hideous gang were buried alive." She scowled at the mention of Gomo, then a thought must have given her hope. She brightened. "Cardassin retrieved the nano-assembler. Cardassin, show Humanus the nano-assembler."

With a grin, Cardassin held up the nano-assembler. "It's still well charged and will serve us for years."

Humanus searched Ariel's calm face, looking for some indication that what she was telling him was being made up as she went along as a way to ease his pain, to explain the unexplainable. "What about the guardian?"

She took both his hands in hers. Her calm dissolved, as though a dark cloud passed over her thoughts. "Justin was wearing the pouch with the guardian when the cave blew. It is buried with him."

Tears welled in Humanus' eyes such was the emotional impact of what he was hearing. Nothing made sense. But they were all alive, except for his mentor. Justin had always wondered why he'd been shifted to this time. Hopefully, before the darkness closed around him, he had realized his purpose.

"And the twins?" Humanus asked.

Ariel smiled, surprised. "How did you know? I never told you we were to have twins."

EPILOGUE

The Shepherd checked his coordinates, checked the time, re-checked his coordinates. His calculations were precise. He was even a bit early-- four million years back from his creation in 1985, the only way he knew to reckon years, and two million of those same years from where he had left Ariel and *Gilomir*.

He maintained a lazy orbit just outside the event horizon of Cygnus X-1. The dark star loomed, invisible in ordinary light, but could be seen as a whirling sink hole in the x-ray spectrum, sucking matter off its blue super giant companion star in a parasitic dance.

The Shepherd felt a slight tick deep in his flesh. The guardian had arrived. Right on time.

"I am here, Master," the Shepherd said. "And so are you, just as you said you'd be. Welcome to the anomalistic locality."

"A moment while I assess the situation," the guardian said.

The Shepherd waited patiently, humbly, for he was in the presence of his creator. No. He was in the presence of much more, the breadth of which he struggled to comprehend. But he had nowhere to go, and nothing pressing to do, so he was content to wait until the guardian told him differently.

"What an anomalous place, this forbidden zone," the guardian said after a while.

"It does have unforeseen aspects."

369

"A cursory scan satisfies me the path to *Gilomir's* salvation will succeed, though it will be long and arduous."

The Shepherd thought this was good news. But how the guardian knew, he had never been able to figure out. "When I left *Gilomir*, he was still trying to find himself."

"But he does find himself. The balance will be restored."

A silence ensued, unnerving the Shepherd. Was he to simply wait for an instruction? He'd come all this way, for what? "What am I to do, now?"

"We have a rendezvous to keep."

"A rendezvous?" Though the Shepherd knew he had no programmed set of emotional responses, the news of a rendezvous seemed to ratchet across his computers. "With whom?"

"An interesting life form. Articulated cells, independently programmable, a female mind, strong maternal instincts. A universal constructor, much like yourself."

"A4-Ni? She ends up here?"

"She does. Unfortunately, or fortunately, depending on your point of view, her polymer tape memory was corrupted during her flight. The Maraia DNA she carried was destroyed. She no longer remembers her origin, who constructed her, or her mission. In her befuddled state she seeks a new seed. Indeed, she will discover and want the *Gilomir* genome I carry."

"So this is how it all begins."

"Isn't that obvious?"

It wasn't obvious. Nothing the guardian did or said was obvious. The Shepherd's computers whirred and tumbled out the inevitable conclusion. "Then you know how it will all end."

"Of course."

"Was that really me back there, in the cave by the river?"

"Yes. There is only one of you."

The Shepherd remained silent for a moment. His computers permutated possible future outcomes. "I sense this rendezvous with A4-Ni will be a fateful one."

"I am certain you will conduct yourself well."

"Thank you for your confidence in me, Master. How long do we have to wait?"

"Two turns around the dark star toward the future will suffice to bring us to A4-Ni."

***

What seemed like moments later, the Shepherd activated an alarm.

"Guardian, A4-Ni is here. She appears threatening."

"Yes, I know.

Such complacency. "Why does she threaten us? She created me. Doesn't she recognize me?"

"You forget your world line is not coincident with hers. She has only just arrived from being created in the distant future. She has yet to travel her world line to 1985 where she will facilitate your construction.

"As I have pointed out, she is confused about her origin and mission. Indeed, she is consumed by a desire to acquire *Gilomir's* DNA. That you stand

371

in the way is of little importance to her. She will try to annihilate you."

The Shepherd's sensors lit up to at a violation of his exterior. "Master, she is attempting to insert a probe into my being. Shall I protect myself?"

"By all means."

The Shepherd satisfied himself that at least he had asked. Was he then being given license to terminate A4-Ni? His sleek surface puckered, loosing gray slugs of matter. Ballooning blasts ripped A4-Ni's insides, reducing her to gossamer strands.

At first, the Shepherd felt a fleeting satisfaction he had succeeded in protecting himself and the guardian. But confusion quickly displaced satisfaction. Obviously, his resistance would fail. A4-Ni must survive if she was to construct him in the future.

A4-Ni turned, reconstituted herself, and despite still being disabled, loosed a pulse of debilitating radiation.

The Shepherd recoiled. Sensitive tissue blistered and blackened. Life-sustaining tubes burst, leaking their fluids. "Master, she has dealt me a terrible blow. My systems are decimated. She returns, and though much reduced, she seems intent on re-inserting her probe."

"Indeed. She doesn't much like what you have done to her."

Desperately, the Shepherd checked his systems. "I can no longer protect myself...or you. What shall I do?"

"Rest at ease. Let her dictate. She is about to launch us upon the path to *Gilomir's* salvation."

"But Master, I--"

"She is done with you. It is me she wants. Not me, personally, of course, but what I carry."

"Is *Gilomir* ready?"

The guardian opened to the Shepherd, enough so he could sense *Gilomir*. "Let's ask him. *Gilomir*, are you ready?"

"He seems shocked at what is about to befall him."

"He might be," the guardian replied.

"You have brought me here," *Gilomir* said, "What am I to make of this situation?"

"You should make the best of it, and we shall see," the guardian said.

"You have told me why I am here, but I do not know where it will lead, and I find an alien life form coveting my DNA repugnant."

"As I said, you should make the best of it."

"I won't do it!"

The guardian closed the door that had given the Shepherd access to *Gilomir*. "Excuse us, Shepherd. I need a moment alone with *Gilomir*."

An interval of silence followed, wherein the Shepherd was left to wonder what was transpiring between the guardian and *Gilomir*.

Then the door reopened.

"I did not understand all I saw," *Gilomir* said, his voice contrite. "Will I survive?"

"That depends on you, of course."

"I shall go insane."

"You will not go insane."

373

"Then what is your advice?"

"Trust your instincts," the guardian said. "Trust the Shepherd. The path to your salvation lies through Earth."

"Earth? I know nothing of Earth. Do I have a choice?"

"No."

A4-Ni inserted her probe and reached for the guardian.

The Shepherd winced, feeling helpless to stop her.

"Do not leave me," *Gilomir* pleaded.

"I shall be close by," the guardian said.

A4-Ni ripped the silvery sphere from the charred tissue of the Shepherd's womb.

"Guardian!"

But only silence met *Gilomir's* cry.

THE BEGINNING

374